Praise for *Parting Gifts*

"Katrina Willis can take a painful experience and offer enlightenment. She can take a hardship and reveal opportunity. She can describe deep despair and make you feel hopeful. How? Through her extraordinary gift of detail and language . . . through her brave willingness to go where others dare not go . . . through her heart that feels deeply and fully. Unlike any author I've ever read, Willis transports me into a moment so I can see, hear, taste, and feel it as if I am there. And when I am lost in one of her stories, I don't want to come back. Because through her stories, I am healed. I am understood. I am fully alive."

—**Rachel Macy Stafford**
New York Times best-selling author
of *Hands Free Mama*

"*Parting Gifts* is a rare treasure, the sort of book that leaves the reader attached to the characters long after finishing the final page. Katrina Anne Willis has painted a family portrait, intricate, and real, capturing what it means to be family, what it means to struggle with both our need to belong, and our need to be set free. *Parting Gifts* cracked my heart open, and reminded me of what it means to be human. I loved this book."

—**Karen Lynch**
author of *Good Cop, Bad Daughter:*
Memoirs of an Unlikely Police Officer

"In *Parting Gifts*, Willis paints the portrait of three sisters with careful and exacting strokes. All three women are seeking to overcome their own personal and shared tragedies, and you will become attached to each one of them as they make their way back home to each other."

—**T. Greenwoo**
author of *Two Rivers, Bodies of Wat*
and *The Forever B*

parting

gifts

parting
gifts

Katrina Anne Willis

SHE WRITES PRESS

Published 2016
Printed in the United States of America
ISBN: 978-1-63152-039-6 paperback
        978-1-63152-040-2 ebook
Library of Congress Control Number: 2015954335

For information, address:
She Writes Press
1563 Solano Ave #546
Berkeley, CA 94707

She Writes Press is a division of SparkPoint Studio, LLC.

To Chris, who makes everything possible.

And to Sam, Gus, Mary Claire, and George,
the best and brightest pieces of us.

before

"A happy family is but an earlier heaven."
—George Bernard Shaw

"We are all so much together, but we are all dying of loneliness."
—Albert Schweitzer

1 *catherine*

Catherine didn't fear the chemo as much as the molasses hours she spent in the infusion room. It took far too long to wait for the Cytoxan cocktail to drip into her veins and search for its target. Time to think about how she'd failed to create the idyllic family she'd so desperately craved as a child, how the poison that was supposed to save her was all but killing her in its noble quest, how very much she'd squandered the forty years she'd been given. Time to wonder whether forty was all she'd ever see.

Her feet were cold. Her feet had always been cold. On the day of her tenth birthday, in a cake and ice cream frenzy, she'd slipped and fallen while running through the kitchen, showing off for her friends, ignoring her parents' vodka-laced indifference, her little sulking sister, Anne. The four layers of socks she'd managed to pull over her feet were thick ice skates on the chilled linoleum; the corner cabinet, unforgiving. Catherine's fingers traced the line of the scar that remained on her forehead.

"Dr. Mathers, can I get you some more water?"

Catherine looked into the eyes of her favorite nurse, Jenna. Young Jenna with the full lips and the fuller boobs. Jenna, who had her entire life ahead of her, stuck in this dreary room with too much sickness and too little hair. Jenna, who respectfully called her "Dr. Mathers" even though Catherine's academic credentials were earned by studying Faulkner and Hemingway while those with her life in their hands were MDs, cutting out chunks of cancer and sewing human bodies back together.

As she commonly did with people she didn't know well, Catherine wondered where Jenna went when she left the confines of this room. What constituted her life outside these walls that smelled of disinfectant and antibacterial soap? Did she work out? Read? Did she have a boyfriend? Someone she slept with on a regular basis? Did she go to church on Sunday? Or did she prefer to sit at home and drink coffee alone on her patio while she listened to John Mayer sing about broken relationships?

All these questions, yet Catherine had never bothered to ask during the past four months.

"Water would be nice."

Outside, a fragile autumn had begun. Yellows here and there, a burst of red, a hint of orange, a promise of cabled sweaters and chai tea. But today the air was hot and thick, Indian summer temperatures with a little extra sizzle. Weather was like that in Indiana. One day you could be sweating in your tank top and shorts; the next, reaching for your favorite IU sweatshirt. Indiana weather was fickle, volatile, equally beautiful and exasperating in its unpredictability.

Catherine glanced at her legs, her pink fuzzy socks. She'd purchased the socks for herself after her first chemo, when she began to grasp the kind of physical havoc the medicine would wreak on her body. She wished someone else had bought her the fuzzy socks. This would have been a warm embrace from a friend, a thoughtful gesture from a lover. "Here," the giver would have said kindly, so as not to jar her cancer-addled body. "They're to keep you warm, to let you know I'm thinking about you. And they're pink—you know, for breast cancer awareness."

But she had bought the socks by herself and for herself at Target. Into the cart went a box of Oreos, two bottles of Cabernet, some frozen Lean Cuisines, a package of Lysol wipes, the latest Julia Glass novel, and the socks. She had placed everything on the conveyor belt—working diligently to avoid the milk condensation left by the young mother in front of her—as the toddler in the cart ahead screamed for a candy bar.

"Not now, Honey. It's almost time for dinner," the mother had said sweetly.

"Now! I want it now!" the child had answered, not so sweetly.

"If you're a good boy, we'll get one and save it for later."

Catherine had wanted to slap them both, to stuff the fuzzy pink socks into the toddler's screaming mouth to silence him… just for a moment. The chemo, it seemed, was rendering her a little less patient, a tad uncharitable.

As Jenna walked away, Catherine's iPhone vibrated in her hand.

Michelle. Her oldest friend, her confidant, her one true-blue.

"Thank God you called," she said, fumbling with the phone. "I need a little Michelle sunshine right this very instant."

"I'm sorry I couldn't be there today, Cat," Michelle said. "If Jake didn't have a basketball game an hour away, you know I'd be with you, right? But there's dinner, and the twins' homework, and…"

"I know, Michelle," Catherine said, "I know. You'd be here if you could. And you'd have brought some damn good Malbec, too, right?"

"Do you have to ask?"

"Then, my friend, all is forgiven. It's the thought that counts. Unless, of course, you're looking for the buzz. Then it's the wine that counts."

Catherine smiled through her infusion haze. Michelle had accompanied her to the majority of her chemo treatments. If Michelle wasn't already committed to driving one of her kids somewhere else, she was there. Catherine would have been embarrassed to have anyone else watch her turn twenty shades of green while she drooled all over herself in a dreamless sleep, but she was always grateful for her friend's presence. Long ago, Catherine had held Michelle's hair while she vomited one too many upside-down margaritas into the Sigma Chi toilet, had stood beside her on her wedding day with a white Calla lily bouquet in a dress she'd never wear again, had attended the births of Michelle's four children. In turn, Michelle had wiped away Catherine's tears as yet another romantic relationship with the seemingly perfect boy imploded, had shared gallons of paint and bottles of wine when Catherine bought her first home, had stood proudly beside her on the day she was awarded the letters Ph.D. Theirs was the one relationship Catherine had somehow managed to sustain, Michelle's picture-perfect family the one Catherine simultaneously feared and coveted. Michelle was Catherine's one and only pink fuzzy sock friend—even if Michelle hadn't thought to buy the pink fuzzy socks. Whether it was through her own clumsy efforts or by the sheer grace of a God Catherine didn't really place much faith in, Michelle was Catherine's one steady.

"I'll bring you a banana shake tomorrow after I'm done volunteering in Molly's class," Michelle promised. "And I'm doing your laundry, so don't argue with me."

Catherine didn't argue. There was nothing more decadent than having someone else wash, fold, and put away your dirty clothes. Not worth the cancer diagnosis, of course, but a welcome consolation prize.

All around Catherine, people in various stages of healing or death—however you chose to envision it—were mired in the sleep of the acutely tired while toxins were pumped into their bloodstreams. Devoted parents, children, friends, and spouses sat beside their loved ones. A baby rested in her car carrier next to her father while her bald mother tucked a blanket around her own ears and chin. They were surviving individually while they struggled to survive together. Some visitors brought books, some watched TV, all looked nearly as broken as the patients they accompanied. Except for that sweet, pink-cheeked baby, smiling in her sleep. Some patients sat alone. It was easier to look at the ones who closed their eyes throughout their treatments. The ones who stared without focus—like the new patient with the white hair who always shared the same corner as Catherine—made her uncomfortable.

But it was the walls that bothered Catherine the most. Why the St. Mark's Oncology Care designers hadn't thought of chair rails was beyond reason. With twenty cheap recliners bumping continually into the beige walls in their deliberate dance, scuffs and chips were inevitable. The resultant state of the walls, however, was unkempt and depressing, a canvas of disregard that left Catherine and her cancer colleagues with a distinct sense of abandonment.

How important were those red exclamation point emails now? How critical was that deadline at work? What they all wouldn't have given for another chance to bend under the weight of an unanswered voice mail. What a luxury to have those things be the worries that filled an eight-hour day.

When Catherine had turned forty, five short months before, she did what every responsible woman her age did. She scheduled her first mammogram and winced as the nurse twisted and flattened her breasts into unfamiliar and increasingly uncomfortable positions. She stared with fake interest at the picture hanging to her left, the purples and blues of the abstract floral painting transforming into a bruise before her eyes. After the second mammogram was ordered, followed immediately by an ultrasound, and then a biopsy, Catherine knew something was wrong. But when Dr. Bingham took her hand and said, with the sad resolve of a man who'd grown too accustomed to delivering bad news, "Catherine, it's Stage II," her heart still skipped a beat. One, then another.

Fuck! Fuck! Fuck!

During those first moments, when she understood her existence would never be the same—that, perhaps, her existence might even be cut short—she noticed the family pictures lining Dr. Bingham's bookshelves. His wife was a lovely wisp of a woman, his daughters smiled from their frames. The girls were both blonde, and they wrapped their arms around each other with convincing ease. Love emanated from those photos. Love and belonging. Catherine thought about her own family pictures. She was certain there were shots of Big Jim and Eva lined up side by side, Catherine, Anne, and little Jessica standing dutifully in front of them. But for a moment, she couldn't remember any pictures. Not one.

As a five-year-old, Catherine would proclaim to everyone within earshot that she wanted to be a horse when she grew up. Her parents' friends giggled into their vodka tonics when her innocent announcement was encouraged at dinner parties, but to Catherine, there was nothing funny about aspiring to be a horse. Horses had strong legs that carried them with purpose and intent. They were exotic, fast, mysterious, and powerful with their muscular torsos and dark eyes. Catherine knew, even at her tender age, that there was more to life than being a good, white, well-educated Catholic girl who someday would grow up to be a good, white, well-educated Catholic suburbanite. But living the charmed suburban TV life she'd never had was still what Catherine wanted most… even now. Never in her childhood aspirations, though, did Catherine say, "I want to have cancer. I want to go through chemotherapy. I want a handsome doctor to lop off one of my boobs before he returns home to his perfectly coiffed wife, his adoring children, and a well-balanced meal awaiting him in his gourmet kitchen."

Later, when she could escape from the circles of her own mind, Catherine found that Stage II (because breast cancer liked to present every patient with a unique bag of tricks) meant the tumor was nearly three centimeters in diameter and had not yet spread to her lymph nodes. A lucky diagnosis, as breast cancer diagnoses go. So Catherine underwent a lumpectomy to remove the evidence and eventually was able to look at the scar left in the wake of the surgeon's scalpel.

Almost unconsciously, Catherine's hand went to her left breast— the damaged mess that landed her in this purgatory of sickness. She glanced down at the port that had been sewn into her chest to make infusion easier.

As if any of this could possibly be easy.

"Here you go, Dr. Mathers," Jenna said as she set a cup of water on the table. Everything here is beaten down, Catherine sighed. Even the cheap-ass furniture.

"Thank you, Jenna," Catherine replied as a wave of fatigue threatened to pull her into semi-consciousness.

"Get some rest," Jenna whispered. "I'll wake you when you're done."

Yes, Catherine thought, allowing her eyes to close. Yes. Just let me sleep until this is all over.

2 *anne*

"Get those shoes on now or there will be no ice cream after lunch!" Anne yelled, even though the mothers in her Willton Tot Moms group swore that yelling was the worst kind of parenting and didn't work, anyway. Anne wasn't worried about yelling. She knew her way around the confessional, was intimately familiar with its dark corners and the shrouded screen that separated her from the priest. She would be absolved.

In a breathless frenzy, Anne raced around the first floor of her three-story home. She opened her walnut cabinets, scanned her Corian countertops. Behind a couch cushion, she found Max's pacifier, a necessity for her eleven-month-old son. From underneath the leather armchair peeked Lila's pink blankie. The car ride would have been intolerable without either one of those traveling necessities.

The early morning sunlight streamed through the family room windows and illuminated the fine layer of dust on all the Jackleys' possessions. Their wedding picture, the one where a fifty-pound-lighter Anne beamed with joy and anticipation, was dotted with sticky fingerprints. On a better day, those innocent reminders of her children might have made her smile. Anne took a brief moment to stare at the youthful face of her husband. His arm was wrapped protectively around her small middle, his eyes were bright and worry-free. She blew on the framed photo, watched the dust settle on the mahogany end table, and sighed deeply. Her focus then returned to the task at hand.

"Absolutely none! And I'm not kidding!" It made Anne feel better to yell. Made her feel heard, noticed. Even when three-year-old Lila continued to ignore her and Max was reduced to tears by the angry tenor of his mother's voice—even then it felt good. And Anne had a hard time believing that all of her fellow Tot Moms never raised their voices. With more than twenty collective children among them, she was convinced that a great deal of yelling occurred behind closed doors. Yelling and probably a vast array of other secrets, too. Anne understood family secrets.

"Momma," Lila chirped, "I don't think I want ice cream today. I think I want yogurt." It took every ounce of Anne's maternal strength not to mimic her daughter's thick "S's" out of an immature and completely unreasonable spite. Especially when every button had already been pushed this morning, and then pushed again. From shirt selection to hair bow placement to oatmeal consistency, nothing Anne had done for her daughter in the hour and a half she'd been out of bed had been right. Only 8:00 in the morning, and already Anne was ready for a nap. Or a magnum of wine.

She glanced at Max as he patiently picked up individual Cheerios and popped them one by one into his mouth. Lila had never been such a content baby. When she was finished with her Cheerios, she'd sweep them off her tray onto the floor. If she didn't want Cheerios but had a taste for Goldfish instead, she'd scream a high-pitched protest that could bring Anne to her knees.

"It doesn't really matter what you want," Anne snapped, "if you don't Get. Your. Shoes. On. NOW. Because we are not leaving this house until you do!"

With an exasperated sigh, Lila stepped into her pink Uggs and smoothed her shirt. She then slung her princess backpack onto her shoulders and proclaimed herself ready for preschool. Thank God for small miracles, Anne thought as she nudged a smiling Max out the door.

The drive to preschool was always made more palatable with a little Guns N' Roses in the background. While Axl sang "Sweet Child of Mine," Anne navigated the Suburban through her neighborhood streets. She kept her windows rolled up and her air-conditioning on so the neighbors wouldn't hear her musical selection pounding through the speakers. There was Bob and Kathy Mansfield's house. Their nine-year-old triplets terrorized the neighborhood on their electric Razor scooters. There was Bill and Lynn Mattison's house. They had two teenage girls who took turns driving a used BMW to high school. Shelby Mattison sometimes babysat for Lila and Max. She was a sweet girl who apparently had no idea how to load a dishwasher, or even to realize that washing dishes was a chore that didn't complete itself. The house that guarded the neighborhood's entrance belonged to Don and Nancy Blackwell. They were both retired and kept their lawn meticulously manicured. Like sentinels guarding their domain, they were menacing in their stoic judgment of everyone else's horticultural missteps. Anne was certain the Jackleys' own dandelion-infested lawn was the bane of the Blackwells' existence. But at least those pesky little bursts of yellow gave Lila great pleasure.

"I love Candy Lions," Lila would say. "They leave yellow marks on my fingers. Max, do you want a Candy Lion?" She'd rub the tip of his tiny nose with the flower, leaving it a jaundiced shade of yellow. Max would grab the dandelion from her fingers and stuff it into his mouth, smiling the whole time.

A familiar pang of guilt gripped Anne briefly as she turned her SUV into the Jackson United Methodist Church parking lot to drop Lila at preschool before attending her own Monday morning Tot Moms meeting. As a staunch and devoted Catholic, Anne worried every day about commingling with those who believed that the Eucharistic host was nothing more than a mere representation of Jesus's body. But St. Andrew's Catholic Church didn't have a preschool or a Tot Moms program, and Anne desperately craved the break and the camaraderie provided by her peer group, albeit her religiously *inferior* peer group. What Anne was after was respite, relief, and a few good movie recommendations. She was already wholly versed in the Father, the Son, and the Holy Spirit. She'd solidified that relationship as a young girl, ever eager to genuflect as expected, kneel when asked, confess when necessary (and even, sometimes, when it wasn't). Pious Anne. Obedient Anne.

"Good morning, Mrs. Daniels!" she said with fake cheer as Lila's preschool teacher opened the car door to greet and escort her young charge into the building.

"So good to see you, Mrs. Jackley!" Mrs. Daniels bellowed, reaching for Lila's hand. "How's our sweet Max today?"

The baby giggled in his car seat at the sound of his name.

"He's perfect as usual," Anne said with a touch of ennui in her voice. Sometimes all the mindless morning chatter wore her down. By the time she dropped Lila off at preschool, she often felt like she'd run a marathon (even though she had absolutely no firsthand experience of what running a marathon might actually feel like). She rarely had anything left to give in the way of chit-chat.

"Have a good morning, Lila," Anne said as she accelerated away with more speed than the preschool staff probably condoned. At least I didn't squeal the tires, she thought. She drove to the back of the church where the Tot Moms meeting was held and unstrapped Max from his seat. Propping his weight on her right hip, Anne felt a wave of sadness rush over her.

This is what I've become, she thought. I'm Mom Jeans and milk stains and piles of dirty laundry. I'm spaghetti with sauce out of the jar and cookie crumbs ground into the carpet. She reminisced about singing Madonna at the top of her lungs into her curling iron microphone. Now the only songs she knew were from the Disney channel. And Disney didn't play *Papa, Don't Preach*.

Anne thought briefly about her carefree college days at Indiana University, when she smoked too much pot and had too much sex. (Surely there was some kind of sin involved with thinking about sex in a church parking lot.) But the pot was good and the sex was even better. After twelve years of Catholic school acquiescence, it had been liberating to try everything she'd formerly believed would send her straight into the depths of hell. For once in her life, she'd decided to dance with the sinners instead of the saints. And it was there that she'd met her husband, Dale. Sexy, smart Dale with the vibrator under his futon—the one he'd purchased and used exclusively for her pleasure. They both waited tables at Nick's and fell madly in love.

"Do you think the dude at table twelve is gay or straight?" he'd whispered as she picked up a tray of wings and breadsticks.

Anne had cast him a sideways glance. Was he talking to her?

"I'll have to look," she said. "My gaydar is never wrong, though, so I'll let you know whether you're getting lucky tonight or not."

Dale had guffawed.

"Well, your gaydar is obviously off right now because I'm not interested in him for myself. I'm checking him out for my roommate."

Anne eyed him suspiciously.

"Seriously, you're much more my type."

Then he'd winked and sauntered away.

Now, fifteen years later, she had Dale, Lila, and Max. And God. She'd begged His Almighty for forgiveness shortly before her first child was born. Anne knew that after her wild-child college days, she was unworthy of being a mother, unfit to shape the course of another human being's life. So she entered the confessional (which in recent weeks felt more like a second home to her), spewed forth all her shame and failure, and begged for God—via the staunch Father Daniel who nodded in agreement as she listed each of her intimate secrets—to forgive her and once again take up residence in her flawed heart.

But somehow, she still felt lonely. Catholicism couldn't fill the ever-expanding void, and the vibrator had been thrown discreetly in the trash a long time ago, wrapped tightly in plastic Meijer bags and tucked underneath rotten banana peels and damp coffee grounds. And then there was Dale. Sexy, smart Dale had developed a bit of a paunch and traveled far too much for her liking. His software sales job kept him on the road at least four days a week. Four long, lonely days and nights with no one to talk to but her sassy daughter and her barely-verbal son. And just to drive the knife deeper, Anne was fairly certain those four days and nights weren't so lonely for Dale. Because of the precedent her philandering father had set, Anne had a nagging suspicion that Dale's vibrator days might not be over—just over with her. And the thought of him with another woman—or numerous women—made her bite her manicured nails down to the quick. These suspicions, of course, were completely unfounded. As far as she knew, Dale had always been true-blue, steady-Eddie. But Anne was always acutely aware—on a nearly molecular level—that things aren't always what they seem. Dale was not her father. Her father was not Dale. But still.

"Good morning, Anna Banana!" her friend Jill called from the parking lot. "Wait for us!"

Jill and her husband, Jim, who'd relocated to Indiana from Seattle just a year before, were strong advocates of attachment parenting. Jill carried her infant son, Jackson, in a new age, granola baby sling. It had become a permanent accessory to her wardrobe. Jackson was, indeed, attached to one of them at all times—on their chests, in their bed, on Jill's nipple. As much as Anne liked Jill and enjoyed her company, the idea of having a baby continually tethered to you seemed exhausting. Did she nurse on the toilet?

"Did you hear about our speaker today?" Jill asked as she sidled up beside Anne, barely out of breath. Jill's slender legs carried her gracefully through life.

"No. Who is it?" Anne could feel droplets of sweat rolling down her back and into the waistband of her underwear. She was irritated by the unseasonal heat of the day. She wanted to remind God that it was supposed to be cooling down, but she had other priorities at the top of her prayer list—like her sick mother, her negative bank account, and the heavy sadness she carried around like an extra child.

"Dr. Jones," Jill said. Dr. Jones was Willton's—and the Jackleys'—most celebrated pediatrician. "He's here to talk about non-violent discipline and behavioral re-direction."

Fabulous, thought Anne. She carried Max into the toddler room where her childcare volunteer saviors awaited his arrival.

If I have to listen to what a failure I am this morning, Anne thought, there had better at least be some good black coffee and a shitload of chocolate chip cookies.

She bent down to give Max a perfunctory peck on the cheek and headed to the Tot Moms gathering room, where she would listen to the numerous ways she could transform herself into Mother of the Year.

3 *jessica*

For Jessica, this mystery remained: what made a man choose to sit in a dark, windowless black hole in the middle of a Tuesday afternoon while his colleagues picked up the slack at work? As she glanced out into her audience, she noticed designer ties—some loosened and askew, some as perfectly knotted as the moment their wearers donned them this morning. So many of these men had money, families, homes, wives, kids. The parking lot almost always had minivans and luxury sedans parked next to pick-up trucks. She could easily spot the family men. They looked the most ill at ease and the most damaged. The regulars were comfortable in their own skin, content with the choices they had made in life. They didn't bother shaving every day, didn't tuck their shirts in, didn't wash the dirt out from under their fingernails. They came, they sat, they drank, they ogled, they tipped, they left.

They kept coming back because of the boobs, Jessica thought. Boobs were the ultimate Achilles Heel. She slid seductively around the pole, strong arms holding her upside down, shapely legs pointing toward the smoky ceiling as she displayed the works of art God had bestowed upon her twenty-seven-year-old body. There were only two girls at the Carousel Lounge who hadn't been altered, lifted, or surgically enhanced. Jessica was proud to be one of them.

"You're so lucky," Desiree had said on Jessica's first night. "Those things won't start hanging until you're at least thirty-five." She'd grabbed her own breasts and hoisted them up a little higher. "I had to get mine lifted when I was twenty-five because they were so damn big. My back hurts all the time. But they pay the bills, right?" And she'd laughed as she'd danced her way onstage, her stilettos clicking their way across the battered stage floor.

Lucky, Jessica thought, was a strange word for Desiree to have chosen. She would not describe herself as *lucky*. She wasn't sure how she would describe herself—alone, unwanted—resilient, perhaps— but definitely not *lucky*. She was independent, for certain, but that was by necessity rather than choice. She'd like to consider herself loved, protected, and safe. But those were adjectives that still eluded her.

"Hey, baby," a faceless voice spoke. "Want to come home with me?"

Jessica smiled at him. Smiling was good for business. She imagined what his home might look like—the dirty dishes, the stained carpet, the mangy dog. The grease in his voice told her everything she needed to know about him.

Intuitive. That was another word that described Jessica.

The afternoon crowd was always a bit smaller and more subdued than the evening crowd. The drinks went down more slowly, the cat-calls weren't quite as loud, the groping was fairly non-existent. But the afternoon patrons' eyes were also different. Sadder, somehow. Emptier.

Jessica noticed these things. She noticed many things. Ever since the day nearly twenty years ago that she'd walked in on her father with his khaki chinos around his ankles, thrusting against the naked back-side of her mother's best friend, Ellen, Jessica began noticing. She was aware of the deceit in Big Jim's every action. She saw the disinterest and disengagement in her older sisters' faces, noticed how Catherine and Anne artfully began removing themselves from the Mathers' day-to-day routine. She never knew, though, whether Eva was aware of Jim's multiple infidelities. And Jessica could not quite decide what was worse—to know and to look the other way, or to live obliviously in the belief that the promises you once made were being honored.

"That's it, that's it…" Jessica could still hear Ellen's voice in the recesses of her mind. She could still see her father's bare, hairy ass, could still recall the strange throaty noises that escaped him. Some things remain. It would be an amputation of sorts to cut this memory from her existence. Who would she be if, at the tender age of eight, she hadn't witnessed her father fucking her mother's best friend?

It was a question Jessica liked to ask. Who would she be? Who could she have been? She'd had so much more than others—a roof over her head, food in the refrigerator, a private education. From an outsider's perspective, she'd had it all. But there are secrets that reside behind locked doors and gauzy curtains. A house might contain all the right accouterments—the pleather armchairs, the chintz pillows, the Corelle "Wildflower" place settings for twelve—but it could still be missing a beating heart.

There were no true connections in a place like the Carousel Lounge. Whatever was spoken had no meaning, and whatever was felt was fleeting and thin. It was comforting for Jessica to recognize this essential truth. She had chosen a livelihood that left her untethered and unattached. It matched her life perfectly. No relationships, no commitment. No commitment, no pain. She was aware that outside the dark confines of these walls, people were in love, were laughing with friends, were cuddling children, were doing more than just screwing their spouses. But in here, it was much safer, more predictable. It might have been darker, seedier, but there were no real risks inside this building. Despite the calloused hands and greasy smiles of the men who professed their drunken devotion to her, and regardless of the amount of times she'd been approached in the parking lot, this life still felt more comfortable than a life of emotional risk-taking. Blackened eyes and bruised limbs? She'd choose those any day over the threat of a broken soul.

Within these walls, it was so much easier to hide. Invisibility was always easier in the dark. She'd learned that with her childhood friends during their late-night games of flashlight tag. Jessica had always been good at hiding, had always been the last to be found.

"Olly olly oxen free!" the neighborhood kids would call when they grew tired of searching. And Jessica would wait just a moment longer, until she could hear the exasperation in their voices. Only then would she emerge from the shadows with a smile on her dirty, nine-year-old face. A smile that conveyed her satisfaction at being the victor again.

"So baby, what's it gonna be? Yes or no?" He was all bad Meatloaf lyrics, this one.

Jessica swung around the pole, stilettos digging into the pocked and dirty hardwood floor. The greasy voice was insistent, but did not pose a threat. Jessica wielded the power here. She was the one in control. It was heady, this knowledge. And when it was her turn to rest backstage with the other dancers, she could disappear once more.

4 *catherine*

"Today, Scholars, I want you to explore your reactions to Dexter Green's idealistic dreams."

Catherine always called her Indiana University students "Scholars." It empowered them, kept their minds on the academic tasks at hand, fulfilled her own need for approval and recognition. After all, if her students were scholars, surely that made her so much more. An academic goddess, perhaps. It felt good to hold such a lofty title, even if it was only in her mind.

She glanced at her students, reveled in their rapt attention. Backpacks were tossed carelessly in aisles and under seats. Baseball caps and ponytails disguised bedheads. A few students slept face down on desks—too many beers at the night before?—but most watched her with anticipation.

Today her literature class was examining Ernest Hemingway. Catherine loved Hemingway. She loved his work, loved the romanticized idea of his existence, his multiple wives and his disintegrating mind, imagined oral sex with him at the top of a mountain—most likely, Kilimanjaro. His lips, his tongue, his literary genius. The oxygen deprivation and climatic impossibilities didn't quell her fantasies.

Her feet ached more than usual today. She removed her baseball cap—still always a bit of a shock to her students, despite the number of times they'd seen her bald head—and sat down behind the mammoth desk at the front of the room. Normally, she liked to be with the class, moving among them. But today, she needed to sit, to lean, to try not to fall asleep with "The Short Happy Life of Frances Macomber" trapped in a puddle of drool.

Before her students could engage in some literary banter, Catherine's iPhone vibrated on the corner of her desk, Anne's picture popping up on the screen. Damn it, she thought. Anne knew her schedule, knew she was teaching right now if she bothered to think. Catherine also knew Anne wouldn't call unless something was happening with their mother. And lately, it seemed, something was always happening with Eva.

"Go ahead and start discussing," she instructed as she grabbed her phone and willed her aching limbs toward the door. "I'll be back in a jiffy."

Her students smiled back at her outdated vernacular. They loved her quirkiness, her quick wit, and her sailor's mouth. She often caught them off guard with an unexpected "fuck" or a passionate "goddamn." She was good to them, respectful of their minds and opinions, and in return, they admired and took care of her. She chose to believe they liked her because she was a fine instructor, not because she had breast cancer and a set of irreparably damaged tits. But either way, she wore their smiles like a protective cloak as she walked to the hallway to take her younger sister's call.

"It's Mom," Anne sighed with the weight of the world on her shoulders.

"Well, hello Anne!" Catherine said, her voice filled with false cheer and sarcasm. "It's so good to hear from you! What's happening in your life? How are the kids? The hubby?"

"Seriously, Catherine," Anne said, "I'm not in the mood for small talk. We need to discuss Mom."

"I assumed as much," Catherine replied. "What's going on?"

"It was the night nurse again. Another *incident*," Anne said. Catherine imagined Anne's pointer fingers creating mock quotation marks around the word "incident." Anne liked to deliver any news regarding their mother as dramatically as possible. "She got combative, threw her dinner tray, and broke the nurse's glasses. It's becoming a real problem, Cat."

Catherine looked at the clock hanging on the wall in front of her. She could hear the tick of the hands as they trudged their way into the next minute, the next hour. She rubbed her head. It was chilly in the hallway. She should have brought her cap.

"She has Alzheimer's, Anne," Catherine said. "Combativeness can be part of it. You know that. They know what to expect at the home. They deal with this every day."

"But it shouldn't be this way," Anne said. "She's our gentle, doormat mother. How in God's name did she become combative?"

Catherine thought about their docile mother and reveled in the knowledge that Eva was finally showing a bit of spunk. Throughout their young lives, Catherine had wanted Eva to stand up for herself, to scream, to yell, to make a scene, to kick Big Jim in his philandering balls. But Eva, instead, had chosen to remain quiet, crying alone in her room and locking the rest of the world out in the chill she left behind. Catherine spent many evenings curled up on the couch, wrapped in an afghan made by her grandmother. She'd poke her fingers through the holes, weaving them in and out. She'd pull the blanket up to her cold nose, attempting to warm herself with her own breath. Their childhood home was always cold. It was their mother's home, after all.

"She just is," Catherine said. "It's who she's become. No matter who she was before, she's different now. You're doing the best you can, Anne."

Catherine liked to throw her younger sister a bone now and then. After all, Anne still lived in their childhood hometown and assumed most of the burden of caring for their ailing mother—tending to the nursing home bills, the physician consults, the obligatory visits. Catherine was pleased that the ninety-minute drive from Indiana University to Willton shielded her from most of the daily shit work involved with taking care of an aging parent. For a while, Anne had even made a valiant effort to take Eva out for lunch, to bring her home for dinner, to get her hair done at her favorite salon. It was a great deal of work and effort that had become a Herculean task. Now Eva spent all her time in the nursing home, and Anne licked her own wounds, festered in woe-is-me. The drive protected Catherine from all of that dysfunction—the self-flagellation, the tedium of the day-to-day, the drama. And that hour-and-a-half travel buffer also allowed her to keep her bald-headed and lopsided-tit secret to herself. She wasn't sure her family (and, of course, she used that word loosely) needed to know about the cancer. Not now. Not yet. She wasn't even sure she wanted to know about it herself.

"I'd really like for you to come stay with us and see Mom," Anne said. "It's been a long time, and soon she's not going to recognize you."

She's not going to recognize me now, Catherine thought.

Anne remained silent.

Catherine couldn't stand the discomfort of a void. Inevitably, she'd fill it with thoughts of death, unpaid bills, men she'd slept with on the first date, and all the other perceived burdens and failures of her life. As different from each other as they liked to believe they were, Catherine and Anne shared this common trait. They were good at keeping secrets, but not so good at keeping their mouths shut in general.

"I'll come after class today," Catherine said. It was Friday, and this was her final class before the weekend. "May I stay with you tonight?"

"We've got plenty of room," Anne said. "Stay as long as you'd like."

Catherine imagined a hint of loneliness in Anne's invitation, but she didn't have the strength to either comfort or engage her sister. Cancer ruled her every action now. Fucking cancer with its bitter blend of fatigue and regret.

"See you soon, Annie."

Catherine addressed her class as soon as she returned.

"Scholars, we're going to wrap today's lesson up early. I have a little family business to tend. Don't forget to read next week's assignment. I'll be keeping my usual office hours if you need to talk to me."

As she was packing up her belongings and loading them into her ancient briefcase, one of her favorite students approached. Julie was a black-haired, black-eyed, willowy beauty with an unmatched passion for the art of letters. She was enamored with the notion that every word in ink was recorded for all eternity. Every single word, a treasure that eventually outlasted every living, breathing creature. And Catherine was inspired by Julie's passion, her devotion to her studies… and—as a bit of a surprise to Catherine herself—those eyes.

"Is everything okay?" Julie asked. Each time she heard the raspy tenor of Julie's self-assuredness, Catherine felt an unfamiliar stirring, one she couldn't quite name. "Is there anything I can do?"

"Thanks, Julie," Catherine replied, "but it's a family matter that needs my presence more than my attention. Nothing serious. I just need to be there."

"Can I take care of anything for you while you're gone?" Julie asked. "Plants to water? Pets to feed? Mail to gather? Laundry to fold?"

Catherine stared at this twenty-one-year-old beauty and talked herself out of believing that she was being propositioned. She—with her ample thighs, her thick middle, and her misshapen, freckled head—was certainly not being flirted with by a beautiful, young coed. But she'd been flirted with before. She recognized the aura, the undertone, the innuendo.

"Well," Catherine said with a voice she didn't quite recognize, "I do have a cat that needs to be fed. He's easy enough to take care of, but he'd probably love a little company." Catherine had left the cat alone overnight before, but was too intrigued by this unexpected offer to refuse help that she didn't really need.

"Done," Julie said, knotting her scarf and buttoning her coat. "What's his name?"

"Dante."

Julie smiled.

Dante's *The Inferno* was one of Catherine's very favorites, her academic go-to. She was intrigued by the various circles of hell with their disturbing and often gruesome punishments, alternately fascinated and terrified by Cerberus, and her blood ran cold every time she read the words, *Abandon hope all ye who enter here.* If Dante's depiction of a tortured afterlife wasn't enough to make someone choose kindness, honesty, love, and acceptance, she wasn't sure what might.

Without a second thought, and more in response to her own current breathlessness than her intellect, Catherine dug through her belongings and handed a spare house key to this virtual stranger. She then stumbled over some sketchy instructions on how to care for a cat that didn't really need tending.

"Let me jot down directions to my house," Catherine said as she pulled a pen from her briefcase. The lecture hall was now empty, and the women's voices echoed throughout the cavernous space. Somehow, all of the other 122 students had slipped out the open doors unbeknownst to their favorite professor.

"No need," Julie said. "I know where you live."

And with that startling revelation (*Did it border on stalking somehow?*), Julie turned on her heel, tossed her Black Beauty locks with grace, and sauntered away without even a single backwards glance. The door slammed shut behind her, and Catherine became keenly aware of the empty space and her insubstantial existence within it.

She was still thinking about Julie and their strange and brazen encounter as she pulled her battered Volvo onto SR 37, and headed north toward Willton, Indiana. She watched the comfort and familiarity of her academic life pass away in her rear view mirror. *Objects in mirror are closer than they appear.* Catherine knew that wasn't true. Indiana University grew smaller and more distant with every mile that passed, with every exit that led her closer to home.

The early fall heat sat heavy on the leaves of each tree, and Catherine found herself feeling sorry for the beautiful oaks and maples that were destined to a life on the side of SR 37. You should be on the grounds of a museum, she thought as a stately beauty sped by. You should be in a schoolyard, surrounded by laughing children. She found herself yearning for the full glory of her favorite season, when the foliage erupted in an autumnal rainbow. The winters in Indiana could be brutal, but autumn made every snowstorm and every wind chill warning worthwhile. To live amidst such natural beauty, to walk in the mornings with a lambswool sweater on her shoulders and a crisp chill on the back of her neck, this was what made life worth living. (Well, she had to admit, it was the perfect trifecta of fall, Dave Eggers, and Dave Matthews that actually made life completely worth living.) Catherine was partial to pumpkin patches and hot apple cider. She loved attending the various fall festivals her state was famous for (the James Whitcomb Riley Festival, AppleFest, and Orchard Days were among her favorites), enjoyed watching children pick the perfect pumpkin (grateful, of course, that the children weren't her own, that she didn't have to carry those dirty vegetables home and stick her arm into their gooey insides), took great pleasure in choosing some phallic gourds to display on her mantel, and was always grateful to be relaxing fireside while listening to her Dave sing about his Dreamgirl. She even forgave Dave for his sketchy grammar. Sex appeal had the power to make her forgive most anything.

As she made her way north toward her childhood home, however, a knot began to develop in the pit of her stomach. She passed the exits for Martinsville, for Beech Grove, for Mount Comfort. When only one exit remained between the relative safety of the Volvo and the unsettling familiarity of Willton, the knot was fully formed and ready for combat. Catherine felt like a foreigner in her hometown. She'd been gone for so long and rarely made the trip back. Although the physical distance between her current life and her childhood was relatively minimal, the emotional distance was ocean-sized. Every year she spent teaching the great American classics made her feel even more like a stranger in a strange land (pun intended). But as she began to pass the familiar landmarks of her youth, she smiled in spite of herself. There was the Dairy Barn where her basketball team gathered after summer AAU games to sip Cherry Slushees and gorge on chili cheese dogs. Across the street was the Land Mark Movie Theatre where John Austin first slipped her the tongue and felt her up underneath her layered Izod polos. A few blocks away stood Jack's Meat Market where her mother always insisted they purchase every slice of meat that passed through their lips. "It's not healthy to buy your meat from a grocery store, girls," her mother said with cool indifference. "You never know how long it's been sitting on the shelf or what they're feeding those animals."

The decline of the town, even though it no longer belonged to Catherine, was still disheartening. Too many buildings on the corner of Harding and Wampler stood empty, boarded up "For Sale or Lease" signs dotting the dirty windows. The cracks in the sidewalk along Main Street were home to far too many dandelions. (Where was weed-gathering Lila when you needed her most?) The courthouse was in need of a good power-washing and a professional landscape contract.

Welcome home, Catherine thought as she pulled into the parking lot of the Regal Manor Nursing Home. A vast array of mums adorned the front entrance, but as the door automatically parted to allow her to enter, the scent of stale urine bombarded her. She entered the single-story brick building and steeled her shoulders.

"There is nothing regal about this," Catherine whispered to no one. "Nothing regal at all."

5 *anne*

"Come on, Mom," Anne begged. "One more bite of green beans. They're good for you. You can't survive on chocolate shakes."

"But I like chocolate shakes," Eva said.

"I know, Mom," Anne sighed, "but you need something healthy, too."

"Oh, for Pete's sake, Anne," Eva said in a rare moment of clarity, remembering her middle daughter's name. "I'm sixty-five years old. If I want to have a chocolate shake for lunch, I'll have a chocolate shake for lunch."

And so Anne readjusted the straw for her mother and sat back in the worn leather recliner.

"When is Jess coming to visit?" Eva asked. It was the same conversation they had during every single visit, but somehow it always seemed to take Anne by surprise. Eva remembered random bits and pieces of her past, but the one thing that always remained consistent was an inquiry about her youngest daughter, Jessica.

"I don't know, Mom," Anne said. "I haven't talked to Jess in a long, long time."

"Well, why don't you just pick up the phone and call her?" Eva asked. "Why not right now?"

"I don't know how to reach her."

"What do you mean 'you don't know how to reach her'?" Eva said, just as she always did. "She's your sister. How do you not know how to reach your own sister?"

And, as always, this line of questioning made Anne stop and take pause, too. Why didn't she know how to reach her baby sister? Because Jess had moved to Los Angeles the moment she celebrated her eighteenth birthday? Because Jess had decided no longer to be a part of the family? Or was it because Anne hadn't tried hard enough? If she'd given a shit—or if any of them had given a shit, for that matter—would Jess have stuck around?

"Tell Big Jim to find her," Eva said, as if channeling her dead husband would solve all their familial problems.

"Mom, you know Dad's dead," Anne said. "He's been dead for five years."

"What?" Eva said, genuinely surprised. With Eva, everything was a surprise. Over and over and over again. It was the Alzheimer's way, the heartbreaking, exhausting Alzheimer's way. "How did he die?"

Watching her mother's confusion and grief play out for the thousandth time was always painful. Anne never thought to play along, though, to attempt to engage her mother in whatever reality she was currently experiencing. Always a stickler for truth, Anne was unable—or perhaps, unwilling—to pretend her way through this unknown land.

Anne gently held her mother's delicate hand as she explained yet again, "Dad had a heart attack, Mom. Doc Peters said it was instant, that he didn't suffer. We had a beautiful funeral for him, and we buried him at Our Lady of Peace."

A fat tear rolled down Eva's face. She reached a hand up to stop it in its tracks, rolled the moisture between her thin fingers.

"Oh."

Eva had no more interest in the shake that sat melting before her. Condensation ran down the sides of the Styrofoam cup and dribbled onto the wheeled dinner tray. Eva touched a water droplet. Examined her finger. Touched another.

The uncomfortable silence expanded into a cavernous void, and Anne grew angry at the thought of her sisters and their lack of responsibility. She was tired of Catherine hiding behind her self-important Indiana University faculty position so she could avoid the realities of her disintegrating family. Catherine rarely showed up to visit Eva, and she was only an hour and a half away. And Jessica. Their little wild-child sister. Off to L.A. at eighteen to find something bigger and better than what Willton, Indiana could offer. Fine, Anne thought. That's perfectly great. But why give up your family? Why sever every remaining tie even if it was just a tenuous thread attached by blood rather than choice? Why try your hardest to pretend your family never existed, to wipe them from your life like bird shit on the windshield? So maybe they weren't the happiest, most well-adjusted group that ever existed. But they were family. Jessica didn't seem to understand or appreciate that minor detail. Selfish Jessica.

"Is she sleeping?"

Anne was startled from her parade of angry thoughts by her sister's voice. She stiffened, straightened her spine.

"Just now," Anne said. She tucked a blanket under her mother's chin and turned to greet her sister.

"Jesus, Catherine," Anne said, sucking in her breath. "Why the hell did you shave your head? Is that some kind of funky English professor statement?"

"No," Catherine replied calmly. "It's not a funky English professor statement. It's an 'I've got breast cancer' statement."

"What?" Anne's mind clouded with confusion.

"I have cancer," Catherine said. "Well, I *had* cancer. They cut it all out—along with most of my left boob and a couple of lymph nodes. I don't technically 'have' cancer anymore, but I'm still going through chemo."

"Why didn't you tell me?"

And that simple question summed up their entire lives.

Why didn't you tell me?

"Because it's not really about you," Catherine said. "Not everything is about you, Anne. Especially this. Why should I have told you? So you'd have a good story to tell at your Tot Moms meeting?"

Anne thought back to an incident in eighth grade when she'd been caught sneaking out her bedroom window to meet up with friends.

They'd planned to walk through Bradley Woods to the old Jones Family Cemetery. Catherine had known where Anne was going, had overheard her making secret plans with her girlfriends. But when Big Jim discovered Anne missing, Catherine had not revealed her sister's whereabouts.

"Where is she, Catherine?" Anne imagined her father's booming voice asking.

"I don't know, Dad," Catherine must have replied again and again.

He'd whipped them both with a belt—ten lashes for Anne for sneaking out, five for Catherine for the lie.

"Why didn't you just tell him?" Anne asked when it was all said and done. "You would have gotten off easy. Why didn't you just say where I was?"

"I don't know!" Catherine yelled back, slamming the bedroom door behind her.

She didn't know.

"That's not fair," Anne said. "That's so not fair. I think, perhaps, you should have told me because I'm family and because I could have been praying for you. The whole congregation could have been praying for you. Even Johnson UMC could have added you to their prayer list."

"Those devil-worshipping Methodists?" Catherine asked. "Do they even pray to the right God?"

Anne felt her cheeks burn red with heat and embarrassment, but opted not to say anything to her condescending sister out of respect for her physical well-being. It was, of course, the Christian thing to do.

"I didn't tell you, Anne, because I didn't want you to know. There was nothing you could have done for me. Your plate is full enough with Lila and Max, and this was my cross to bear."

"But you had surgery," Anne said. "Who was with you then?"

"The doctors and nurses," Catherine said. "And I do have a few friends, Anne. Michelle has been great."

"But what about your family? What about us?"

"Anne, Honey, it's done," Catherine said. "We can't go back and change it. My boob is history, gone forever. Time to move forward."

"It's just not right," Anne said, shaking her head. Because for Anne, there was always a Right and a Wrong. There was always a Black and a White. There was always a Good and a Bad. Fuck the middle road. Screw shades of gray. Anne was committed to an all-or-nothing kind of life—one that didn't allow for any variations or exceptions. Profanity, yes. Anne gave herself permission to abuse that singular vice. (After all, general cursing—without using God's name in vain— was a venial sin, not a mortal one. Those were the far less dangerous kind.) But everything else was either A or Z.

"Who are you?" a frail, but firm voice inquired from the bed. "And what happened to your hair?"

6 *jessica*

The Hoosier Hops liquor store was empty at 2:00 on a Friday afternoon. Jessica roamed the aisles aimlessly, looking for something to dull the ache in her chest. She couldn't quite put her finger on the pain, but she was fairly certain the root of it was loneliness. Life alone was hard. Jessica preferred it, though, to life surrounded by those who hardly noticed you existed. She'd decided it was infinitely harder to be discarded by others than simply to keep her distance. Her heart couldn't be broken if she never took it out of the box for anyone to admire. But she wished, sometimes, for a little more noise, for something to anticipate.

She plunked a bottle of cherry vodka on the counter and forced a smile.

"That it for you?" the androgynous clerk asked.

"Yes."

She fumbled in her purse for the right amount of ones, threw the change in a plastic tray on the counter. She put the brown-bagged vodka in her car and walked across the street to Walgreens.

For nearly twenty minutes, she stood staring at the rows of boxed hair color on Aisle 3. What did she feel like becoming today? A platinum blonde? A redhead? So many opportunities to become someone else. Same soul, different exterior.

Settling on red, Jessica walked to the candy aisle for gum and made her way to the cashier.

The pimply faced boy behind the register rang up a prescription, a box of Kotex, and a King Size Snickers bar for the young woman in front of Jessica. The woman's face glowed red with embarrassment at her array of purchases while the boy went about his job obliviously.

Jessica set the gum and hair dye on the counter. She'd been red before, but it had been at least a decade prior. Left to her own devices as a child, she'd experimented with make-up, hair dye, and ear piercings done with an ice cube and a needle. No one seemed to notice or care that she meandered through her childhood, chameleon-like, changing her exterior on a whim.

By the time she'd reached double-digits, her sisters had already left for college, for life. And Big Jim and Eva had always been inaccessible. Looking back, Jessica realized that her mother couldn't afford to give Jess any of her love and attention when she was trying so diligently to keep her marriage afloat. And in all honesty, Big Jim never really cared about anyone but himself. Jessica easily recalled the lonely ache of her childhood. As a freshman in high school, she'd claimed she made the volleyball team, just so she wouldn't have to come home after school and face the emptiness.

"Congratulations, honey," Eva had said distractedly at the announcement. "We'll have to come see you play."

"All of our games are away," Jessica had lied. And no further questions were asked.

Throughout the entire season, she'd hung out at the mall instead, watching the happy couples, the laughing families purchase baubles and trinkets and clothes in which to adorn themselves and their lives. It had all seemed so pointless to her then. Still did. After countless afternoons in the food court chewing on greasy French fries and eavesdropping on others' conversations, she still didn't understand the human condition.

The Walgreens cashier scanned Jessica's items.

"That'll be $14.96."

Jessica handed him her debit card.

As the cashier handed her bag to her, she heard a male voice say, "Jessica? Jessica Mathers?"

She wasn't ready to be recognized in her home state. She'd done her best to remain anonymous, to stay under the radar. She turned slowly to see who was calling her name and felt her breath quicken when she realized who it was.

"Dale?" she asked. She contemplated running for a brief and fleeting moment, but couldn't coax her feet into movement.

Her brother-in-law was holding a super sized package of Pampers and a gallon of skim milk. He'd put on a few pounds since she'd last seen him thirteen years before, but he was still handsome, his face still kind.

"It *is* you," he said. "It's been so long, I wasn't sure. But you look so much like Anne—your face, I mean. Obviously, your hair is different." He stopped rambling, took a breath. "What are you doing here?"

They fumbled in their awkwardness, neither quite knowing what to say or do.

"I moved back," Jessica said, not revealing how much time had actually passed since her exodus from California.

"You did?" Dale asked. "Does Anne know? Catherine? Does anyone know?"

"Not yet," Jessica said evasively.

She stared at the diapers in Dale's hands. Were those for his child? For her niece or nephew?

"No one knows you're here?" Dale asked incredulously.

"No," Jessica said. "Well, you know now."

"Jessica, that's kind of crazy," he smiled. "I mean, I'm sure your sisters would love to see you."

Jessica wasn't so sure.

"Would you like to join us for dinner?" Dale asked. He wasn't sure what prompted him to invite his wayward sister-in-law over for dinner, but once he'd said it, there was no turning back.

Jessica laughed nervously.

"No. No, thank you," she said, inching toward the door. "I don't think that would be a good idea."

"Sure it would," Dale said. "You can meet our kids—we have a boy and a girl—catch up with Anne. She could use a little diversion," he said as an afterthought, his tone tinged with sadness.

Jessica noticed the heaviness in Dale's final sentence. His voice was flat and without affect, a sound without a soul. She toyed with the notion that her sister had managed to suck the life out of her husband, that in thirteen years, she had killed his spirit. Anne had always been good at that. In an attempt to fill herself up, Anne used others to feed her insatiable need. Throughout Anne's high school years, Jessica distinctly remembered a parade of different friends marching through her life.

"Jess, this is Judy. We're going to listen to music, so leave us alone."

"Mom, I'm going over to Leslie's house. I don't know when I'll be back."

"Shut up, Catherine! Molly Jo is my best friend! You wouldn't understand."

Before any of the Mathers had an opportunity to know Anne's friends, she'd moved on to the next one. Friend du Jour, Catherine would remark. Jessica didn't know what that meant at the time, but it always sent Anne into a rage.

"You *wish* you had so many friends!" Anne would scream.

"You wish you had one *true* friend," Catherine would calmly counter.

"Thank you, Dale," Jessica said, gripping the Walgreens bag tightly. "But I already have plans tonight." It was a lie, of course, but one that prevented any further inquiry.

"Okay," he said. He hesitated, looking confused and unsure of what to say next. "Can I at least get your number?"

Dale readied his phone to type in Jessica's number, and Jessica rattled it off without really thinking about the possible ramifications.

"Thanks," he said. "It was good to see you, Jessica. Welcome home." He looked at her strangely, still apparently confused by the surprise of their encounter, and headed for the automatic doors.

Jessica watched the door close behind him. She clutched the bag in her hands with a death grip. And she cried when he turned the corner. She hid her red eyes behind dark sunglasses as she walked to her ratty 1983 Saturn, and she cried all the way back to her studio apartment—which was really just a fancy name for a dirty room above her landlord's kitchen. She cried as she made Kraft Macaroni and Cheese from a box, and she cried as she spooned thick, calorie-dense bites into her mouth.

Anne. Catherine. Big Jim. Eva. Her family.

Once, they were all she ever wanted. Just a moment of recognition, a hint of interest in her young life. But instead, she got babysitters. And short visits from her sisters when they returned home from their college glory days for vacations. And a secret about her father's infidelity that was far too heavy a burden for a child to bear. And an angst-filled relationship with her broken mother, the one she could not fix, the one who most needed fixing.

Her childhood consisted of a series of stories she'd invented to make her own life look more appealing, to stave off the loneliness that always threatened to pull her under. Before she hurtled headfirst into her disconnected teenage years, Jessica loved to crawl off into the woods behind her house with a book, a blanket, and a flashlight. She'd read for hours, lost in the make-believe that separated her own reality from the fantasies she preferred. She'd devour her books into the night, until the flicker of the flashlight indicated a low battery, until the mosquitoes threatened to devour her whole, or until one of her parents actually noticed that she hadn't come in for dinner.

"Jessica!" her father's gruff voice would reverberate through the darkness. "Jessica! Time for bed."

Still dressed in his high-powered C-Suite suit and tie, he held a Scotch in one hand and a cigarette in the other. When she brushed by him on her way inside, shaking the twigs from her hair, she inhaled the scent of his aftershave. She wanted to linger there in the smell, wanted to breathe in the nicotine, but she knew she wasn't invited to share that space with him. So she made her way to her beautifully decorated bedroom, glanced briefly at the shadow of her mother on the living room couch in front of the TV, and tucked herself into the soft and welcome escape of her canopy bed. Later, she would tiptoe to the kitchen for some peanut butter and jelly crackers to combat the growling in her stomach.

It was five years ago that Jessica read her father's obituary in the *Indianapolis Star*. One short year after she'd moved back to Indiana, she'd seen his handsome face in the smeary ink of the Sunday paper. The obituary was a generous tribute to a powerful and philanthropic businessman. She read about her mother, her sisters, herself. *Daughter, Jessica, who resides in California.* But by then, she was already back in Indiana, and California seemed like a faraway dream. The obituary didn't mention Big Jim's philandering, didn't highlight his multiple affairs and the slow, steady demise of his family, didn't list the names of the women he'd screwed in her mother's bed. Jessica cried when she'd read about her father's passing. Although she knew he'd never really been and would never be a father to her, no longer having him part of this world was so final. She'd cried more for herself than for him. She supposed that was the way grieving worked for most, really. The ones left behind still had to carry the detritus of the ones who were granted freedom and absolution from the universe. She'd cried until her eyes were raw and swollen, and then she'd wiped her tears, blown her nose, and gotten back onstage.

Jessica wasn't entirely surprised that she'd finally been found. She'd moved back to Indiana six years ago fully understanding the high probability of someone discovering her. As the months in her home state turned into years, however, she'd convinced herself that she'd once again perfected the art of hiding. But to be found by Dale? Her brother-in-law? At a random Walgreens? That was a reunion she was most definitely not expecting.

Dale and Jessica barely knew each other. Jess, of course, was at the wedding that took place thirteen years prior, but she was only fourteen then. And at fourteen, Jessica was all about Jessica. The fact that she had to wear a stupid yellow junior bridesmaid gown made her want to vomit. In fact, when the wedding was over, she'd cut the dress into shreds, refashioning the material into hippie-style headbands and fabric bracelets. She wasn't old enough to attend the bachelorette party, and she wasn't allowed to stay late after the rehearsal dinner. She was expected to show up for fittings, chat with Anne's boring friends, and stay as far in the background as possible. But that part had been easy for Jess.

The background was what she knew best.

7 *anne*

What was most interesting about having her older sister stay with her, Anne decided, was that for a college professor with numerous degrees, publications, and academic accolades, Catherine was so completely clueless about life. She didn't help with dinner, wouldn't know what a garlic press was if it was up her ass, and she conveniently disappeared whenever Max needed a diaper change. Catherine slept a great deal. Although Anne assumed that was probably due to the chemo, it still managed to piss her off.

And just to add fuel to the fire, Dale came home late for dinner. Again.

"Sorry, babe," he offered as he put the fresh gallon of milk in the refrigerator, kissed Anne on the cheek, and tossed baby Max up into the air.

"He just ate," Anne said. "You're going to make him throw up."

"He's fine," Dale replied. "Aren't you, Big Guy? Aren't you, Big Guy?" And over and over, Dale tossed his son until Max did, indeed, barf down the front of Dale's shirt.

Anne did not say, "I told you so." Whether or not she contemplated saying it—whether or not she bit her tongue (hard) in order to avoid saying it—was a moot point.

"Is that Catherine's car in the driveway?" Dale asked, mopping up baby vomit with a kitchen rag.

"Yes. I asked her to come after Mom broke the night nurse's glasses.

We need to talk about what comes next. Mom's getting worse. I can't keep doing this by myself." She grabbed the dish rag from Dale's hands. "And would you please not clean up vomit with the same washcloth I use on our dishes?"

"So what do you want Catherine to do for you?" Dale asked, ignoring Anne's admonition. She rarely spoke anymore without chastising him in some way. It was as if her mind couldn't complete a thought until she'd corrected some fault of his.

"Well, I want her to help. With something. Anything."

"Maybe you should be a bit more specific."

"I'm so overwhelmed, Dale, I don't even know what kind of help to ask for," Anne said. "Oh, and by the way, she has breast cancer."

"What? Your mom has breast cancer?"

"No, dumb ass," Anne said. Early in their marriage, she wouldn't have been able to fathom calling her husband something as disrespectful as "dumb ass." Now it was just part of their everyday vernacular. So overused, in fact, that it didn't really affect either of them anymore. Dale never resorted to such cruel name-calling, but for Anne, it had become second nature. Just one additional way to spit out all her repressed anger and frustration. "Catherine has cancer."

Anne remembered saying her sister's name in a much different way, an affectionate way, decades ago. She thought back to the family vacations they used to take with the McPhersons. Big Jim, Eva, Ellen, and Dave would line their beach chairs up side-by-side, slowly sipping Vodka mixers, half-watching the kids play in the Florida surf. Catherine and Joe would dive into the waves, would swim dangerously out to reach the next sand bar. Anne and Lucas built sandcastles on the shore while they nervously watched their older siblings grow smaller and smaller against the blue landscape.

"Catherine," Anne would call in her tiny voice, "come back!" But her words were always swallowed in the swell of the sea and in the loud, half-drunken laughter of the adults in the sand behind them. Somehow, Catherine and Joe always made it back to shore safely. They were never eaten by sharks or pulled under by riptides.

"It scares me when you swim out in the ocean too far," Anne admitted to her sister as they settled into their rented beds. The smell of aloe was fresh and strong, and Anne's pink nose was tender to the touch.

"I'm a good swimmer, Annie," Catherine had assured her. "And Joe's always with me. He won't let anything happen to me."

But Anne knew that bad things did happen and that no one could really prevent them. She heard her Mom and Dad arguing in the late night hours. She saw the amount of Scotch her father consumed. She knew her Mom didn't just "fall asleep on the couch," but that she'd instead made a conscious decision to sleep as far away from Big Jim as she could. She understood that most mothers didn't spend hours alone, locked in the silence and escape of their private bedrooms, while their children were left to fend for themselves.

"Catherine has cancer?" Dale asked. "Really?"

"You'll believe me when you see her."

As if on queue, Catherine came sauntering down the stairs with a pillow crease on her left cheek.

"Hi Dale," she said, hugging him gently.

"Catherine," Dale said, "how are you?"

"Well, I'm bald and half-titless, but other than that, I'm great."

"Do you have to be so crass?" Anne asked as she wrinkled her nose in disgust. "Titless? In front of Max? Really?"

The baby giggled from his spot on the kitchen floor where he was busy gagging himself with a wooden spoon.

Lila ran in through the back screen door screaming like a banshee. She'd been sitting on her bike—the new one with training wheels—on the back concrete patio, attempting to balance, but afraid to actually work the pedals.

"Mooooommmmmmmmaaaaa!" she wailed. "I fell off my biiiiiiiiiiiike!"

"Oh, Sweetie, let me see," Anne cooed as she scooped up her daughter.

"Right heeeeeeerrrrre!" Lila continued to scream as she pointed to her knee. A single drop of blood was squeezing its way into the sight line of the three hovering adults.

"Looks like you're probably going to live," Anne said. "Let's get a Band-Aid and fix that right up."

"I want Daaaaaaadddddyyyyyy!" Lila screamed as she squirmed her way out of Anne's arms. Max stared wide-eyed and slack-jawed at the scene surrounding him.

"Come here, Pumpkin," Dale invited as he opened his arms. "Let Daddy fix you all up."

"Lila," Anne finally snapped, "stop your wailing! I don't want to hear you scream like that unless something is broken!"

"But Mooooommmmmmyyyyyy," Lila screamed, "something *is* broken! My knee is broken!"

"It's not broken. It's cut," Anne said. "Let Daddy put a Band-Aid on it, and it will be good as new."

Lila's wails settled into sniffles as Dale tended to his daughter's knee.

"Why were you so late tonight?" Anne asked, the thought of her own philandering father never far from her mind. Snapshots of Big Jim flashed through her head—his hand a little too far down Ellen's back, his laughter at another woman's joke a little too loud. Big. Booming. Lecherous. Her father had been all of these things. And in the background stood Eva, watching him out of the corner of her eye, pasting a smile on her face, and pouring herself another martini. Anne knew it wasn't fair to suspect Dale of cheating, to almost expect it of him. He'd never given her any reason to think he was unfaithful. In fact, if pressed, Anne would have to admit that Dale was a good husband. He was responsible, hard-working, and gentle with her continuous mood swings. In comparison to all the other men she knew, he was beyond kind and attentive. He was everything she wished her father would have been. But Anne, much like Pavlov's dog, was conditioned to believe the worst from the men in her life.

"Just work, honey," Dale said. "And I picked up some diapers and milk at the store. How was your mom today?"

"Well, she refused to eat anything but a chocolate shake, she asked about Jessica again, she cried about Dad dying, and she didn't know who Catherine was."

"Really, Anne, you can't blame her for not recognizing me," Catherine said, trying to lighten the mood. "Sometimes when I look in the mirror, I don't even recognize myself. More than once, I've walked by a store window and shocked myself with my own reflection. It takes some getting used to."

"Your hair doesn't matter, Catherine," Anne said. "She's just losing it. Every day, it's a little bit worse than before. Every day, she's a little more confused, and a little farther gone." Anne felt the need to explain the gritty details of their mother's demise to her older sister. *This is harder for me than it is for you*, she wanted Catherine to understand. I'm here. I'm sitting in it. I live this every single day while you hide behind your grading and your students and your tall vanilla lattés from the bookstore café.

"That's the way Alzheimer's works, Annie," Catherine said.

Anne bristled at Catherine's know-it-all nonchalance. "I know, Catherine. I get that. Don't you think I've researched all of this ad nauseam? I'm the one who's here, remember? But she's our mother. She's my mom. And I'm not ready for this. I don't know what to do with this." Anne held her hands out awkwardly as if returning a gift that she didn't really want.

Catherine took Anne's shaking hands in her own. "Ready or not, Annie, it's here. We're losing her a little every day. We can't stop it, we can't reverse it, we can't change course. We're just here for the ride. We need to love her and accept her, no matter who she becomes in the following days or months or years. There are no returns or exchanges here. She's our mom."

Anne was simultaneously comforted and irritated by Catherine's soliloquy. It was good to hear someone else's words describe their mother, was reassuring to know that what was happening was real and palpable to others as well. But the shopping metaphor? Jesus. Sometimes Catherine's stupid analogies drove Anne right over the edge. For a career academic, Catherine didn't always sound very smart.

"Trust me, Catherine, I know," Anne said. "I see her every single day of my life. Hell, Lila and Max see her more than you do, and Lila is deathly afraid of the patient in Room 145. I have to practically drag her down the hallway to get her to see her Nana."

"What's wrong with the patient in Room 145?" Catherine asked. Avoid the accusations, run interference with questions that don't really matter. Anne watched Catherine play the Mathers family game.

"She yells for her daughter all day long. 'Ruuuuuuth! Ruuuuuuth! Where are you, Ruuuuuuth?' But no one ever comes to see her. It's pathetic, really. But that's not the point. The point is that you need to come see Mom more often."

Catherine smiled half-heartedly and nodded her head in agreement. Smile and nod, smile and nod.

"Anne," Catherine said pensively, "don't you feel like we lost Mom a long time ago?"

Anne glanced sideways at her sister, aware of what Catherine was attempting to say, but acknowledging that neither of them had ever had the guts to talk about it before.

"What do you mean?" Anne asked.

"I mean, where was she when we were growing up? Did you ever feel like she was really around? She was there, but she wasn't really there. Even when I look back through our pictures, she looks far away. Did you ever feel—I don't know—connected to her? Like a daughter should be connected to a mother?"

Anne thought about Lila, knew exactly what Catherine was alluding to. Anne's love for her own daughter was something she couldn't quantify. It was bigger, more intense, more frightening, and more powerful than Anne had ever thought herself capable of feeling. Anne had never felt that kind of love from Eva. Never.

"I don't know, Catherine," she admitted. "I don't know whether Mom knew how to really love. She cooked and cleaned and poured drinks and chatted with the neighbors and attended a few PTA meetings. I think she thought that was enough."

"Did you think it was enough?" Catherine asked.

"I don't know. I wanted to think it was. It was all we had. I wanted it to be enough."

"Me, too," Catherine said. "Me, too. And poor Jessica. She got what was left of the leftovers. That wasn't much."

"Maybe," Anne said, unwilling to cut her wayward baby sister any slack, not noticing as Dale's spine stiffened at the mention of Jessica's name.

"Wherever Mom may be in her own mind right now," Catherine said, "I'm sure she's grateful to see you and Dale and her grandbabies. Thank you for being there for her."

8 *jessica*

B ecause she wasn't scheduled to work the following day, Jessica decided to stay home and obsess about her niece and nephew. Dale had only mentioned them in passing, had thrown that little tidbit out as a tease, but it was the one morsel of information Jessica couldn't dismiss, the one she could not push into an empty corner of her mind. A niece and a nephew. Anne's kids. Pieces of herself she'd never met, that she never even knew about. Shared flesh and blood.

Jessica sat in her tiny kitchen and imagined them first blue-eyed like their mom and their Aunt Catherine and then dark-eyed like their Aunt Jessica. They probably didn't even know they had a second aunt. Jessica drummed her fingers and ran through a litany of possible names. Was the girl named Alicia? She once overheard Anne talking about the name Alicia. Was the boy Jacob? Zachary? Jessica thought about Anne as a mother. It was difficult to imagine her as anything much more than detached, judgmental, and loud. She was probably a yeller and a spanker, Jessica thought. But she also considered the notion that Anne might look in on their sleeping faces at night and regret the critical words that could never be unsaid. Maybe—just maybe—she held those babies tightly and told them bedtime stories about fairies and dragons and happily-ever-afters. Perhaps Anne had found what was missing inside her once she became a mother.

Because ultimately, Jessica thought, we're all searching for something. An escape, an apology, forgiveness, reconciliation, absolution.

Forgive me, Father, for I have sinned.

Jessica had been on her knees begging forgiveness far too many times to remember. She had offered a lifetime of Hail Marys in exchange for the black mark that stained her own soul. Taking her clothes off in front of strangers was nothing compared to what she'd done in L.A. seven long years ago. Nothing compared to what had been done to her and what she'd chosen in response.

To distract herself from her California memories, she decided instead to search through her small bundle of pictures, the ones she'd taken from her childhood home so many years ago. High on her closet shelf, behind a pile of rumpled hoodies, she found them. They were wrapped in a delicate gold ribbon, an unexpected touch of grace and sentimentalism that was not normally Jessica's style. But the pictures were all she had of her family, of her roots. Here was a shot of Big Jim and Eva on their wedding day. Big Jim was handsome and self-assured in his jet black tux. Eva was elegant, graceful, angelic in her white satin gown. They looked happy, content, young, and blissfully unaware. Next was a close-up of Eva holding a smiling baby Anne while Catherine toddled in the background. Eva looked a bit wearier in this one, a bit older, and more than a bit sadder. Is this when it began? Jessica wondered. Could this have been the precise moment when it all started unraveling? Was Eva's emotional undoing behind those eyes, just out of reach, waiting to make its appearance and alter their family's existence forever? She turned her attention to a family portrait on the beach. Catherine was probably eight or nine; Anne, three years younger. Their youthful faces were sun-kissed and freckled. Big Jim stood to the right of Catherine, Eva stood on Anne's left side as an unknown passerby snapped the seemingly perfect family shot. Jim and the girls were smiling at the camera, but Eva's focus was elsewhere. She looked wistfully at something beyond the camera lens' reach, something no one else could see. Jessica had only one picture of herself. She was sitting on her pink gingham canopy bed in the midst of what seemed a million stuffed animals. Still a pig-tailed toddler, she grinned broadly at the photographer. She'd found out years later that her babysitter, Daisy, had taken the photo. Daisy was the only person for whom Jessica would smile willingly.

"Jessica! Jessica!"

A startling knock and a gruff voice pulled her from the tangle of her memories.

"Jesus, Harvey! You scared the shit out of me," she said, hands trembling, as she opened the door for her landlord. And there stood greasy Harvey Menker in his sweat-stained undershirt and his dirty blue jeans.

"Rent's due," he said as he simultaneously sucked some leftover food through his front teeth and scratched his old-man balls.

"Here," Jessica said as she dug through her purse for a hefty wad of ones and a few twenties. She counted out exactly what she owed him and reluctantly handed it over.

"Wish I could see where that's been," Harvey said, baring his gray teeth.

"Fat chance," Jessica replied.

"Maybe I'll just become an honest, paying customer," Harvey said. "Then you'd have to show me."

"Maybe I'll become a nun," Jessica said. "Then I won't have to show anyone but God." She shut the door in his face. "Goodbye, Harvey."

She wasn't bothered by dirty old men and their endless litany of sexual remarks. She'd grown used to it over the years and had learned how to separate herself from their animal instincts. What really bothered her was that every one of those men was once someone's child. She imagined Harvey as a little boy burning worms with a magnifying glass and using stray cats as BB gun targets. Then she saw him standing in the background waiting to be the last one chosen for a pick-up game of backyard baseball, his little-boy heart breaking and his pride crushed as the other boys rolled their eyes at the prospect of having to choose him as a teammate. Day by day, that broken little-boy heart hardened and solidified into a grown man's heart, one that had been rendered incapable of compassion and civility. *We're all such products of our past,* Jessica thought. *We're all so stuck in our stories, in what we've been conditioned to believe about ourselves.*

Jessica knew that she was more than her story.

She just didn't know how to tell it any differently.

9 *dale*

Dale was fixated on his run-in with Jessica. He couldn't stop thinking about her, couldn't stop contemplating what his next step should be. Or if he should step at all.

As a young boy, what Dale wanted most was to be a big brother. Hunting crawfish in the creek without a partner was lonely business. And baseballs didn't throw themselves. But Dale's parents hadn't obliged. What they'd chosen to give him, instead, was a broken home. Before his sixth birthday, they'd divorced, a legacy of angry words left in their marital wake. Dale lived with his mom who had never chosen to remarry. He would have taken a step-brother just as easily as a blood brother, but siblings were not destined for him. It was unfathomable to him then—always had been—that the Mathers sisters chose lives of isolation instead of connection. Sure, growing up with Big Jim and Eva might not have been easy, but why the girls didn't turn to instead of away from each other remained a mystery. When he would discuss it with Anne, she'd brush him off, say he didn't understand. And she was right—he didn't.

This new family twist made him uncomfortable. He didn't want people to feel excluded, ever. It was not in his nature. And yet, he didn't want to invite Anne's anger if he intervened. Should he tell Anne that Jessica was back in town? Should he call Jessica first? Would she run again? Had she already?

"Dale!" Anne yelled from their upstairs bedroom, interrupting his thoughts, "Max needs to be changed! I've got Lila in the tub. Can you please take care of it?"

Dale grabbed a box of Pampers wipes and headed down his beige hallway to contend with a diaper full of shit.

He stopped outside the bathroom door to glance at his wife and daughter. Lila played happily in the bathtub while Anne sat next to it, staring at the pink and green striped walls. She turned to look at him, to look through him.

"What?"

"Nothing," Dale said. "I just wanted to look at my girls."

"Well, here we are," Anne said, turning back to the wall where a cartoon frog leapt over a mushroom.

"Hi, Daddy!" Lila called. "Watch this!"

His daughter plunged her face into the soapy water and came up laughing and sputtering.

"You're so brave, Lila," Dale said.

"I know!" Lila shrieked. "I love blowing bubbles!"

Their daughter splashed and played noisily as Dale looked at the empty shell of his tired wife. There she sat, overweight, dressed in a food stained t-shirt, farther and farther out of his reach. He loved her still, loved who she was and who she was capable of being in her elusive moments of happiness, but he worried that she was slipping through his fingers.

"Anne," Dale said quietly as Lila continued to play, "what's happening to us?"

"What's that supposed to mean?"

Dale could feel the air thicken with Anne's defensiveness. It almost always happened this way. When he felt strong enough to talk, a fight ensued. Most of the time, it was easier to continue on their silent paths, contributing to the running of the household, tending to the kids, sleeping as far away from each other as their bed would allow, holding their tongues and building barriers around their hearts.

"I mean…," he hesitated. "I mean… you just don't seem to be happy anymore."

"Life isn't all fun and games, Dale," she snapped. "It's a lot of work taking care of this house and these kids."

"What can I do to help you?" Dale asked.

"Make more money. Be home more often."

He smiled sadly at the impossibility. To make more money, he'd need to be gone more often. He knew Anne understood that. She was suggesting unreachable goals, deliberately setting him up to fail.

"What is it that would make you happy, Anne?" he asked. "Is it really more money? Because if that's it, I'll do it. I'm just afraid I could make a million dollars and you still wouldn't be happy. I'm worried that what makes you sad," he hesitated, "…is me. And I don't know how to fix that."

"Watch me, Mama!" Lila yelled, splashing water onto the fuzzy throw rug and into Anne's lap.

Dale turned away and moved on to a now-wailing Max's room, thoughts of Jessica clouding his mind.

At promptly 9:00 the next morning, after Anne and the kids had hurriedly left for preschool and Tot Moms, Dale jumped into his Nissan Altima and began driving to his scheduled appointments. A 9:30, a 10:30, a 1:00, and a 2:30. Big day ahead of him, lots of software to sell. He had to make quota this month. They needed the money, and his boss was less than pleased with last month's performance.

"I need you to step it up a notch," Mr. Jay had said. "I used to be able to rely on you for 110% of quota every month. Now you're barely scratching by. What can I do to help?"

Fix my marriage, Dale thought. Figure out my wife. Dale felt the slow burn of busy days, of a life unfulfilled.

"Nothing, really," Dale said. "I'll make sure I'm where I need to be. Thanks, Mr. Jay."

At 9:10, Dale cancelled his first appointment and pulled into a Waffle House parking lot. He sat for a while, staring at the number on his phone. Jessica's number. Twice, his finger hovered over the "Call" button. Twice, he stopped. On the third attempt, skin touched phone, and he was connected. His stomach lurched and tumbled. He had not thought about what to say.

"Hello?" the female voice on the other end answered, the lilt more unknown than familiar. Jessica had grown from teenager to woman in the time she'd been gone. She was a stranger to him, to his wife, to everyone he loved. But she should be known, he thought. The little girl that was never taken care of needed to be tended.

"Jessica?" he said tentatively. "It's Dale."

The silence on the other end was deafening.

"Your brother-in-law, Dale," he said stupidly.

"I know who you are," she said.

"Of course. Yeah. I just… I thought I'd call. Do you have a minute?"

"What do you want, Dale?" she asked. It was neither warm nor dismissive, just a succinct and pointed question.

"What do I want? I don't want anything. Just to talk to you. Find out what's been happening in your life. That's all."

"That's all? Really? Because if this is some kind of weird 'seduce the little sister' thing, I'm not interested."

"What? Are you…? Jesus, Jessica! Are you kidding me? That's not at all what this is about! You're my sister-in-law. You're here. No one knows about it but me. I guess I feel responsible for you in some way."

"I'm perfectly capable of taking care of myself," Jessica said.

"I never said you weren't," Dale said, flustered by his inability to guide the conversation into a positive place. "I just wanted to reach out to you, to let you know that you still have family that cares about you."

"Cares about me? Ha! That's a good one, Dale! I haven't talked to my family for years. How in the world does that constitute care?"

"I don't know, Jessica," Dale answered honestly, ashamed that he played a silent part in the abandonment of his wife's sister. "I don't know. I'm just sorry that it happened this way. I am. I want to open that door if you'll let me."

"I don't know if that's a good idea," Jessica said. "I don't know if I'm ready for that."

"I hope you'll think about it," Dale said. "I really do, Jessica. You can call me any time. I won't tell your sisters until you're ready."

"What about my mom?" Jessica asked. "Will you tell her?"

Dale's voice softened. "It won't matter if I do," he said. He paused, the weight of the information he was about to share with his sister-in-law heavy and burdensome. "She has Alzheimer's, Jessica. She's in a nursing home. She asks about you all the time, but she doesn't really understand. Some part of her hasn't forgotten, though."

Dale thought he heard Jessica's breath catch.

"Where is she?"

"Regal Manor."

"Thank you for telling me," she said politely.

"You're welcome. I'm here if you need me."

"Thank you, Dale. Goodbye."

And she was gone.

10 *catherine*

Often times, the intensity of the pain made Catherine want to crawl into a hole and stay there until chemotherapy was nothing more than a memory. Her colleagues asked how she was feeling, and she wanted to scream.

"I feel like SHIT!" she wanted to yell. "I feel like my bones have been crushed and stomped on and glued back together by a five-year-old in a kindergarten art class! I feel like I want to DIE!"

But instead, she wore a brave smile while the very marrow in her bones ached.

"I'm hanging in there," she'd say. And she'd return her attention to the piles of papers waiting to be graded. What else, really, was there to convey? They didn't understand, didn't truly want to know. The concern in their eyes would instantly turn to horror if she told them she'd rather rip her own eyeballs out of their sockets than sit in that cold infusion room for one more second. "Only a few more months."

And so, the inquiring minds would be happy with her progress and satisfied with her Pollyanna report. They would return to their own windowless offices and their own hand-me-down desks, and they would mark their piles of papers with red-inked corrections and encouragements.

Fucking cancer.

As Max pulled himself into her lap, Catherine experienced a wave of nausea and fatigue that threatened to pull her under. He handed her a slobber-stained board book, the corners thickened and damp, and it took every ounce of strength Catherine possessed to read to him about the plucky little engine who persisted with *I think I can. I think I can.* Irony at its best. Just shy of three days into her stay at Anne's, and already she was beyond exhausted. Catherine loved her niece and nephew fiercely, but they required so much effort.

When she finished reading the final page of Max's book, she kissed the top of his sweet-smelling head and whispered, "It's time for Aunt Cat to go home now, Sweet Pea."

And because he was as compliant and good-natured as his sister was sassy and hot-headed, he climbed obediently from her lap and toddled to his waiting mother.

"Do you really have to go back already?" Anne asked. "It seems like you just got here. And we really didn't come up with a game plan for Mom."

Catherine wasn't sure what kind of "game plan" Anne intended to concoct, but she knew for certain that it wasn't necessary. Life would continue with or without a plan. Anne would yell at her children and argue with her husband. Catherine would teach class, comment on half-assed compositions, and endure chemotherapy. Eva would lose what little remained of her memory, slowly, surely. Catherine would watch her mother's demise from afar, unable to do anything to stop the journey that had long ago been set into motion. The plaques in Eva's brain would grow, and her cognitive abilities would lessen. Eventually, she'd forget how to eat, how to breathe, how to live.

Unlike most of her contemporaries, Catherine would say goodbye to her mother three times within a single lifetime. Eventually, Alzheimer's would claim Eva's body, but they'd really already lost her to the disease that had stolen the connections—albeit tenuous at best—to the lives of her children. And the goodbye all three girls would struggle with indefinitely? The long, painful goodbye that comes from letting go of the mother they all thought they wanted, the one they all thought they'd deserved. The one who might have looked *at* them instead of *through* them. The one who showed more than just a passing interest in them as human beings, as daughters.

"I have a class to teach tomorrow, Annie, and Mom's where she needs to be."

"What's that supposed to mean?" Anne asked.

"It's not supposed to 'mean' anything," Catherine said. "She has Alzheimer's. She's going to get worse. Regal Manor is doing everything they can for her. You're doing everything you can for her. It's not going to get easier, and we can't fix it."

"Well, you certainly can't fix it if you keep running away from it."

"Anne, I don't want to fight about this. I love you. And I appreciate what you're doing for Mom. But I'm not going to let you make me feel guilty for having a life and a career. Cut yourself some slack. Live your life, too, Anne. Mom would want it that way."

Anne's anger gave way to a sudden sadness. "It just sucks, Cat!" she cried. "In every possible way, it sucks. And you. You fucking have cancer. Jesus. When did things go so wrong?"

"It's what we call life, Annie," Catherine said, her eyelids suddenly very heavy. "We can't do anything but move forward, right? Let's not get stuck."

"How can you be so optimistic when you don't even have hair anymore?" Anne asked. It was a strange and awkward question, and Catherine had to bite her tongue to keep from laughing.

"Hair is overrated, Annie," Catherine said. "I'm still alive. And I intend to stay that way. It will grow back."

Catherine remembered how it felt to have Anne crawl into her bed during a childhood thunderstorm, recalled the warmth of her little sister snuggling in beside her. Catherine would rub her fingers lightly over Anne's arm while she whispered sleepy "shhhh's" until fatigue overtook them both. As young sisters, they fumbled their way through familial love, not quite knowing how it should rightfully look or feel. More often than not, they turned away from each other rather than toward one another. And as they grew older, so did the distance between them.

When Big Jim died, five years ago, Catherine thought she would feel a great void in her life. But as she said her final goodbyes to her father, she realized the void had always been there. Big Jim's death didn't fix or exacerbate it. When he clutched his damaged heart and dropped to the floor, Catherine fully expected to feel his pain in her own chest. But she didn't. When she studied the face in his casket, she cried for what should have been. But she wasn't any emptier than before. He seemed somehow diminished lying in his outrageously expensive, silk-lined final resting place. In life, he had been foreboding, loud, big. In death, he was simply an empty, waxen shell of broken promises and unfulfilled potential.

And Eva. When Eva stood beside her husband's casket, Catherine was startled by the emptiness in her mother's eyes. Perhaps Catherine thought they'd all grow closer once Big Jim was gone, that Jessica would return, that they'd figure out how to be a family at long last, but when she looked at her grieving mother, she realized, instead, that what remained of Eva was now more unreachable than ever. Catherine would insist to anyone who would listen that Alzheimer's took Eva's hand the day Big Jim died. And Eva, without her husband, willingly grabbed hold and let it guide her.

Lila cried as Catherine threw her small overnight bag into her Volvo and kissed everyone goodbye.

"Don't leave, Cat!" Lila yelled. "Take me with you! Mommy yells too much!"

Catherine stifled a laugh.

"That is not fair, Lila!" Anne yelled, true to form.

"Is too!"

Then Lila's attention flipped back to her aunt. Her small hand reached out for Catherine's bald head, and Catherine bent over to let her touch it. Lila rubbed the smooth surface over and over, her tiny fingers tracing a circular path.

"Aunt Cat?" she asked innocently. Catherine could sense her young niece stalling for time. "Were there grocery stores when you were little, or did you have to hunt for your food?"

"Lila!" Anne gasped.

"Well, Lila Bear," Catherine said, standing up and marveling at how many syllables her niece was capable of inserting into the word *stores*, "there were grocery stores, but sometimes, we'd find wild animals roaming through them." She crouched down in imitation of a hunter. "We'd take our bows and arrows and shoot them right there on the spot! Bam!" Lila jumped. "Then we'd load them up in the car and cook them for dinner."

"Catherine!" Anne said.

"Goodbye, my loves!" Catherine called as she closed her car door. "See you soon!"

The moment she hit the open highway, the tension in her shoulders eased a bit, but the pain that seemed to touch every nerve ending in her body swelled to epic proportions. She popped some prescription-strength ibuprofen into her mouth, turned up the Billy Joel ballad on her Sirius station, and thought about nothing but her waiting bed.

When she arrived back at the Indiana University campus and opened her front door, she was greeted by the surprising smell of beef stew and the sound of Dave Matthews on her iPod player. Julie greeted her with a smile and a gentle hug, her young arms wrapped purposefully around Catherine's middle.

"How was your trip?"

Catherine struggled to hide her surprise as she pulled quickly from Julie's embrace. The skin on her arms prickled with an unfamiliar charge of electricity.

"It was fine."

"You look so tired," Julie said. "I made my mom's famous beef stew. I know it may be a little early in the season for stew, but it's just so damn good, I knew you wouldn't be able to resist. Let me finish up the dishes, and I'll get out of your way."

Catherine stood speechless. Who was this brazen young girl, breaching her personal space, cooking in her home, and chatting as if they were old friends? She'd wrapped her arms around Catherine's waist without warning or invitation. Catherine was taken aback and intrigued and generally perplexed by Julie's odd—and somehow welcome—behavior. Dante curled around Catherine's legs, winding his way in and out of the familiar landscape.

"He and I became fast friends," Julie said. She dried a cutting board, slipped it into its resting place beside the oven. Catherine watched, unable to process what was happening, her brain foggy in the way only chemotherapy could render it.

"Can you stay for dinner?" Catherine asked when she found her voice. "I'd love the company." And she really did want the company. Not just any company, but Julie's self-assured, easy presence. The fatigue she'd been battling during the drive home didn't seem quite so incapacitating in the light of Julie's sunshine.

"I'd love to," Julie said without hesitation. "May I pour you a glass of wine? Can you drink during chemo?"

"Within reason," Catherine said. "It hasn't slowed me down yet. And if the cancer doesn't kill me, I'd rather it be the wine." She laughed awkwardly at her own bad joke.

And so professor and student shared a bottle of red and a bowl of stew over engaging conversation and laughter.

"Have you read *Olive Kitteridge* yet?" Julie asked.

Catherine nodded.

"I love Olive so much," Julie said. "She's so blunt and flawed and altogether fascinating, don't you think? I want to be like her. She's a gravitational force, I think. Even as a secondary character, you just know she's *there.*"

"I think, maybe, you two might share some of those more compelling traits," Catherine said. "Except Olive is a big woman, and you certainly couldn't be described in those terms... physically at least. But I'd say personality-wise, you're pretty big. You definitely hold your space in the world."

Julie laughed. "My parents always used to say I was larger than life—a little more than they bargained for!"

"I'd have to agree with them," Catherine said.

And the conversation continued, compelling and engaging and more than enjoyable.

Catherine let the Cabernet warm her lips, the elusive taste of pepper lingering on her tongue. The spices in the beef stew were more intense, Julie's wit sharp in the night air. Catherine was present in a way she hadn't been for many months. She sank into the moment, chatting about Adele and the best local grocery stores. This was a space she'd forgotten how to inhabit. Typically, her days were filled with fear and angst and uncertainty, but during her evening with Julie, she forgot about all those things. Instead, she focused on the curve of Julie's lips as she spoke and the way Julie's hair fell over slender shoulders. Her senses heightened, she was hyper-aware of the smell of Julie's body lotion, the lingering scent of onion in the kitchen.

When the last drop of wine had been drunk, Catherine's fatigue had traveled from her body to her face. It was the side effect of alcohol and chemo, the numbing fatigue. Once it hit, she was powerless in its wake.

"Go to bed, Professor," Julie said. "I'll clean up and show myself out."

"Nonsense," Catherine said. "I'll help."

Catherine steadied herself to stand, and Julie gently placed her young hand on the hand that was just beginning to show the fine wrinkles of accumulated days.

"Please. Just let me do this."

Julie leaned over, brushed a gentle kiss across Catherine's forehead, and turned to the kitchen. Catherine knew she should be shocked at her student's show of affection, but she was too tired—or too intrigued— to protest. Affection was a complete unknown in the Mathers' home, but the ease in Julie's effort convinced Catherine that her student's was a family formed with love and intimacy and unabashed physicality. The warmth from Julie's lips spread to Catherine's cheeks. And if she was truly honest with herself, that kiss wasn't as shocking as it might have seemed. It was, instead, comforting. It was kindness wrapped in a beautiful, silver package and topped with a purple bow. It was an unexpected gift, the treasured one that sat on your mantel and made you smile every time you walked past.

With the last of her strength, Catherine conceded and headed toward her bedroom, her forehead warm and damp.

"Goodnight, Professor."

Those were the final words she heard as she rested her head on her pillow and faded off to oblivion.

11 *anne*

The numbers didn't add up. No matter how many times Anne added, subtracted, rearranged, and prayed about them, there were too many debits and not nearly enough deposits. Every month, it was the same story. With each passing day, their checking account balance dwindled. She'd learned the fine art of robbing Peter to pay Paul. Too often, Anne used their bank's overdraft protection service to make ends meet. Take $500 out of a non-existent balance for the low, low fee of just $35? What a bargain. The next deposit was coming in a mere fifteen days, after all. And she had to feed her kids.

Dale never looked at the checkbook, never logged into their online account to see what was happening with the money he made, always assumed he was providing what his family needed. So Anne had become creative with the bills. She didn't pay a utility until a disconnect was imminent. She called it the Red Bill Payment Plan—a little levity so she wouldn't be crushed under the weight of her reality. The panic didn't settle completely in until their lights were about to be turned off. And for the first time ever, she skipped the monthly mortgage payment. Lila's preschool bill was due, and there wasn't enough money to cover both. Because she had to look the preschool director in the eye every day, and because the mortgage company was just some faceless name across the country, Anne ripped up the mortgage bill and vowed to make it up next month. She counted on Dale's commission check to cover the deficit.

She wasn't sure where the money was going, except to the kids' seemingly endless expenses. Swim lessons, teachers' gifts, birthday parties, diapers, new shoes, dance classes, doctor bills. She didn't buy with reckless abandon, didn't have a closet full of designer clothes. Hell, she didn't even have clothes that fit her ever-expanding body anymore. Just paying the mortgage, the grocery bills, the school tuition, the occasional babysitters, that alone was enough continually to drain their checking account. College savings? An emergency fund? Vacation money? Those frivolities didn't even register on Anne's radar.

Just recently, though, creditors had begun calling. And they were unrelenting. A few late credit card payments, a couple of medical bills turned over to collections, and suddenly, Anne felt like a fugitive on the run. She avoided answering the unknown numbers, turned the ringer down during the day, stayed up in the middle of the night with numbers—always inadequate—racing through her brain.

Often times, she thought about her unused college degree and the extra $50,000 a year that could tip the scales in their favor if she went back to teaching. But when she factored in the childcare expenses, the necessary new wardrobe, the dinners out, the convenience costs that would inevitably come, the profit margin decreased substantially. And so she continued staying home with her kids. She was there to feed them three times a day, wash their clothes and their dirty necks and feet, drive them wherever they needed to be, tuck them into bed each and every night. She was there to fret over the constant lack of money, to eat every ounce of chocolate she could glean from their meager pantry. She wanted life to be good; she aspired to enjoy these moments with her young children. And yet the stress of her secrets weighed so heavily she often found herself gasping for air.

"Lila, Max, we're going on an adventure today," Anne said, tucking her mother's pearl ring into a small, drawstring bag and dropping it into her purse. "It's kind of a treasure hunt."

"Ooh, I love treasure!" Lila squealed. "Will there be pirates?"

"Maybe," Anne said, thinking about the characters they might soon encounter.

After a bit of online research, Anne had located a pawn shop close enough to her house to be somewhat convenient, but far enough away to render them anonymous. She'd agonized for days about her decision, but knew in her heart that Eva would rather she keep a roof over her children's heads than cling to some jewelry the Mathers girls' philandering father had once gifted.

It's come to this, Anne thought. Pawning my sick mother's jewelry for cash to make my mortgage payment.

Perhaps it was some kind of self-sabotage. Perhaps she was being tested like Job himself. Plagues of locust didn't hold a candle to the pressures of suburbia. In the land of plenty, it felt like they had so little. When she peeked into the lives of her neighbors, Lila's friends' parents, her church acquaintances, they seemed to have it all. From shiny new cars to oversized McMansions to all the right clothes and vacation destinations, they never seemed to want for anything. Professional landscaping that transformed the neighborhood into a movie set, leather sectionals too big to fit in her childhood living and dining rooms combined, TVs as centerpieces above fireplaces that turned on and off with the flick of a switch. Of course, it could all be a façade. After all, Anne herself put on a pretty good show. Lila's Baby Lulu dresses always had matching bows, didn't they?

Anne pulled into the pawn shop parking lot. The gaudy "We Buy Gold" sign flashing in the window tripped the start of a headache.

"Is this where the pirates is?" Lila asked with obvious disappointment.

"Where the pirates *are*," Anne said. "And yes, if there are any pirates, this is where we'll see them."

Anne unbuckled Max from his car seat as Lila crawled out the passenger's side and stood on the sidewalk.

"Stay where I can see you, Lila," Anne said. She didn't know much about pawn shop clientele and this particular section of town, but she wasn't willing to take any chances with her daughter.

A tinkling of bells greeted them as they opened the door and stepped into the dark and cluttered room. Anne was pleasantly surprised to see a bearded man smiling at them from behind the counter.

With his leathery skin and faded denim, he was just pirate-esque enough.

"Can I help ya?" he asked.

"I've got some jewelry to sell," Anne said tentatively. "Do you buy jewelry?"

"Depends. Let me see whatcha got."

Lila and Max pressed their noses against the glass display case as they gazed with rapt attention at the jewelry, watches, knives, and guns on display. This was the world they inhabited: Bowie knives beside diamond necklaces, inches away from three different Glocks.

Anne pulled the small bag from her purse and dumped three rings into the waiting pirate's hand. First was an emerald her father had brought back from a business trip to Hawaii. Anne doubted the trip had anything to do with business and was certain the ring had been a marital peace offering. Even so, it felt like a betrayal of sorts to pass the evidence into the hand of a stranger poised to calculate the market price of her father's infidelity. The emerald clinked against a black pearl offset with opals and landed next to the coup de grâce: a diamond anniversary band that had marked Big Jim and Eva's first twenty-five years together. This offering, perhaps, made Anne's skin crawl the most, but she comforted herself with the memory of her mother's words as she'd passed the ring on to her middle daughter.

"Your father bought this for me because he knew I was mad at him," Eva had explained. "We didn't have the money, so he cashed in part of his retirement account. For a ring! Can you imagine? I never wore it, always thought it was too flashy, and I was always mad at him for putting our future at risk so he could give me something glittery— something that made *him* feel better about our marriage. You take it, Annie," she'd said. "Catherine will get my engagement ring someday. You take this and make something good out of it."

And that's exactly what Anne was doing, right? Did it matter that she had put herself in this position with her own piss-poor planning and lackadaisical budgeting? Ultimately, she was doing what needed to be done. Her justifications made her hands shake a little bit less as she dropped the empty drawstring bag back into her purse.

The pawn shop pirate examined Anne's wares under his high-powered microscope, jotted some figures down on a dirty, dog-eared note pad, and belted his offer out to her anxious and waiting ears.

"Fifteen hundred for all three," he said.

Anne's heart sank. Fifteen hundred? The anniversary band alone had to be worth at least $5,000.

"That seems a bit low," Anne replied. "I know my father paid at least $5,000 for the diamond ring."

"This ain't retail, honey," the pirate said with a smile. "I can only give you what I know I can sell 'em for. Ain't nobody gonna walk in here and give me $5,000 for that ring."

Fifteen hundred wasn't quite enough to cover the late mortgage payment. Anne was hoping she'd be able to pay a couple of medical bills, too. But she was desperate—desperate to get the mortgage monkey off her back, desperate to make sure Dale never found out about her fiscal mismanagement.

"Okay," she sighed.

And when she walked out of the store with her children's hands in her own and fifteen $100 bills in her purse, she felt like she'd not only sold her ailing mother's rings, but a little piece of her soul as well.

12 *jessica*

The crowd was small when Jessica's Carousel Lounge shift ended. A couple of stumblers, a handful of business men chatting over beers. The fewer, the better. A small crowd meant less opportunity for men to follow her out to the parking lot. It wasn't that she couldn't handle herself. In fact, she was a formidable opponent, a small but mighty purveyor of caustic words and threats that weren't always empty. The men who were dumb enough to follow her to the parking lot were often blindsided with her fiery temper and her fierce sense of self-preservation.

But Jessica hadn't always been that way. When she was an eighteen-year-old fleeing the dull and dysfunctional confines of her Indiana home to pursue a Los Angeles adventure, she was carefree, invincible, and no longer bound by the unwritten rules of her childhood: stay quiet, stay invisible, stay out of the way. She had her entire life ahead of her, her disconnected family behind her. Anything was possible.

Anything.

Jessica waited tables with all the other young hopefuls on the Golden Coast. She made friends with the Beautiful People, the ones full of promise, not yet jaded, willing to do anything to follow the dreams of their youth. They partied as one day became the next, drinking themselves into oblivion, trying out the latest designer drugs with the tip money they'd earned. Jess made lots of friends, but always kept herself at arm's length from any real relationships. Breadth, not depth.

She'd lived by herself in a cramped studio apartment in a semi-seedy part of town. Her tips barely covered the rent, but it was her own place. Her respite, her refuge, her sanctuary. She was perfectly content eating Ramen noodles and watching *Friends* on her small color TV. Jessica was fascinated by other people's relationships and their willingness to put their hearts and souls so casually on the line. She loved waiting tables, listening to her customers interact, inventing the stories of their lives.

And then one evening after she'd cashed out her tickets and rolled napkins for the next day's business, she'd decided to forego an evening of TV and run a three-miler instead.

With the warm wind in her hair and Nelly on her MP3 player, Jessica watched the world stretch out before her. She'd just turned nineteen, was strong, fast. She had the power to be whatever she wanted, to do whatever she pleased. She'd left her childhood home abruptly and without any lengthy goodbyes, severing the ties that loosely bound her to her older sisters and her uninterested parents. At nineteen, her life was finally her own. With no past to speak of and a future without boundaries, she raced through the City of Angels.

And when she stepped back into her apartment—sweaty, spent, exhilarated—that fire was extinguished by a stringy-haired man with a knife, the one who stealthily caught the door with his foot and forced his way in behind her. The one she hadn't noticed as she fumbled with her key and adjusted the volume on her MP3 player.

For the following hour, she slipped outside herself and floated, untouchable, on the ceiling. She watched with detached curiosity as the scene unfolded beneath her and busied her mind with the creature comfort memories of her childhood, the taste of orange Jell-O, the way the grass smells after a hot summer rain, the sweet surprise of the gum in the center of a cherry Blow Pop.

The stranger held the dirty knife against her throat—perhaps a little too closely, she thought as small beads of blood appeared against the blade—while he instructed her to remove her running shorts.

"Don't scream. Don't fight. I will kill you if you do. No one will ever know, Jessica, will they?"

She was stunned into submission by the use of her name. Did she know this pale stranger who reeked of cigarettes and cheap beer? Had she waited on him before? Smoked weed with him at a party? Confusion clouded her mind as the girl on the floor lay still and motionless, not fighting, not screaming, not resisting. Ceiling-Jessica wanted to scream out in anger.

Fight back! she wanted to yell at the girl who looked so much like her reflection in the mirror. *Why aren't you screaming? Kick him! Run. Do something. Anything.* But the girl on the floor didn't make a sound. Her eyes were wide with terror, her body unresponsive.

"I've been watching you," he said as he fumbled with the zipper on his blue jeans. "I've been watching you for a while now. You're so beautiful, Jessica. Such a pretty girl."

As she looked down from the ceiling, Jessica noticed a tear rolling down her cheek. She didn't feel it, but she saw it mix with the salty sweat residue leftover from her run. It charted its own course as it dripped from her face to the carpet. There was the stain from the red wine she'd spilled last week. There was the spot where she'd dropped her entire bowl of Fruit Loops.

She glanced at her apartment, her safe haven, the place from which all her dreams were going to take flight. There were no framed pictures of her mom and dad, her sisters, her former life. She was grateful for this small blessing. No matter what she felt—or didn't feel—about her family, she wouldn't have wanted them to witness what was happening on her L.A. floor.

From the ceiling, she breathed in the remembered scent of her mother's burgundy lipstick, waxy and sweet. She tasted the hint of leftover tobacco in the minty gum squares at the bottom of her mother's purse, traced the veins of her father's hands—thick, ropy—with her mind.

Close your eyes, she would have whispered to her parents if they'd been observing from their black lacquered frames. *Don't watch*, she would have said as the stranger forced himself into her mouth, as she gagged in response.

Don't listen, she would have cautioned while he moaned.

She continued to watch as he spread her legs with careless indiscretion and tore her resistant flesh with his thrusts. She noticed the knife was always in his hand, always too close to her face, always shining in the glow of the exposed light bulbs. She also noticed how still she remained, how compliant, how quiet.

When he was finished, he whispered in her ear.

"Do you want to die tonight?"

It seemed a redundant question, because Jessica was fairly certain she already had.

She lay perfectly still as the residual stickiness wet her inner thighs. Was it blood? Semen? She couldn't be sure.

"I don't want you to die tonight, Jessica," he said as he traced the outline of her breasts with his knife. "But I could kill you if I wanted to."

From her eight-foot vantage point, Jessica noticed him getting harder as he talked about her possible demise. And still, she lay perfectly motionless. She thought about playing hide-and-seek with her babysitter as a young girl. She'd burrow herself into the back of her mother's walk-in closet and cover her eyes with her hands, believing, as young children do, that if she couldn't see Daisy, then Daisy couldn't see her. It was her giggling that always gave her away.

"I hear something," Daisy would tease. "Could it be Jessica? Where could she be?" And Jessica would close her eyes tightly, would press her fingers against her face to block out the light. Where was Daisy now? She would have been twenty-six? Twenty-seven? They might have been friends today, Jessica and Daisy.

I can't see you. I can't see you. She repeated it again and again in her mind to block out the sound of the stranger's heavy breaths.

He leaned over to whisper menacingly in her ear. "I won't kill you tonight. But remember that I always can."

With those two short sentences, Jessica's entire California existence changed. She knew then that his eyes would always be on her, his scent forever in her skin. She understood that wherever she went, he would not be far behind. Even when he wasn't sharing the same street with her, he would be around her, inside her, consuming her.

He turned her over and raped her from behind. She could feel the carpet burning her face. She continued to watch from the ceiling, saw the rhythmic bobbing of her ponytail.

"Don't call the police, Jessica," he said. "Don't call anyone. I know where you live. I know where you work. I'll be watching."

He grabbed a chunk of her ponytail and sliced it off with his blade.

"I'm keeping this as a little souvenir."

Her face was still in the carpet when she heard the door click shut. The scent of ground-in dirt and old dog hair assaulted her nostrils. She wasn't sure how long she remained there—possibly an entire lifetime—but when she finally got up, she journeyed directly out of her nightmare and into the shower.

Jessica—not usually a girl to do as she was told—heeded the stranger's warning and remained silent. She was silent as she waited her tables, silent as she stuffed her meager tips into her apron pockets, silent as she bought the pregnancy test at the pharmacy down the street two and a half months later. She was silent as she urinated on the thin white stick and silent as the line turned blue. She wept silently in her bathroom as she made her decision. She spoke only to schedule the procedure at the women's clinic, gave them just enough information to confirm her appointment. And again, when the doctor spread her legs to insert the suction that would remove the stranger's fetus from her body, she wept without a sound. She thought about the picketers outside the clinic, holding their hand-lettered signs and demanding her to reconsider, heard their monotone voices singing, "Jesus Loves the Little Children." She looked sideways as a nurse carried away the remains of what might have been, what never should have been.

"You'll have some cramping," the doctor said with purpose rather than kindness when the machine was turned off and quiet. "If you pass any large clots or bleed excessively in the next two weeks, I need to see you." He was cold. And his eyes never met hers as he removed his no-longer-sterile gloves and tossed them carelessly into the hazardous materials bin. Jessica wondered what was so hazardous about the contents of that plastic container. Perhaps it was human hands that should have been considered the contaminants, the ones that could inflict such pain and loss. Perhaps there should have been a hazardous materials bin for human beings. They were the dangerous ones. The gloves, after all, were harmless.

Jessica knew she wouldn't be back here in two weeks. And in the silence she'd recently grown accustomed to, she made arrangements to return to the home state she'd tried so desperately to escape.

Over the next ten days as her body first bled and then began to heal itself, she packed her meager belongings in boxes she'd salvaged from the restaurant next door. She worked with all the lights on, survived only because the harsh glare of the hot bulbs kept her awake and moving. When she slept, her dreams were crowded out by nightmares of epic proportions—dead bodies floating in the bay, shadows lurking in the bushes, babies whose mouths opened in anguished cries, but whose voices could not be heard.

Once—just once—she thought of calling Catherine. She wanted to talk to her big sister, wanted to find solace in the inherent familiarity of a blood relation. But she couldn't decide what to say, couldn't script an appropriate conversation in her ringing head.

Hello, Catherine, it's me. Jessica. I know we haven't talked in a long time. I know you never really knew me. And I know I didn't make much of an effort either. But here's the thing, Catherine. I was raped. And I'm scared. And I'm lonely. And I want a mother to talk to, but I never really had a mother to talk to. You didn't either, did you? So I thought maybe we could talk to each other. Oh, and there's this other thing, too. I had an abortion. I'm not sad that I did it—I couldn't have had that baby—but I just kinda want to talk about it. To someone. To you, I guess. You're my sister, after all.

But the conversation never gelled in her mind. It never took the shape she wanted or needed it to. The silence, instead, became her comfort zone. Her co-workers questioned with their eyes—and occasionally with their voices—but they couldn't break down the wall Jessica had built between herself and the rest of existence.

"This is just the next step in the disaster that is my life," she whispered to herself in bed at night. Shit begets shit, she thought. And although she had glimpsed the fleeting promise of a life that, perhaps, might have offered her a bit more, she knew she couldn't stay where she didn't belong.

Less than two weeks later, her Saturn loaded down with the detritus of a small, sad life, she started the drive back to the place where she'd begun.

13 *catherine*

She didn't mean for it to happen. With all her other relationships, there had been some kind of plan. Pursue, catch, release. She couldn't really pinpoint the exact moment that it happened, and looking back, it wasn't one of her most stellar career moves, but Catherine's relationship with Julie was so satisfying, so sensuous that she couldn't imagine her life existing in any other capacity.

It had begun, it seemed, almost without her rational knowledge. The day after their unexpected dinner together, Julie had returned to Catherine's house to check on her professor. (And she did, admittedly, think of Catherine as *her* professor now.) They'd ended up spending most of the day together, talking, laughing, sharing another bottle of red along with bits and pieces of themselves. Catherine learned about Julie's parents in Wisconsin, about growing up as an only child, the beloved progeny of two highly respected surgeons. Julie was a daughter of privilege, a recipient of all the best. And she'd left home—and straight into Catherine's life—to begin something new and different.

"My parents are wonderful," Julie explained. "I've never wanted for anything. New clothes, pretty homes, fabulous vacations—I had it all. But my parents also like to be in control. I needed to go away to school to find out if I was capable of controlling my own life for once."

"And what have you discovered?" Catherine asked.

"So far, so good."

They discussed God and atheism, cancer and natural healing,

politics and literature. They went on long, leisurely walks through wooded parks resplendent with fall color. They wrapped their heads and hands in woolen mittens and scarves as the Indiana temperatures began to plummet.

They first kissed under a canopy of red in Brown County State Park. They'd stopped walking to rest beside a small stream, to stick their bare feet into the icy cold surprise of the water. They'd splashed each other like children, screeching with delight at the moment, at the chill of the stream on their hands. Julie had wiped a droplet of water from Catherine's cheek, deliberately tracing the gentle curve of an early wrinkle with her young finger. Catherine, who had always loved the feel of a gentle touch on her face, held her breath in an attempt to stop time, to capture the here and now like a butterfly and pin the moment to the display board of her life so she would be able to revisit this feeling again and again. And then Julie had traced that finger along the line of Catherine's lower lip, slowly, slowly until Catherine stopped breathing altogether. When Julie leaned in to press her cool lips against Catherine's, there was never a second thought, never a moment of doubt. When she parted Catherine's lips with her soft, searching tongue, Catherine did not resist.

Julie had willingly dropped Catherine's Hemingway course, promising that she'd pick it up next semester with another professor, ensuring Catherine that her academic plate was already full enough, anyway.

And because Catherine's head was anywhere but in a place of logic and reason, she'd agreed. Catherine knew she was tempting fate, that the tenure she'd worked so hard to attain was at risk, that beginning a relationship with a student was irrational—foolhardy, even. Late at night, when she was alone and able to think clearly, she sometimes broke out in a cold sweat, knowing she was pursuing a path that could lead directly to her professional demise.

Yet, less than a week after their kiss in the park, Julie had a toothbrush in Catherine's bathroom and clothes hanging in the closet. When Catherine wasn't teaching and Julie wasn't learning, they were together.

Julie wasn't the first student with which Catherine had entertained a relationship. Julie wasn't even the youngest. Sweet, soulful Jack had been barely legal when he and Catherine started sleeping together. He was angst-ridden and poetic and fantastically hot in bed. And while it lasted, it was good. Catherine took care of Jack. She cooked for him, loaned him money when his checking account was empty. And he, in turn, thanked her graciously with a generous supply of orgasms. The story with David was strikingly similar. The conversation was enticing, the sex earth-shattering. Catherine was not unfamiliar with the lure of the hot, young student.

But Julie was her first girlfriend.

Catherine had always touted her liberal theory that lesbianism was the most natural trajectory. After all, she'd explain to those willing to listen, a child first falls in love with his or her mother. Whether born male or female, most every child—at least those lucky enough to be born into waiting arms—has experienced that primal mother-love. It only stands to reason, then, that a return to that primitive female love was a natural—even predictable—progression.

What did it mean, anyway? Lesbian. The word was nothing more than a label in a world full of meaningless labels. Gender was a social construct, the idea of femininity and masculinity as assigned by humans. So she loved a woman. So what? She loved her mother (as much as she was allowed), loved her sisters (in theory), loved Michelle and her other female friends, even loved herself every once in a while. What did it mean to add a physicality to that love? What she had with Julie couldn't be condensed into a labeled filing cabinet drawer that would hold the vast range of emotions she was experiencing.

Who am I? Catherine wondered. Cancer patient. Lesbian. Professor. Sister. Daughter. Labels, all of them. She could create whatever existence she wanted to create by redefining her classifications. Sage. Seductress. Compassionate caregiver. What did she want to be?

With Julie, she was more open, honest, and trusting than she'd ever been with anyone in her life. As young as Julie was, she possessed wisdom that exceeded her years, had the insight of one who has fearlessly examined her own heart and her own mind. Catherine wanted to be that brave. She admired it, longed for it. And the pull that Julie had was undeniable. From their first moment together, Catherine knew. There was a bond, not created by time or familiarity as so many are, but by something much bigger than both of them. It captivated Catherine, kept her awake in the wee hours of the morning with a core longing. It scared her a bit, this near-obsession. The intensity of their connection was vast and overwhelming and all-encompassing.

"Haven't you ever been hurt?" Catherine asked as they shared a bottle of Cabernet by the fire. "Aren't you afraid it's going to happen again?"

Julie absentmindedly stroked the back of Catherine's bald head. Her fingers were cool and soft.

"Of course I've been hurt," Julie said. "Brandon Gentry broke my heart in tenth grade. He swore he loved me, but he really just loved blow jobs. I loved him, though. I truly did." She paused. "Who hasn't been hurt? Pain, fear, disappointment—they're all part of life, right? But if you dwell on what *might* happen, how do you ever move forward?" She took another sip of wine. "I loved Brandon, and the truth is, he didn't love me back. Once I stopped crying and writing sappy love poems, I realized how important it was to learn that lesson—that love isn't always reciprocated. But that doesn't mean you shouldn't give it."

Catherine was lost in the glow of the fire, the touch of Julie's fingers.

"Why would you choose to spend your time worrying about what might go wrong? Then whatever moment you're in has already gone wrong."

Intellectually, Catherine understood that what Julie was saying had merit, but she wondered how you actually made the moment-by-moment conscious decision to remain present. As a child, Catherine always felt like she was hiding, scheming, trying to chart a clear and simple path for her younger sisters. She had created a life out of if/then. If I find Dad fucking his secretary, then I will close the door and take Anne to the park. If I find Mom crying in her room, then I will cook dinner for Dad and pretend Mom is taking a nap. If Anne falls off the swing, then I will bandage her knee so Mom won't be bothered. If Mom and Dad have another baby, then I will run away to college and never look back. Being present was impossible in the wake of so many plans.

"What are you thinking about?" Julie asked gently, pulling Catherine from her reverie.

"My family. My mom."

"Tell me about them," Julie said.

"That's a long, sordid story," Catherine laughed. "I'm not even sure I know how to tell it." But she told Julie her story as best she could. The parties, the fights, and the interminable, crushing silence that shadowed everything else.

"You deserved to have a good Mom and Dad," Julie said. "I'm sorry you didn't."

"Julie?" Catherine asked, shifting her weight and the conversation.

"Yes?"

"How long have you loved women? I mean, after Brandon, what happened next?"

Julie paused. She rarely answered a question right away. First, she thought about her words, then she framed them in her mind, and when she was sure her semantics conveyed precisely what she intended to communicate, she shared them. Catherine was the exact opposite. Quick to speak and without a filter, she was forever sticking her foot in her mouth.

"I've always been a lover," Julie said. "I'm not sure I consciously choose to love anyone based on gender, race, hair color, or fashion sense. I just love."

"Why me?" Catherine asked.

"It was most definitely not your sense of fashion," Julie said. She took Catherine's face in her hands and turned her head so they were eye to eye.

"You are beautiful, Catherine," she said. "You are kind. You are brilliant. You are strong and wounded and irreverent and funny and engaging. You are so much more than you know."

Catherine leaned into Julie, found the soft of her lips, weaved her fingers into the inky blackness of Julie's hair, and felt a warmth spread throughout her tired body and settle comfortably in the bottom of her stomach. With her wine-stained tongue, she parted Julie's lips, explored her soft upper palate. Catherine's hands traced the sharp outline of Julie's cheekbones and wandered down her neck to her slim shoulders, then to her smooth, young breasts. Julie's nipples were firm and Catherine longed to touch them with her mouth.

This, she thought. This is what it means to be in the moment. To be present. To be loved. To love. This was not a hard, sweaty fuck with a young, male student and his always-ready erection.

But this.

This tenderness, this trust, this emotion. She loved Julie. Loved her mind, loved her body, loved her soul. It was not a familiar love forged from time and trust and experience, it was something deeper, something almost ethereal. As Julie tenderly ran her hands under Catherine's shirt and across the scar left behind by her surgeon, Catherine felt tears roll from her eyes, down her cheeks, and into Julie's open mouth. Taste them, Catherine thought. Eat them. Ingest them. I want them to be a part of you. I want to be a part of you.

14 *anne*

"What do you mean, 'We don't have the money'?" Dale asked. The question, obviously, was rhetorical—much more of an accusation than an inquiry. "How can we not have enough money to fix the air conditioning in my car?"

Anne scrubbed the kitchen sink with increased intensity as a nervous sweat trail made its way down her back. She used more Lysol cleaner than necessary—washed, rinsed, repeated. All the while, she avoided Dale's eyes. Her focus, instead, was on the dried and hardened egg remnants and the peanut butter on the counter.

"It's just been a bad month," Anne said. "Lila's preschool bill was due, the kids needed new clothes…" She looked away.

"Then we'll take it out of savings," Dale said.

There aren't any fucking savings, Anne thought. If we had savings, we wouldn't be a month behind on our mortgage right now.

"Dale, let's just wait until next month," Anne said. "It will be easier then. And the weather's turning, anyway. You won't need air conditioning much longer."

"That's not the point," Dale said. "I make enough money to get my air conditioning fixed when I want to have it fixed. What's going on, Anne?"

"Nothing. It's just bad timing."

Anne turned back to the dishes and scrubbed the leftover meatloaf out of her Pampered Chef pan with a vengeance. She could feel the heat of Dale's frustration in the air behind her.

"Anne," he said, "I need to know what's going on."

"And I need to know why you're always working late," she countered. Deflect, deflect, deflect. *I'm rubber and you're glue, whatever you say bounces off me and sticks to you.* She was a master at avoidance.

"Jesus, Anne, I'm out working to support this family. What do you want me to say? That I'm fucking a couple of housewives on the side? Would that make you happy? Keep you off my back? Don't you know me any better than that?"

"I don't know you at all any more!" Anne shouted. "*That's* the problem!"

"If you don't feel like you know me," Dale replied, "it's because you don't want to know me, Anne. I don't know what to do to make you happy. I don't know what to do to make things right between us again. You don't talk to me, you won't have sex with me, you barely even look at me."

"Oh, of course, it always comes back to sex, doesn't it?" Anne lashed, snot running from her left nostril. "I'm tired, Dale. Tired. You might be working hard, but at least you get to have lunch with other human beings. At least you get to talk to adults. At least you leave the goddamn house every day!"

"Anne, I know taking care of the kids all day is tough. I know it's a big job. I want to help you, but you won't let me."

"What are you going to do to help me?" Anne shouted. She was growing more desperate by the moment, grasping at the straws she thought might save her. "Are you going to quit your job so you can drive to preschool? Are you going to leave work early so you can make dinner every night?"

"You're being ridiculous," Dale said, but his voice was more tired than accusatory. "Of course, I can't do those things every day—unless you want to go back to work full-time. But I can do them sometimes, Anne. I can help you. We're partners in this. At least we used to be."

Anne stifled a sob as she thought about her own silences, her hidden secrets, her trip to the pawn shop. They couldn't be partners—true partners—if she wasn't willing to be honest and forthright with him. But the lies had gotten so easy, they'd piled up so effortlessly, and now she was trapped under the weight of them.

"I'm just worried about our finances," Anne said, wiping her nose with the back of her hand. "We never seem to have enough. No matter what you make, we end up spending it."

"Then we need to sit down and look at where it's going," Dale said gently. "Maybe it's time for a budget."

The word struck a chord of fear in Anne's heart. Budget. Accountability. She felt the financial noose tightening around her neck. What if a new budget meant no more new shoes? What if she wanted to go on a girls' weekend with her friends and Dale said the flight was too expensive? What if she needed a new Dyson vacuum cleaner and Dale said they should get a Hoover instead?

She thought about her own childhood of secrets and lies, remembered how Eva would spend money without a second thought, would emerge from her own bedroom with red-rimmed eyes, a smile plastered to her face, and her purse on her arm. Big Jim might have controlled everything else in their lives, but the Mathers had never lived on a budget. Whatever Eva wanted to buy, she'd buy. Wherever Eva wanted to go, she'd go. It was Big Jim's unspoken concession—I'll screw whomever I want, you spend every penny I make, and we'll both look the other way.

"Come on, girls!" she'd say with fake gaiety, absentmindedly arranging the contents of her purse. "We're going to the movies tonight!"

And off they'd go, Eva, Catherine, and Anne. They'd buy a large box of popcorn, various and sundry candies, and three giant Cokes and lose themselves in the darkness of the theatre cocoon. They'd laugh and cry and rub their buttery fingers on their jeans. And Anne always knew that it was a lie, that they were at the movies because their father was with a woman who wasn't his wife, that all her mother had left was the money Big Jim made. It was a poor substitute for his love and devotion and fidelity. But it was what she had, her consolation prize.

"Don't hog all the Twizzlers," Eva would say to the girls as they passed the package back and forth.

"Catherine ate the last one," Anne complained.

It made her nauseous as a pre-teen to imagine her father naked, to think about him sticking his dick into another woman. Anne knew how it worked. Her friends at school kept her well informed. It was bad enough to imagine her own parents doing it, but the thought of her father with his hair graying around the temples and his freckled arms wrapped around another naked middle-aged woman made the bile rise in her throat. It was too much for her young and impressionable mind. Every time that particular image bored its way into her brain, Anne said a Hail Mary and asked for forgiveness.

Now, as a mother and wife, she felt a mixed bag of emotions and insecurities. It was impossible to know whether she was raising her kids properly, whether she was being a good wife, whether she was being true to herself. So perhaps Eva hadn't been privy to those answers, either. Perhaps she'd known about Big Jim's philandering and had looked the other way. Perhaps maintaining the illusion of her perfect family was more important than kicking her asshole husband to the curb.

And perhaps Anne was following directly in her mother's foot-steps. After all, she'd already proven how adept she was at maintaining illusions.

"Do you want me to go back to teaching?" Anne asked, afraid of Dale's answer.

"Do you want to go back?"

"No, not really. But I think we might need the money. It's huge, though, Dale. The prospect of finding a job, finding daycare, working out all the logistics—it's overwhelming."

"Well, then think about one thing at a time," Dale said. "Think about whether you'd enjoy working again. And if you think you would, then start looking for a teaching job. Maybe even something temporary or part-time to see if it might work. But if you don't want to go back, let's look at the numbers. Let's see how we can make it work on just my salary."

Anne didn't want to look at the numbers, didn't want to think about going back to work. She just wanted to sleep.

For a million years. Maybe more.

15 *jessica*

Dale was tenacious. She'd give him that much. She understood that for some strange reason, he felt responsible for her. And she had to admit, she enjoyed the notion that he hadn't given up on her as easily as she'd expected. But she was still guarded, still tentative, and still unwilling to participate in the sisterly reunion Dale kept envisioning. To her surprise, though, she looked forward to the easy conversations she had with Dale on the phone. He called faithfully between 9:00 and 10:00 a.m. every weekday morning to check on her, to learn a little more about her.

And she'd finally agreed to have coffee with him.

They were sitting in Jessica's tiny kitchen at 10:35 a.m.. The morning sun illuminated the cigarette burns on the laminate countertops and the years of accumulated grease under the cabinets. Both Dale and Jessica clutched cups of coffee like caffeinated life rafts.

"Stripping?" Dale asked incredulously. "Really?"

Jessica wasn't shy about her choice of livelihoods. She was, in fact, more than a little proud of her independence and her ability to evoke such intense desire from complete strangers. There was power in her sexuality, and onstage, with burly bouncers and plain-clothes police officers nearby, that power was safe.

"Why not?" Jessica answered.

"I can think of plenty of reasons *why not*."

"And?"

"Well, for starters, it doesn't seem very safe. Or clean. Or even lucrative for that matter. I mean, is it? Lucrative?"

Jessica ignored his question. "Have you ever gone to a strip club?" she asked.

"Of course," Dale said.

"So what keeps you safe and clean while you're there?"

"It's different for me," he said. "I'm not on stage."

The dirty bathrooms, the ever-present bodily fluids. There was a great deal of sweat and spit and various and sundry other unhygienic substances that permeated a place like the Carousel Lounge. The stage was probably the cleanest place in the building. The girls, after all, were the only ones allowed up there.

"I do it because I can," Jessica answered. "My body works, it pays the bills, and I'm not afraid or ashamed of anything anymore."

"Is that what life in L.A. will do for you?" he asked.

The coffee grounds in Jessica's cup swam around and around. "Yeah. Something like that." Life in L.A., she thought, will do lots of things for you. And *to* you.

"Why did you leave?" Dale asked. "We all thought you'd never come back to Indiana."

Plans change, Jessica thought. Every single moment, plans change.

"It's a long story," she said. "But this is home. It was time to come back."

When Jessica first returned to Indiana, she found her apartment and talked greasy Harvey $100 down on the rent. And then she sat in her empty new home and cried for days on end. Wadded balls of tissue decorated every surface, and the few boxes of her personal belongings—the small collection of a life void of all but the most basic material possessions—sat untouched. There were moments when she wanted to reach out to her family. She imagined Anne's voice on the other end of the line, brash and abrupt. But she'd soften when she heard her little sister's nearly forgotten voice... wouldn't she? Idyllic childhood dreams aren't so easily laid to rest.

The first—and last—time Catherine and Anne had come home

from college for a Mathers family Thanksgiving, Jessica remembered little more than large amounts of turkey and Scotch. Her sisters had eaten quickly, wrapped themselves back up into their winter coats and scarves, and headed out to visit with old high school friends. Jessica washed the dishes and went to bed early, her parents retiring to their respective places: Eva to her bed, Big Jim to the TV in the den. In the wee hours of the morning, Jessica heard the National Anthem play, followed by the familiar static drone of the station sign-off.

Less than six months after she arrived back in Indiana, while the hum of the doctor's suction machine still rang in her ears, Jessica read her father's obituary in the paper. She felt numb when she read about Big Jim's professional accomplishments. His sixty years on earth looked good on paper. According to the Indianapolis Star, he was a devoted husband and father to three beautiful girls. He was respected and admired by his employees and his colleagues. He was well-educated, handsome, involved in his community. And he was dead. Memorial contributions were directed to the American Heart Association. His fragmented heart—with pieces at work, pieces on the golf course, pieces with his mistress, pieces in the bottom of his bottle of Scotch, too few pieces at home—had finally given way. His heart was unable to remain whole and healthy when its chambers were so drastically divided.

"So now that you're here, why haven't you contacted your sisters? Why won't you let me tell Anne?"

"Why would I want to?" Jessica asked without a trace of bitterness. "We're more strangers than we are sisters. We've never really known each other."

"What about your mom?" Dale asked.

"What about her?"

"Well, don't you think she'd like to see you?"

"She had eighteen years to see me," Jessica said. "And she never looked."

Eva was the tragic heroine of her youngest daughter's life. Jessica watched her mother inhabit the background, a sponge for sadness. Eva's tears were drowned in vodka tonics and swallowed with the pills that helped her sleep. Big Jim was so big he consumed all the oxygen in Jessica's childhood home. Eva got the leftovers, the air that had already been breathed, the body that had already been fucked. Jessica got nothing.

"Does she remember anything?" Jessica asked.

"Very little. Just flashes here and there." A pause. "She asks about you."

"She does?"

"Every time Anne goes to see her, she asks about you."

Jessica chewed on that news for a moment. For most of her young life, she'd been invisible. The notion of being seen—of being missed, even—was a desert rife with land mines.

"Is she healthy?" Jessica asked. "I mean, can she still walk? Get around on her own?"

"Yup. Her memory went fast, but her body is still strong, relatively speaking. When your dad was still alive, he took good care of her. She was slipping, but we didn't really understand just how quickly. Once Jim died, her mind went fast. Early onset, they called it. But she's physically healthy still. She'll probably outlive us all."

In her prime, Eva was beautiful—dark-haired, dark-eyed, her body lithe and graceful. As a child, Jessica ached for her, needed her in a way that now seemed weak and clingy. On the rare occasion when Eva would hold or hug her youngest, Jessica clung tightly, willing her mother's distant soul into her corporeal form, prayed for it to inhabit her arms, her hands—the ones holding Jessica. But Eva was busy wishing the same of Big Jim. She pined for him, for something more than a sliver of his attention.

"Jess?" Dale asked, stirring his coffee.

"Hmm?"

"Where are you?"

"Just thinking. Remembering. Tell me, Dale, what's my sister like today? What's she really like?"

"That's a loaded question if I ever heard one," Dale said. "What do you mean?"

"I just remember her as selfish and self-righteous and lonely. What made you fall in love with her?"

"Well, she probably is all those things you described," Dale said. "But that's just a fraction of Anne. She's also smart and sexy and funny and devoted and confused… Aren't you lots of little pieces, too, Jessica? Aren't we all?"

"And Catherine? Do you ever see her?"

"Sure, we see her quite a bit. She's an English professor at Indiana University and her students love her. She hasn't gotten married yet—no serious prospects, either."

"What about your marriage?" Jessica asked. "The kids?"

"My marriage is the most important thing in my life," Dale said. "But I'm not sure I'm very good at it, at us. I don't want to leave Anne. I don't want the kids to grown up in a broken home. But I'm not sure how to raise them in the home we have right now, either. I love her, Jess. I do. I don't always love the way she acts, but I love who she is—the core of her. Lately, though, we just argue and pick and yell. And neither of us knows how to stop it… or fix it. I'm afraid that pretty soon, we're going to stop trying."

"That sounds familiar," Jessica said. "She learned those marital lessons well."

"But I do love her," Dale said. "That's the difference. I don't know whether your dad was capable of loving anyone but himself. I know he was your dad and all, Jess, but damn—that man was a one-person wrecking crew."

A sad smile. "Life with my dad was never dull," Jessica said. "Never happy, never carefree, never safe, rarely sober. But certainly never dull."

"Jess," Dale said, standing and stretching his legs, "I have to go to work. I'm never going to make quota this month if I don't get focused. And God knows we need the money right now."

"Go," Jessica said. "Take care of your family. Take care of you."

They hugged, first awkwardly, then with conviction.

"You're a good man, Dale," Jessica said. And with sad resignation, she admitted he was probably the only man she'd ever known who fit that description.

16 *catherine*

Michelle tucked Catherine into bed and set a steaming cup of tea on the table beside her. They'd just returned from another round of chemo, and Catherine was eager to sleep off the sweat and the sadness.

"What would I do without you?" Catherine asked.

"Probably drink a lot less tea," Michelle replied. "Want me to turn the TV on for you?"

"No, I'm going to sleep," Catherine said. "Can you sit with me for just a minute?"

"Of course," Michelle said, rubbing Catherine's cold hand with her warm ones.

"Tell me about the kids," Catherine said. "What are they involved in right now?"

"Well, there's nothing but basketball for Jake," Michelle said. "We eat, sleep, and breathe basketball. He's trying out for the middle school team this year, so we're in heavy-duty preparation mode. And the twins are playing volleyball and loving it."

Catherine enjoyed the notion of those blue-eyed beauties playing the sport she once loved. Mara and Molly had just turned ten, were graceful and athletic like their mother, and eschewed anything and everything girly. They had always preferred to dismember their Barbies rather than change their tiny high heels. From day one, Michelle had been perplexed by her little tomboys.

Even their birth was a surprise to Michelle and Tony. Mara had been hiding behind Molly for nine months. And because Michelle opted for as little medical intervention as possible when it came to childbirth, Mara took everyone by surprise when her little head of curls crowned.

"And Danny?" Catherine asked.

"We're just trying to keep him out of jail," Michelle said. "He's more interested in girls than any eight-year-old should be, and we'd prefer to transfer that focus to things like multiplication tables and spelling. At least he loves his teacher this year. Mrs. Adams is straight out of college, has more energy than all six of us combined, and has the most beautiful green eyes imaginable. I think Tony has a thing for her, too. You know… the apple and the tree."

"I miss them," Catherine said. "Let's get together for pizza soon. I want you to meet my new friend, Julie, too."

"You've mentioned Julie a few times," Michelle said. "Tell me about her. Do you two teach together?"

"Actually, no. She was my student, but she transferred out of my class early in the semester."

"Not tough enough to handle Dr. Mathers, huh?"

"Something like that," Catherine said. She paused, unsure of how to continue. "You're going to love her, Michelle. She's smart and beautiful and fun."

"She's not my BFF replacement, is she?" Michelle laughed. She bent to adjust Catherine's pillow.

"Psh," Catherine said. "Replacement? For you?" Catherine gestured to her disheveled room, the dirty clothes on the floor, the wigs scattered on her dresser, the empty cups lining her bedside table. "Who else could so gracefully handle all this glamour and excitement?" Catherine sat up to take her next round of medication. "Hand me my tea, pretty please?"

She swallowed her pills and leaned back into her pillow.

"Here's the thing, Michelle," Catherine said. Her mind swirled as she held the words in her mouth. "Julie is my girlfriend."

"Okay," Michelle said, not fully comprehending the semantics. "Then I'm sure she'll be my girlfriend, too."

"No, Michelle, she's my *girlfriend*. We're dating."

Michelle blinked. A wave of understanding washed over her face.

"It wasn't anything I planned or expected," Catherine said. She filled the room with a quick burst of words, her most reliable defense against the threat of an empty silence. "I certainly wasn't looking for a relationship in the midst of chemo. It just happened. And it's been so wonderful, Michelle."

"I don't understand," Michelle said, her face screwed up with confusion. "Are you telling me that you're gay?"

"I don't think I'm telling you anything like that," Catherine said. "I'm just telling you about Julie."

"But she's a girl, right?" Michelle asked. "And you're a girl, right? And you're in a relationship, right? Is this your 'coming out of the closet' moment?"

Catherine had not considered it any kind of moment. She understood this was a new normal for everyone, herself included. Yes, there were questions, concerns, reflections. But she hadn't expected this reaction from Michelle, this sudden cooling. The path they had just been walking together seemed to diverge—Michelle choosing one path, Catherine choosing the other. Catherine reached across the divide with her words, chosen softly, carefully.

"I'm not calling myself anything," she said. "But I'm in love with her. And it's a different kind of love than I feel for you. You're my I'd-run-in-front-of-a-speeding-train-because-you're-my-best-friend kind of love. I'm *in* love with Julie. She's my I-think-I-could-spend-the-rest-of-my-life-with-her kind of love. One's not better or worse than the other. They're just different. I know it may not make much sense right now. This whole thing doesn't make much sense when you take it apart and examine it from different angles. But here it is."

"So are you having sex with her?" Michelle asked.

Catherine and Michelle had never been shy about discussing their sex lives with each other. Every crush, every one-night-stand, every intimate detail—nothing had ever been off limits. This, however, felt dangerous. The question was not so much an inquiry as an accusation, a judgment, a challenge to be navigated with caution.

"Yes, Michelle, we have a physical relationship. And it's pretty much what you'd imagine it to be."

Michelle sat. The silence between sentences was a crevasse.

"I know," Catherine said. "I know it seems crazy. It does to me, too. But Michelle, I am so happy. So much happier, so much more fulfilled than I've ever been with anyone else."

"But are you a lesbian?" Michelle asked again.

"I don't know what I am," Catherine said, wishing instead that Michelle had simply said *If you're happy, then so am I.* "By definition, probably. Maybe bisexual. I don't *know*, Michelle. I don't know what to call myself. And you know what? I don't care. I care about Julie. I love her, Michelle. I really, truly love her. I have something with her that I've never had with a man."

Michelle shook her head, erasing the Etch-a-Sketch picture from her mind.

"Catherine, this is crazy."

"Yes. Maybe. I know it's hard to understand. I don't even know if *I* understand."

"I can't get my mind around it," Michelle admitted. "I don't know what to say."

"Say you'll come have dinner with us," Catherine said. "Bring the kids. Bring Tony. Meet her, talk with her, get to know her. I know you're going to love each other."

Michelle stood awkwardly.

"I don't know, Catherine. I don't know. What do I tell Tony? What do I tell the kids? I just don't know about all this."

"I'm not sure what you're asking," Catherine said. "Why do you have to tell them anything? And if you feel like you have to tell them something, why not tell them the truth? Or tell them we're having chili for dinner. It doesn't seem that difficult."

"Well, it's a little more complicated when you're talking about kids," Michelle said. "I'm not sure I'm ready to discuss this when them yet. I mean, Jake just turned thirteen. He's going to be dating soon."

"And you're afraid he might turn gay if he sees me with another woman? Are you kidding me, Michelle? Are you hearing yourself? What if Jake's already gay? Have you thought about that?" Catherine was a little surprised at the vitriol in her voice, but not as surprised as she was by the unanticipated reaction of her best friend. For the past twenty years, they'd shared everything. From shoes to jeans to late night talks to date details to God, there was no subject that ever threatened to divide them. Until now. Catherine felt the stability of her world wobble beneath her.

"What about Michael?" Catherine asked, referencing their mutual gay friend, the one who lived in Baltimore with his partner of ten years.

"That's different," Michelle said. "He's not a part of our everyday lives or of our kids' lives. Catherine, please," Michelle said. "Don't make this harder than it has to be. I need some time to think. You just dropped this out of nowhere, and I don't even know what to say. Surely you can understand that?"

"Surely you can understand that I didn't expect this reaction from my best friend," Catherine said. "You've known me for twenty years, Michelle. Twenty years. You know everything about me. What makes this so different?"

Michelle laughed, though neither was amused. "What makes this different? What makes this different? Everything makes this different, Catherine! This *is* different. I didn't know my best friend was gay. That's very different."

"And so, am I different now?" Catherine asked. "If you have to put a label on me, does that label change how you *feel* about me?"

"Come on, Catherine, you have to admit this is a little weird. And it's complicated. It's all very complicated."

"That is the worst cliché I've heard in a long time," Catherine said. "I wouldn't have expected it from you."

"Then I guess we're both surprised by each other, huh?" Michelle said. She brushed her hands over her jeans, grabbed her purse.

"I need some time to think, Catherine," Michelle said. "I just need some time."

Catherine heard the click of her apartment door closing. She glanced at the tea cup—just out of her reach—and closed her eyes.

17 *anne*

Paying attention to her daughter was more than challenging when Anne's mind was solely focused on her bank account. She sat in the shade on the patio, enjoying an unseasonably warm fall day, while Lila went down the slide again and again and again. The play set may have cost a pretty penny—one that Anne desperately wished she had back at this particular moment—but it kept Lila entertained longer than any of her other minor distractions. Worth every cent, Anne thought as she tallied up this month's overdraft fees. $35 + $35 + $35… Oh, and there's another $35 for a $3 cup of coffee. Pecking quietly at her laptop, Anne felt a lump form in her throat.

It was inconceivable they'd gotten so far behind on their bills and their bank account had so little to show for the hours Dale labored on the road. Anne typed the numbers on her calculator one more time as the baby monitor stirred beside her.

"Please don't wake up," Anne begged quietly. "Please don't wake up." It had only been forty-five minutes since Max had fallen into a fitful slumber. If he didn't nap his requisite two hours, the day would fall apart at the seams. Of this, Anne was certain.

She was growing more certain, too, of another inevitability: she had to return to work. They were digging themselves into a financial hole that was going to swallow them if they didn't make a near-immediate change. She'd run the numbers many times, and as much as she'd hoped the associated costs—daycare, work wardrobe, convenience meals—would render this possibility unfounded, it had become more and more apparent that her return to the classroom was a necessity. Anne was equally disheartened and relieved about the conclusion she'd already drawn in her mind. She'd always loved being in the classroom, but the thought of juggling two small children and a full-time job was more than overwhelming. A positive bank account, though? That was the reality that rendered all other options obsolete.

"Mama, watch!" Lila demanded as she crawled up the final step to the landing. "Watch me slide!"

Anne had grown weary of watching Lila slide.

Watch *me*! Anne wanted to yell back. Watch me take care of all of you and wash your laundry and make your meals and scrub your toilets and buy your groceries. Watch me do everything so your lives can be easy and worry-free. Watch me lose a little bit of myself every single day.

There was a great deal of guilt in owning these thoughts, but she felt powerless to stop them. Wasn't this what parenthood was all about? Hadn't she signed up for this? She knew there would be sacrifices. She loved her husband, loved her children. On better days, she understood the depth and significance of this truth. But her own life? Not so much. She'd forgotten what it felt like to be a woman first, a wife and mother second.

"Watch me, Mama!" Lila called again as she waved to her mother from the top of the play set.

But at the moment Anne reluctantly looked up, Lila lost her balance. Anne watched in horror as her daughter's skinny arms circled wildly in a cartoonish attempt to regain her footing. And before Anne could finish sucking in a terrified breath, the taste of a warm breeze on her tongue, Lila thumped to the ground in a still and silent repose. Her tiny body splayed out, a stranded starfish.

Anne could not move quickly enough. In some parodied semblance of animated slow motion, she shoved her laptop to the ground, pulled herself out of her chair, and ran. It felt funny and foreign, this running. Her thick legs didn't quite remember what was expected of them.

"Lila!" she yelled. "Lila!"

But her small daughter didn't respond.

It took a lifetime for Anne to reach her girl. As she plodded across the yard, Anne recalled the scent of Lila's freshly washed infant head, the feel of Lila's paper fingernails, the weight of her own responsibility as a mother. She first noticed the dirt on Lila's forehead, the delicate veins in her eyelids. Then she saw the trickle of blood that flowed from under Lila's curls.

"Please be okay," Anne cried. "Please breathe. Please be okay."

Anne knelt over her child and listened as Lila made a grunting sound, a challenged gasp for oxygen.

"That's it," Anne said. "Breathe. Breathe. Breathe."

Anne realized her cell phone was on the patio end table. Her expired CPR certification had taught her never to move a patient with a head injury. But Anne also couldn't fathom leaving her daughter's side.

"Help!" she screamed into the afternoon sunshine. "Help me!"

She prayed for a neighbor to hear her cries, willed someone to open a sliding glass door and run to her. But all she heard was Max crying on the monitor.

Anne ran—as fast as her body would allow— to the patio and dialed 911 with trembling fingers.

"Send an ambulance. Now. My daughter…"

Somehow, she was able to provide the dispatcher all the pertinent information as she ran back to Lila's side. Name. Address. Phone number. Yes, she's breathing. No, she's not moving. Yes, there's blood. No, she's not responding. Max was safe in his crib, she decided. He would be okay. She would not leave Lila.

Anne thought about the precious package her daughter was on the day of her birth. She was perfect in every way—ten fingers, ten toes, a beating heart, lungs full of breath. What a miracle it would be to traverse this life without breaking the perfect packaging we're delivered in, without a stitch or a cast or even a Band-Aid. But the moment we arrive, the world begins pushing us around. It challenges and knocks us to our knees. Even the youngest and most innocent are not spared this initiation. And it continues forever, the bruising, the scarring, the hurting and healing.

As the sirens wailed to a stop on the front street, Anne's neighbor ran over with her infant son in tow.

"Oh, Anne, what happened? What can I do?" she asked.

"Max," Anne cried. "Take care of Max. Please, Connie. He's in his crib. And call Dale."

Anne climbed into the ambulance beside her daughter. Oxygen mask, gauze, bandages, blood pressure cuff. She looked so little on that long expanse of white stretcher.

"God, please let her be okay," Anne prayed. "I will do anything. I will be anything. Please, please, please."

The EMTs worked with precision as Anne began a litany of Hail Marys. "Blessed art you among women and blessed is the fruit of your womb, Jesus. Holy Mary, Mother of God, pray for us sinners now and at the hour of our death. Amen." Anne shuddered as the word *death* passed from her lips. Not death. Not death.

"Lila, can you hear me?" the young EMT asked. No response.

For Anne, the seven-minute drive turned into a cross-country venture. The siren was too loud, the lights too bright. Her prayers to Mother Mary continued without fail.

Time collapsed in on itself when Lila's gurney was wheeled through the emergency room doors. Anne was escorted to the waiting room by a kind nurse wearing pink scrubs. At some point, Dale was by her side. When had he arrived? Too many minutes ticked by, and still no word from beyond the automatic doors.

"What happened?" Dale asked.

"She fell," Anne said. "She waved to me. And then she fell."

Dale hugged his wife, and Anne could feel him tremble.

"She's going to be okay," he said. "She is." But his shaky hands were not convincing.

Together they stood, supporting each other. There were empty chairs, but the thought of sitting had not occurred to them. The hospital buzzed with afternoon activity and an undercurrent of urgency.

"Mr. and Mrs. Jackley?"

"Yes," they replied in unison as a graying man in a white jacket extended his hand.

"I'm Dr. Denton. I've been taking care of Lila."

They looked at him wordlessly.

"Your daughter is going to be fine," he assured them. "She has five stitches, a minor concussion, and we're going to keep her overnight for observation. But there's no evidence of internal hemorrhaging. She's conscious, she's alert—but medicated—and she would very much like to see you."

An unattractive croaking noise escaped from Anne's throat.

"Thank you, Doctor. Where is she?"

Dr. Denton turned and motioned for them to follow.

In the darkness of the small room that would serve as her overnight sanctuary, Lila gazed groggily at them from her metal bed.

"Mama," she said. "Daddy."

"Oh, sweet girl," Dale said, rushing to envelop her pale hand in his own. He always moved more quickly than Anne. Always knew the right thing to say. Dale never second-guessed his own instincts, never gave his gut reactions a second thought. "What an adventure, Lila-Bear. You've sure made this an exciting day." He kissed her fingers as Anne awkwardly rubbed Lila's blanketed leg.

"My head hurts, Daddy," Lila said. "I'm tired."

"I know, baby," Dale said. "Try to get some rest. Mama and I are right here. We won't leave you."

Anne stood in silence, her mind busy with God and the Virgin Mother and brightly colored plastic slides. Other than the standard childhood illnesses—flu, fever, earaches, colds—her children had always been healthy. They'd never been to an emergency room, had never been stitched, had never broken a bone. What did a concussion mean? Shouldn't Lila stay awake? How would her stitches be removed?

And when? Caught up in a flurry of all the questions that didn't really matter, Anne found it impossible to focus on the moment at hand.

"What now?" Anne asked.

"What do you mean?" Dale said.

"What happens now?"

"We stay with her."

"Well, I get that," Anne said. "But then what?"

Dale looked at her with obvious confusion. "I don't know what you mean, Anne. We sit with her. We wait. We listen to what the doctor says. There's no master agenda for this. We don't have a playbook. We just get to be here with her."

Just be. It was a foreign concept. Anne's life consisted of movement, of planning, of worrying, of scheduling, of driving, of cooking, of cleaning, of shopping. She wasn't entirely sure how to just be. It sounded intriguing in many ways, but she didn't know how to accomplish that task, to check it off the list, to evaluate and grade it.

Anne felt like she was unraveling. Her life had become ragged around the edges. Memories of Eva rushed at her—Eva taking to her bed too early in the afternoon; Eva staring out the window for what seemed like hours at a time; Eva looking through Catherine and Anne, not comprehending their simple childhood questions, unable to have even the simplest of conversations. Had Eva unraveled, too? Was this a Mathers family trait, a curse? This inability to act—to move—in the face of the unknown or, sometimes, even the known. Anne sat down on the faux leather couch and put her face into her hands, hiding out from the clamor and urgency inside her mind.

18 *catherine*

When you lose someone, Catherine thought, they tend to go in pieces. The first fracture she felt when Michelle began stepping away was the silence of her day-to-day routine. The random drop-bys ceased, and her phone no longer buzzed with texts. When Catherine heard a great throwback on the Sirius eighties station or finished a book that begged to be shared, she looked longingly at her phone.

Give her space, she thought. Give her time.

And so the silence expanded. And the distance grew.

When Julie was in class, Catherine drove herself to her chemotherapy appointments. She was fine alone. She could entertain herself, was willing to drool without an audience. But the steady cadence of Michelle's presence in her life was missed.

Next, she began to feel the absence of Michelle's family. Jake continued to play basketball games without Catherine cheering in the bleachers. She longed to hug the twins. She wondered every day whether Danny had ended up in the principal's office again. She missed sharing a Scotch on the rocks with Tony, the steady hum of a busy family kitchen on a weekend evening. But she didn't call.

This is Michelle's choice, she thought. I can't alter how she feels. I can't crowd her, can't convince her, can't change her.

Julie was there. Julie served the tea Michelle had always made, filled many of the empty hours with games of Scrabble and glasses of wine. But Julie wasn't Michelle. There was only one Michelle, and she had continued to walk away. Step after step. While Catherine's arms and legs ached from the chemo, her heart ached with loss. Many evenings, she'd lay still and silent, her head in Julie's lap, tears on her cheeks. Why did loving one mean losing the other?

At times, she was angry, even livid. There were moments when her self-righteousness reared its ugly head. Who was Michelle to judge? To determine a universal right and wrong? To force everyone else to play by her arbitrary rules? Catherine was appalled that this moral crossroads was enough to stop a twenty-year friendship in its tracks. But most of the time, Catherine was just sad. The loss of her best friend was palpable. Like an amputated limb, Catherine could feel Michelle's absence. Ghost friend. Ghost pains.

When Catherine woke in the mornings—when Michelle's face first surfaced in the foggy remains of her dreams—Catherine's heart beat a little more quickly. It was a different feeling than chemo. It was loss, her body's recognition of it.

"Maybe you should call her," Julie said. "Talk to her."

"I can't," Catherine said. But that wasn't entirely true. She could call. She was capable of calling. She wanted to call. She thought about calling at least every half hour of every day. But whenever she reached for the phone, the tiny pin prick of a headache began. "Well, actually, I guess I won't. This is her issue to work through. This is her choice. Ultimately, it really doesn't have anything to do with me, does it?"

"Not really," Julie said. "But the hurt is yours. How Michelle feels has everything to do with her and her own heart. You're just the impetus for those feelings right now."

"As a control freak," Catherine said, "I have to admit it's tough not to take this one on. I have my soliloquy completely rehearsed. I'm ready to present my case."

"She'll come around." Julie took Catherine's hand in her own. "Or she won't. What's that awful cliché? Friends are there for a reason, a season, or a lifetime?"

"Maybe. But what do you do when you think it's a lifetime and it turns out to be only a season?"

"I guess you're grateful for what you had and the lessons you learned," Julie said. "You chose her for a reason. She chose you for a reason. If those reasons have been fulfilled, maybe that's all there is."

The weight of Julie's words was barely disguised by the tenderness in her voice. Could that really be it? After twenty years, could a relationship end so unexpectedly? So abruptly? Should she just let it burn out, that flame that once sustained? It broke her heart into a million little pieces to consider what life without Michelle would be—the missed vacations, the silent phone, the kids' milestones, the weddings, the funerals, the heartaches and the celebrations, the growing older, the retirement home luncheons and outings. But she trusted Julie's innate wisdom, and she trusted her own broken heart. She couldn't change Michelle's mind. It wasn't her mind to change. She could only love her, whether up close or from a distance. And although her anger and disappointment shadowed her love of late, Catherine did, indeed, hold Michelle tightly in her heart. She would always love her friend. Always. Right or wrong or indifferent, it didn't matter. Perhaps things would never return to what they were, or to what Catherine always thought they would be, but the love remained.

"If she comes back, I can't pretend nothing happened," Catherine said.

"Then don't. You have that choice. You both have choices. Choose what's right for you. She'll choose what's right for her."

It was beyond Catherine's current comprehension to consider that she might not be the right choice for Michelle, that twenty years of friendship hadn't made an indelible mark on Michelle's life. The pain was still too new, the abandonment still too fresh. But Catherine tucked Julie's words away in the back of her mind to revisit when the hurt wasn't quite so raw.

The phone rang beside her. Catherine reluctantly picked it up, looked at the caller's name, decided to answer.

"Cat," Anne said, "It's Lila."

19 *jessica*

"Those shoes don't come off while you're on stage," Lou said. "It'll come outta your pay if they do."

The Rules of Stripping, Jessica thought as she watched the Carousel Lounge's newest dancer take the floor. There were fines for everything here. Had to perfect a signature move by week two of your employment, had to have your shirt off by the time you reached the second pole, had to bring at least two men (or women) into the VIP dance area every shift. Leila, Lou's newest hire, was only eighteen and had a two-year-old daughter, Jade. Jade's father was a married bartender who didn't even know his daughter existed. Leila had chosen not to tell him. She didn't want the hassle, the money, or the custody battle. It had just been a one-night stand, after all. It wasn't meant to be a life sentence. But Leila wanted her baby, was certain even at the age of sixteen—still, in many ways, a baby herself—that she'd be a good mother.

Because of her own choice, her own loss, Jessica couldn't hear enough about Jade. She interrogated Leila at every opportunity. What did Jade look like? How much did she talk? Which words did she speak first? Who did she stay with when Leila was at work? What was her favorite color? Her favorite food? Jessica knew in the way only a mother understands that the baby she'd lost was a girl. Half of her, half of a monster. And yet, not one day went by that Jessica didn't think about a daughter, about her daughter. Would she have been able to love her? Would she have been able to look into the eyes of her baby and not see a dirty knife and greasy hair? She saw those things every day, anyway. In her dreams, in her waking hours, in her thoughts, in her memory. Would being responsible for another human being have ameliorated the burden of her past? If she lost herself in the act of brushing silky, dark curls, would she have somehow been healed?

As the time separating Jessica's present from her past grew, so did her regret. She was capable of love and forgiveness—it was part of her basic constitution. She could have raised a child conceived in violence and turned it into love. But that was knowledge that came to her in her twenties. At nineteen, she hadn't known.

What is real and right and possible changes with age and perspective. What was once a *never* could so easily become a *maybe someday*. She had created an unexpected relationship with her brother-in-law. She was an aunt. She was home. All things, ultimately, were possible.

"You're on next, Jessica," Lou said. "Get your ass ready."

Lou was harsh and crass and rough around the edges, but he made Jessica—and all the other dancers—feel safe. He took care of his girls. When the patrons were snide or vulgar or when they overstepped their boundaries, Jessica knew Lou would step in. There was something paternal about Lou, and something else that drove him to protect and defend his greatest assets. No matter what the motivation, Lou took care of them.

Big Jim, in contrast, had never possessed anything resembling a paternal protectiveness. Jessica's father had always been too concerned about satisfying his own restless libido to worry about his daughters.

Or his wife, for that matter.

Their hearts had been left out in the open, exposed to the elements, at the mercy of whatever happened to come their way. By the time she was ten, Jessica had lost count of the number of times she'd witnessed Jim crossing the line with other women. From seemingly benign ass smacks to awkward absences at a New Year's Eve party (*"Have you seen your father?"*), Jessica had experienced her share of her Big Jim's infidelity. At first, she hadn't understood. She was, of course, too young to fully understand. But what she did know was this: her father loved women, even—and perhaps even especially—those to which he was not wed. That realization posed its own unanswered question. Did Eva know? Did she honestly not see? Or did she choose to look the other way? The power, after all, rested with the choice. Those who willingly sacrificed their power no longer had choices.

When her sisters both left for college—first Catherine, then Anne—Jessica wondered what secrets they took with them. She was quite certain, even at her tender young age, that Big Jim had been fucking other women all his life. She knew a great deal about fucking despite the best efforts of her Catholic school nuns. Jessica spent many of her unsupervised hours in the library, expanding her mind as well as her sexual literacy. She cut her teeth on Judy Blume's *Are You There, God? It's Me, Margaret* and was thrilled to discover *Wifey* and *Forever* in the adult fiction section. Next, she devoured *The Thorn Birds* and *Flowers in the Attic*. She recognized there was something insatiable—almost predatory—in her father. For Big Jim, the thrill was in the hunt, satisfaction in the conquest. And he was handsome. He was charming. The women, Jessica was sure, were eager to give themselves to him. Even her mother's best friend. Even Ellen.

Ellen and Dave were married the same year as Jim and Eva. Their sons, Joe and Lucas, were a few years older than Catherine and Anne. The adult foursome had been inseparable when Jessica was young. From vacation to bridge club to summer barbeques, the two families were more like one—in so many ways. Jessica didn't know whether Eva and Dave knew about Jim and Ellen. Perhaps the four of them were all co-fucking. Jessica doubted it, though. Her mother was too loyal, too quiet, too timid, too eager to please her larger-than-life husband. And Dave seemed to genuinely love Ellen. Sure, there was tense sexual banter, there were lewd jokes and comments made in a drunken stupor that were inappropriate at best. But Jessica was fairly certain the broken vows were shared only by Big Jim and Ellen.

Once on a joint family trip to Hawaii, the adults came tumbling drunkenly into their shared suite after a night out. Jessica was the only one of the five children on the trip, the only one still young enough to be living at home. Earlier in the evening, she'd retired to the suite after too many hours of watching a pig turn on a stick. She'd fallen asleep on the couch watching late night movies.

"Shhh...." she'd heard Big Jim whisper, certain he was spitting through his clenched teeth. "Jess is sleeping." And the couples had retired to their respective bedrooms, doors clicking loudly behind them.

Later, Jessica had woken groggily to a clatter of ice in the kitchen.

"Just needed some water," she'd heard Ellen whisper.

"I think you need something more than that," her father had answered.

She heard heavy breathing and a rustling of clothes. Jessica pulled a pillow over her head, disinterested in hearing whatever was happening a mere twenty feet away. Her nose was sunburned, and she could still feel sand in between her toes. Hawaii was a million miles from home, but she could never travel far enough to escape the sins of her father.

As Jessica danced her way to the second pole and simultaneously removed her bikini top, she wondered if Big Jim had ever come to a place like the Carousel Lounge. She didn't know much about him, about what he did when he wasn't at home. For her, he was no more than the one who paid the bills and put her food on the table. He never let any of his daughters into his heart. His proclivity toward sex never extended to them, either. No, Big Jim was not a molester. His greatest fatherly sin was not in touching his girls inappropriately, but in never touching them at all.

There was no shame for Jessica in topless dancing. She knew there was a stigma associated with it, knew that people judged her and prayed for her and wondered how she could choose such a profession. But Jessica was good at what she did, and she made enough money to support herself, to be debt-free, and to even secure a small savings account. There were no expectations of friendship or work camaraderie here, either. She could remain aloof, detached, alone without being criticized for not being a "team player." And although she had the intellectual wherewithal to succeed in any given profession, the thought of sitting in a stuffy cubicle all day long made her gasp for air. She was much more content to walk into a work environment where naked pictures of women in compromising positions were stapled to the entrance walls. She'd never been one for conformity.

No, her shame was not in her chosen profession but in her inability to love and be loved. Survival alone was what she understood. Many evenings, she stayed awake as the night became day wondering what made her unlovable, wondering why parents continued to have children they didn't want. She knew other families were different than her own; she was always able to recognize that the way Dave and Ellen looked at Joe and Lucas was fundamentally different from the way Big Jim and Eva regarded her. She supposed she should have been grateful that all her material needs were met, that her canopy bed kept her warm and relatively safe, that there was always enough food in the kitchen if she was willing to prepare it herself. But she would have sacrificed any of those creature comforts for the warmth of a mother's arms or the safety of a father's lap.

When Jessica moved to California, Big Jim and Eva simply let her go. They didn't beg her to stay, didn't try to find her, didn't hire a private investigator to check on her well-being. She imagined the Indiana conversations that took place after her departure.

"You know Jessica!" Big Jim's voice rang in her ears. "She's always been the restless one, has always had a foot out the door. She's got to find a grand adventure before she'll ever be able to settle down."

Eva would concur. "Of all the girls, she's the most independent. She raised herself, really. Didn't need us for much of anything. Can't hold that kind of spirit back."

Her sisters were just as disinterested. It wasn't normal. Jessica understood that on a base level, but she always questioned how it came to be. Were some human beings so egomaniacal that self-preservation became the number one goal in life? Or was that just a Mathers trait? Jessica guessed that when hurt, some hurt back. And when betrayed, some sealed themselves off so nothing could ever get inside again. But in this choice lived a bitter concoction of solitude, loneliness, denial, and pain. It perpetuated itself, became a cancer that gnawed away at the bones.

20 *dale*

Dale knelt in the tiny hospital chapel, his middle-aged knees popping and cracking with every shift of his weight, and stared at the Crucifix before him. The room was lit only by the glow of electric candles and a few strategically placed lamps. Catholics, he thought, were so odd with their gory depiction of Jesus' tragic life and painful death. The Crucifix itself had always been disturbing to him with the blood at Jesus's hands and feet, the gaping wound in his side, and the thorns encircling his head. He imagined scores of Catholic school children staring faithfully at the image in churches across the world and wondered which ones had nightmares as a result.

It had been a long time since Dale had prayed. He wasn't even sure how to do it anymore. He was certain, however, that he needed to do it, that his life was unraveling. A short elevator ride away, his daughter rested with stitches in her head. By her side sat his wife, the one whom he hardly knew anymore. Life had taken a couple of hard left turns, and he was still trying to figure out where he was. What was he doing in a hospital, for heaven's sake? His kids were strong, healthy. His family, intact. And yet, they weren't.

The year before, Anne had cut her hair a little shorter than usual.

"What do you think?" she'd asked.

"It's different," he said. "I have to get used to it." No judgment, no disappointment in his words.

"Jesus, Dale!" she'd cried. "How do you think that makes me feel?"

"I like it, Anne! I do. It's just different."

"Well, of course it's different," she said. "That's the whole point."

"You know you're always beautiful to me, no matter what you do with your hair. You know that, right?"

"Well, sometimes it's nice to hear it!" She'd wiped her tears and stormed out of the room, leaving Dale silent and shell-shocked.

Last month, he'd grown a goatee. He'd tamed and trimmed it, shaved it into a manageable shape. Anne never even noticed. She didn't notice when he grew it, didn't notice when he shaved it. In fact, he wasn't entirely sure she looked at him at all any more.

Anne was a mess. He knew it. He knew she was slipping away from him, knew there was a well of hurt that he couldn't touch. He felt fairly certain he wasn't the source of her pain, but he wanted to fix it, and he didn't have any idea where to start. So he went to work every day and tried to provide for the family he'd created, tried to do the right thing. His life, however, scared the shit out of him. He was responsible for the safety and care of three other human beings. He provided food, shelter, clothing, and security for a family of four. It was a daunting thought, really. How had life charged so quickly forward when he still wasn't sure he was ready to be an adult? He'd been so good at being young, at being carefree and fun and the life of the party. Now the universe expected him to be something different, and he felt like he was making it all up as he went along. It wasn't that he was necessarily unhappy with the choices he'd made. He loved his wife, loved being married, loved being a father. It was just all so much. The weight of it all—the adult-ness of it—was overwhelming. And too often, he felt like he was letting everyone down.

"Hey, God," he whispered, the sound of his own voice jarring in the chapel's silence. "It's me. Well, I'm sure you know it's me because you're God and all..."

What was he saying? Anne did this so easily, so naturally, so... often. Treading on unknown prayer waters was still foreign to him. It made him feel like an unworthy supplicant to throw his supernatural requests into the air willy-nilly. But perhaps, he thought, that was the point.

He closed his mouth and opened his mind. *Help me*, he thought. *Help us. Please.*

He bowed his head into his hands and muffled the cry that lodged in his throat.

21 *anne*

At the precise moment Dale bowed his head to pray, Anne stepped quietly into the chapel. The stained glass and candles were her comfort, her hope, her home. And there knelt Dale. What was he doing here?

The juxtaposition of her husband kneeling in front of Jesus made her head spin.

And then she noticed Dale's shoulders shaking. Was he *crying*?

The doctor had told them that Lila would be okay. In fact, they were going home tomorrow. But Anne wasn't sure she, herself, was okay. Wasn't sure Dale was okay. Wasn't sure they were all going to be okay together. And Dale's posture suggested that he might feel the same way.

She watched her husband's shoulders slump and felt like an intruder. She'd walked in on something she didn't expect and didn't understand. Anne was alternately softened by his kind heart and burdened by her own selfish thoughts. Could she share her Jesus? Could she share her Dale?

With all the grace and stealth she and her extra fifty pounds could muster, Anne backed quietly out of the chapel and left the two men in her life to work out their own details.

Lately, Anne's dreams had been crowded out by a God who came to her in the form of a woman. She'd always imagined God as a man in a flowing white robe with matching white facial hair. Charlton

Heston-esque, she supposed. This God-as-a-Woman notion was new and unnerving to her. She didn't like to think about God morphing and changing like the rest of the world. She needed Him to be the stable, all-knowing force that anchored her life to this earth. And her dreams had become disturbing enough in the recent weeks without God appearing as a goddess. Too often, she found her subconscious self standing at the edge of a dark precipice. Her heart raced as she leaned into the abyss, a little further, a little further. The wind whipped through her hair, the weight of her body threatened to offset the balance just enough for her to tumble into the blackness below. Most nights, she woke up in a cold sweat, saved from the fall by flailing arms and legs. But the next day, she was always off-balance and under water. She cried too easily. She wanted to crawl back into bed. More and more, she felt like sleep was her only respite from the everyday demands of her life. She sought it as often and as fully as she could.

When she returned from the chapel to Lila's room, she found Catherine sitting by her daughter's bedside. And on the couch in the corner was a young, dark-haired beauty. Lila giggled drowsily at something Catherine had whispered in her ear, and the dark-haired girl smiled warmly as Anne entered the room.

"Cat," she said with gratitude, "thanks for coming."

"Wouldn't miss a chance to see my Lila-Bear. Especially with her fashionable new headwear."

Lila giggled again as she tentatively touched the gauze on her head.

Catherine stood and hugged her sister. The dark-haired girl stood as well, and Catherine made introductions.

"Anne, this is my friend, Julie. Julie, my sister, Anne." Anne extended her hand, but was surprised as Julie wrapped her in a hug instead. Anne stood stiffly, taken aback by Julie's easy show of affection and her total disregard for Anne's personal space.

"Nice to meet you, Julie," Anne said, awkwardly extricating herself from Julie's arms. "Are you a student of Catherine's?"

"I was," Julie smiled.

"You're pretty," Lila said.

"Why, thank you, sweetie," Julie said. "But I'm not half as pretty as you are. And you're smart, too. I can tell just by looking at you."

"Really?" Lila asked. "Just by looking? You must be smart, too." Lila smiled and closed her eyes.

"What are the doctors saying?" Catherine asked.

"She's going to be okay," Anne said. "She has a concussion, and they're keeping her overnight for observation. But she's going to be fine."

"Thank God," Catherine said, flippantly throwing Anne's savior's name into the conversation.

"Where's Max?" Catherine asked.

"He's with our neighbor, Connie."

"Why don't you let us stay with him tonight?" Catherine offered. "Then you and Dale can both stay here with Lila."

Anne looked at Julie. It seemed odd that Catherine's friend was in for an overnight. But still, she appreciated the offer and knew that both she and Dale would want to be with Lila until she was discharged.

"Thanks, Cat. That would be perfect."

"I cancelled class tomorrow," Catherine said. "Take all the time you need. We'll go back to campus when you're all settled back at home."

Anne smiled gratefully. "What are you studying, Julie?"

"I'm a double major: Philosophy and Biology."

"Interesting combination," Anne said.

"When you think about it, it's really not so strange," Julie explained. "The great philosophers were problem-solvers at heart. They looked at everything—questions about existence, values, language, the arts. Biology just completes the circle. From the philosophical to the physical, I've got it all covered." Julie flashed her brilliant smile.

"I'd say you do," Anne agreed, eyeing Catherine's new friend warily. She was apprehensive about this girl with her charm and her ease. She carefully noted how Catherine approached this girl who was so comfortable in her own skin, so sure of her place on this earth. Catherine seemed noticeably different around Julie, almost smitten. It was unsettling for Anne. She trusted Catherine to take good care

of Max, but she didn't necessarily trust Catherine to make good decisions about her own life. Anne wasn't sure what to think of Julie, but
didn't have time to contemplate much beyond the care and keeping
of her injured daughter right now. Her judgment would have to wait.

22 *catherine*

When they were all certain that Lila was asleep, Catherine and Julie left to get Max. They sat side-by-side in the Volvo and enjoyed the soothing sounds of Dave Matthews and Tim Reynolds.

"Your sister's pretty," Julie said. "She looks like you."

Catherine reached to turn the Sirius station down as she flipped her left turn signal on.

"You're not going to dump me for her, are you?"

"Why? Has that happened to you before?"

"No, thank God. We never dated the same guys when we were younger. We had enough baggage without adding *that* to the mix."

"She's not you," Julie said. "But she is pretty. You two look very similar."

"We both look like our Dad," Catherine explained. "Our youngest sister looks like our Mom."

"Wait…," Julie said. "I thought you only had one sister?"

Catherine was taken aback. In all of their late night conversations, was it possible that she'd never mentioned Jessica to Julie? Jessica had so completely slipped out of their lives that she'd also managed to slip out of their everyday vocabulary.

"I have a younger sister, too. Her name is Jessica," Catherine said. "She's what you'd call a 'surprise' sibling. Our parents had her when I was thirteen and Anne was ten. I never felt like I knew her well because I was busy with my own self-centered teenage existence when she was little. And then when she turned eighteen, she moved to L.A."

"Where is she now?" Julie asked.

"I assume she's still in California."

"But you don't know for sure?"

Spoken from the lips of a family outsider, it seemed an accusation of sorts. Catherine was embarrassed to admit she didn't know her baby sister's whereabouts. She couldn't imagine Julie ever letting a human being disappear from her life like that. But between Jessica's departure and Julie's question, an entire lifetime had transpired.

"We don't know for sure," Catherine said. She thought about the sister she barely knew. Her memories of Jessica were like an old movie that you half-watched while you played a game of Scrabble with your friends. You remember bits and pieces of the movie, but what stands out in your mind is the game, the friends, the laughter. Jessica was a background character in Catherine's story, a member of the chorus. She could barely conjure up what Jessica looked like as a child, could not remember the sound of her sister's voice.

"Jessica wanted to disappear. She was done with us. She was done with Indiana."

"That's crazy, Cat," Julie said, arranging her skinny legs on the leather passenger's seat in a criss-cross applesauce pattern. "She disappeared? And you all just let her go?"

Catherine's face burned with embarrassment.

"Yes," she said. "But there's so much more to it." A memory washed over Catherine, a snapshot of Jessica's solitary childhood, peppered with babysitters and stuffed animals and a family that wasn't. "It's probably best for her. She was pretty lonely growing up. Mom and Dad had their own issues, and Anne and I left for college without a second thought. We were all trying to escape. Jess was just more successful than the rest of us."

The two women sat in silence for a moment. The turn signal interrupted the quiet with its insistent, staccato beat.

"Do you think about her?" Julie asked.

Catherine was ashamed to admit that she didn't think about her youngest sister nearly as much as she should. And with every passing year, she thought about her less.

"Sometimes," Catherine said.

"What do you think she's doing?

"I don't know. I hope she's going to school or working or living with someone who's taking good care of her."

"Did your parents ever try to find her?"

Catherine felt the weight of Julie's innocent interrogation pressing down on her chest.

"I think they did. For a while. I hope they did. I'm not sure how hard they tried. And Jessica didn't want to be found," she reminded Julie.

"Do you know if she's alive?"

A quickening. Jesus, Catherine thought as she realized how inappropriate and uncaring her honest answer to that question was. She didn't even know whether her little sister was living.

"I don't."

The silence in the car was thick and weighty with disappointment.

Catherine was relieved when they arrived at Connie's house mere moments later to claim baby Max. And she was grateful for the feel of his small, warm body in her arms, relieved that his physical weight helped counterbalance the crush of her own guilt.

Throughout the evening, the two women busied themselves with toddler care. Thoughts of Jessica, however, were never far from Catherine's mind. Once Max had been fed, bathed, and put to bed, Catherine stretched out on the sofa and rested her head in Julie's lap.

"He's such a sweet baby," Julie said.

"Pure happiness, that boy," Catherine agreed. "He's so easy to love. It would be nice, wouldn't it, if every relationship was that easy? If everyone was so unassuming?"

"Are you still thinking about Jessica?" Julie asked. Julie was not afraid to ask the questions that so obviously needed answers.

"I am," Catherine said. "And Michelle, too. I'm losing her, Julie. It's so surreal. I never imagined a life without Michelle, and now here I am, living it."

"How does that make you feel?" Julie asked.

Catherine raised her eyebrows and glanced skeptically at her lover.

"What are you, my therapist?" Catherine asked.

Julie grinned. "Nah. I've got no interest in psychoanalyzing you. I just want to know how you're feeling about Michelle. I mean, if she's no longer a part of your life because of me, I think we need to talk about it."

"She's no longer a part of my life because of *her*," Catherine said.

"I get that," Julie said. "I do. I understand that Michelle's beliefs have nothing to do with you or me. In fact," she smiled, "I think I'm the one who told you that. But how do you *feel* about it?"

Catherine's chest tightened with a dull ache. Her bald head was cold and felt strange under the slight pressure of Julie's soft hand.

"I feel sad," Catherine said. And then the tears began. "Sad. And angry. And disappointed. And sad all over again. She was my best friend. I never imagined a moment without her in my life. There's a big Michelle-shaped hole in my heart."

The empty space where Michelle used to abide ached with the enormous weight of her absence. Catherine felt something akin to grief—the hopelessness, the angst, the sensation of being trapped underwater for just a few seconds too long. Her heart alternately hurt and flared with anger. Such a waste of twenty precious years.

Perhaps, Catherine thought for the first time, this was how Jessica felt.

When Catherine and Anne were young, it would have made sense for them to gravitate toward each other for companionship, for solace. But they hadn't. They'd chosen instead to take divergent paths, to go it alone. Catherine would have welcomed memories of giggling under blanket forts and riding bikes with colorful streamers flying from the handlebars. But in the Mathers' house, it was every man for himself—or more appropriately, every girl for herself. They'd bought into that precedent hook, line, and sinker, and their blood tie had become nothing more than genetics. Likewise, in all of Catherine's young friendships, it had been cut and run. No connection, no pain. Michelle had been Catherine's first true companion. The sting of losing the one person she'd been willing to trust was a knife in her heart.

"I wish..." Catherine said as she searched for the right words. "I wish that she loved me more than she loves feeling 'right.'"

"My mom once called that an 'article' conversation," Julie said, sipping a glass of Pinot Noir. "She didn't believe in 'the' way, she believed in 'a' way. 'Life is too short to worry about who's right and who's wrong,' she'd say. And I agreed. We waste so much time and energy trying to get people to see things our way. In the end, does it really matter?" Julie asked.

"I guess there's something to be said about the power of your convictions and beliefs," Catherine said. "But ultimately, I'd like for love—not righteousness—to rule my life."

"You can't change how she feels about our relationship," Julie said.

"I know."

"You just have to love her where she is."

Catherine sighed. She did love Michelle. Michelle was her right-hand girl, the sidekick to her superhero. They shared so much history, they had so much future. But Catherine was also angry and hurt and victimized. This was new terrain for her, too. She would have liked a best friend with whom to traverse this unknown landscape. But she felt abandoned, judged, and hung out to dry. And she felt tired. Always so fucking tired.

Catherine had written a letter to Michelle last week.

My Dearest Michelle,

I'm not sure how we reached this crossroads. I'm not sure how we move forward. All I know is that I miss you desperately. Every moment of every day, I feel a piece of me has gone missing. I don't know if it will ever be found again. I don't know whether tomorrow exists for us or not.

Here's what I do know: I love you. I have always loved you. You are the friend who has walked beside me through every hill and valley of my life. When I've needed a shoulder, a laugh, a glass of wine, you have always been the one I've turned to. My life is different without you. My life is less without you.

Here's what I don't know: how you could give me up so easily. I feel blindsided, cut off at the knees. And for what? Because I fell in love? Because you're afraid of what your kids might think or see or learn? Do you not know that I love them like they're my own? Do you not realize that I would do anything in my power to protect them, to guide them, to nurture them? Do you trust me so very little?

I keep thinking about our Outer Banks vacation two summers ago. I can still vividly recall how the sun felt on my skin, how warm the sand was between my toes. You and I sat side-by-side in our beach chairs with our Vodkas and grapefruit juice while the kids built a sand castle with Tony. Do you remember? We talked about how we'd retire to Boca Raton someday and drive around in a convertible together while Tony golfed with his old-man friends. We planned to catcall the young boys, eat sushi, drink too much red wine, and bake our old, wrinkled faces in the Florida sun. Your kids were going to bring your grandbabies to visit us, and we were going to spoil them rotten and send them home. Do you remember? We had plans for the future. This wasn't part of our plan.

I'm sad that you've chosen not to know Julie. She is kind and good-hearted and patient and beautiful and brilliant. In any other situation, in any other given moment, you would have loved her, too. It makes my heart hurt to think that because we have a physical relationship, you have chosen not to have a relationship with either one of us.

The choice is yours. I realize that. I won't try to change you, and I won't apologize for how I feel. And my feelings run the gamut. Yesterday, I was sad. Today, I'm angry. Tomorrow, I will weep over the loss of you, my friend.

I will always consider you my friend. You know that, right? At every juncture in my fucked-up life, you have been there. You have been the one I've turned to, the one I've laughed with, the shoulder I've cried on. I am equally devastated by the void you've left in your wake and angered by the self-righteousness that made you choose the way you did.

But here's the thing… I don't want to be angry. I've never wanted to be angry with you. At some point in my life, however, I have to choose what's best for me. You have Tony. You have Jake and Molly and Mara and Danny. Your life is so full, so complete. And now I have Julie. I never knew I was looking for her, never knew I needed her. But I do now. And I can't imagine life without her. I wish you respected that. I wish you approved. But I realize that wishes don't create reality.

There is nothing I want more for you than happiness and good health and laughter and love. I am choosing the same for myself. Be well, my dear friend. Be free. Be at peace.

Love always,
Catherine

When the ink and the tears had both dried, Catherine folded the letter into tiny squares and buried it deep in her office trash can. What she needed to say didn't matter. Decisions had already been made, judgments already rendered.

She felt Julie shift beneath her as they rested together on Anne and Dale's couch. The damp warmth of Julie's breath on Catherine's neck lulled her into a dreamless sleep. Her last thoughts before fading off into oblivion were of Michelle's kids' smiling faces.

Catherine and Julie were both awakened by the sound of the garage door opening at 8:00 a.m. Dale, Anne, and Lila stumbled into the family room as Catherine sat up and stretched her achy body.

"Well, good morning," Anne said awkwardly as her eyes scanned the scene before her. Julie sat up without any semblance of hurry or alarm. She adjusted the couch cushions behind her, fluffed her hair, radiated confidence and ease.

"Good morning," Julie said. "You're home early."

"They released Lila after morning rounds," Anne said stiffly. She paused.

"Obviously, you weren't expecting us so soon."

Catherine detected the familiar contempt in Anne's voice and steered the conversation in a different direction.

"No, no, we're so glad you're home. I'll get some coffee on." Catherine continued talking. "Max was an angel. He went to bed without any fuss and slept all night. Still snoozing, in fact."

"May I please talk to you alone?" Anne asked.

"Of course," Catherine said, feeling the dread of Anne's unspoken accusations settle in her chest long before she rose to follow her sister into the kitchen. She heard Julie introduce herself to Dale as the sisters walked from the room.

"Isn't she pretty?" Lila asked her father as the sisters walked out of earshot.

"What the fuck is going on?" Anne asked through clenched teeth.

"What do you mean?"

"Don't be coy with me, Catherine," Anne said. "You know what I mean. Are you having a *relationship* with that girl?"

Catherine was growing weary of this particular conversation, fraught with condemnation.

"Yes, Anne, I am having a relationship with that girl. And her name is Julie—in case you forgot." Catherine fought to keep her voice from shaking. Anne's proclivity toward high drama was imminent, and Catherine intended to keep the calm and rational upper hand.

"I remember her name," Anne said. "What I want to know is what you're doing with her? What kind of relationship are you having? What in the hell does that even mean?"

"It means I love her. I fell in love with her. She's smart, she's beautiful, she's kind, she's fun. I love her. That's it."

"That's it? That's it? What does that mean? Are you a lesbian now?"

Despite her best efforts, Catherine couldn't help but smile in amusement. She was learning so much lately about the societal need for labels, about the perceived safety and security that came with putting everyone and everything into its proper place. It was exhausting, really, this desire for everyone to define every single moment of an existence.

"I don't know what I am," Catherine said. "Except in love."

Anne paced back and forth in her kitchen, wringing her hands nervously.

"Jesus, Catherine, what about the Bible?"

"What about it?"

"The Bible clearly states that homosexuality is an abomination," Anne said. "Read Leviticus."

Catherine felt her cheeks flush with anger as she tried her best to keep her voice calm.

"It also clearly states that the name of the Lord should not be used in vain. And while we're quoting the Bible, how about that little issue around eating pork? Have you had bacon lately, Anne?" She didn't wait for a reply. "And how about your friends and neighbors who are cheating on their spouses? Are you scheduling their public stoning?"

"Don't be ridiculous," Anne said. "I'm trying to make a point here."

"So am I," Catherine said. "And my point is that you're a fucking hypocrite. I'd rather you not throw your judgmental God at me. I prefer my God—the one who loves us all despite our flaws. I choose the God who embraces love instead of condemning it. That's the God I want in my life."

"Well, that's pretty convenient for you, then," Anne said. "That lets you off the hook easily. Why don't you go ahead and rob a grocery store? Your God will understand, right? And why not murder all of your problem students, too? You can just ask forgiveness later."

"I'm done with this conversation," Catherine said as she walked toward the family room. "Thanks for letting us take care of Max."

Lila folded herself into Catherine's arms as she rounded the corner. "Did you see my balloon, Aunt Cat?"

"I did, sweet girl. And I'm so glad you're home."

"I'm glad you're here, too," Lila said.

"But we have to go back to school now," Catherine said sadly. "Aunt Cat has to teach tomorrow and Julie has class. Promise me you'll take good care of yourself while I'm gone? No more jumping off the play set?"

"Silly Cat," Lila said. "I didn't jump. I felled."

"No more felling then," Catherine said. She hugged her niece closely, careful not to touch her bandaged head.

Julie hugged Dale as she rose from the couch and grabbed her purse.

"It was so nice meeting you and your family," she said.

"You, too," Dale answered, glancing nervously toward the kitchen.

Catherine kissed Lila once more, hugged Dale, and very deliberately took Julie's hand as they walked toward the door. Anne never came into the room to say goodbye, but Catherine could feel her sister's eyes watching every minute detail of their departure.

23 *eva*

When her oldest daughters were little, Eva dreamed about nothing more than living the white-picket fence life she saw on TV and read about in glossy magazines. Her own childhood—full of wooden spoon bruises, angry words, and empty bourbon bottles—had left her wanting for something she'd been denied. After her single mother drank herself into an early grave, Eva carefully chose Big Jim. His rugged good looks, charismatic appeal, and self-assured smile seemed the perfect trifecta for the head of a strong household. And Eva was certain he would be able to create what she'd wanted and never had. Sure, she loved him. But she also loved the *idea* of him. With his mathematically-inclined mind and his Engineering degree from Purdue, Eva knew he'd provide for all their family's material needs and most of their material wants. And he was fun. He was witty, loud, the life of the party. When Big Jim was around, everyone knew it.

Eva was proud to be his wife, proud that he'd picked her from all the other vying, young coeds, proud that he had lifted her veil to say *I do* instead of lifting Mary Anne Maguire's. Of course, he'd lifted Mary Anne's skirt enough times when they were on the West Lafayette campus, but Eva was the one who'd won him in the end. And when her beautiful, blue-eyed babies had arrived—the ones who looked just like Jim despite all the work her uterus had done to grow them into perfect human beings—she felt very strongly that her idealized fairy-tale life was most certainly becoming a reality.

It wasn't until Big Jim began coming home late smelling vaguely of Chanel and cigarettes that Eva first felt a pang of doubt.

"What were you working on tonight?" Eva would ask once Catherine and Anne were tucked safely in their beds, small hands gripping worn blankies and stuffed bears.

"Big project for Fletcher," Jim would respond. And then he'd eat the meal she'd reheated in the oven, the one she'd choked down for the girls' sake while they waited for their father's return.

"Big project for Fletcher" began to conjure up images of loose women with short skirts and red fingernails. The scenes that played out in Eva's mind gripped her, haunted her, left a dull ache in her chest. Big Jim's naked body underneath another woman, his chest hair gripped in her hands, the familiar curve of his neck being licked by someone who gave him something that Eva herself could not.

And still she welcomed him back into her own bed. Still she ran her fingers through his hair, took his cock in her mouth, fucked him breathlessly. All the while thinking, "See me. See me. Love me. Let me be enough."

It was difficult, however, for Jim to see anyone but himself, challenging for him to notice that his wife had forgotten how to smile, that his daughters were growing into sullen, moody adolescents. Big Jim focused on himself, his own needs, kept a keen eye on his professional success and his trim waistline.

The day Eva found out she was pregnant with Jessica, she sat down on her bed and wept. She hadn't wanted more children, was emotionally ill-equipped to feel enough for the two she already had. She never hit her girls, but she stayed far enough away to quell the constant temptation. She'd heard that women who were once abused, whether as children or adults, often looked for an escape route. Eva knew she would never be able to escape, but she was continually torn between her duties as wife and mother and her desire to get the hell out. This new baby cemented her role firmly and with finality in suburbia. Her only option now was to make the most of the cards she'd been dealt, to try to salvage what was once a viable union, or at least a pretty picture of one.

"What's wrong, Mom?" Catherine had asked when she walked in on her crying mother.

"It's nothing," Eva had wept. "Go play with your sister."

It was nothing, really. A foolish misstep that now became a last-ditch effort to save a marriage that had never amounted to much more than semi-peaceful cohabitation. Eva wept for her idealistic dreams, for the life she'd once envisioned. The Mathers family looked perfect from the outside. To any unsuspecting passerby, they had it all. They were like a decadent dark chocolate bar that you bit into, expecting a thick, rich, substantial adventure. But in reality, the bar is hollow and the chocolate breaks off into little, unsatisfying pieces in your mouth. Bits of it taste good, but overall, the experience is disappointing, lacking, not what you'd expected.

Eva knew it was too late to make a change, though. Her girls were growing up, another was growing in her belly. Big Jim would provide food, shelter, clothing. Eva would pack their school lunches and safely usher them to the bus. But neither Jim nor Eva knew how to unlock their hearts to give their daughters what they really needed. As they continued to polish their skills in disappointing each other, the Mathers adults had also forgotten how to love. Eva Mathers had forgotten many things in her lifetime—especially over the past few years—but that one element was undoubtedly the most important. And there was a sliver of hope, somewhere in the mysterious recesses of her failing brain, that her daughters would someday forget just how much she had failed them.

"Oh, my God," Eva prayed, the memorized words rolling from her tongue, even as so many others eluded her. "I am heartily sorry for having offended thee. And I detest all of my sins because of your just punishments, but mostly because they offend you, my God, who art all good and deserving of all my love. I firmly resolve, with the help of your grace, to sin no more and to avoid the near occasion of sin." She made the sign of the cross and hoped that it was enough.

Even though she knew it wasn't.

24 *anne*

As so often happens during an Indiana fall, the atmosphere abruptly changed from beautiful reds and yellows into cool grays and browns. The leaves that had been so vibrant just last week blew aimlessly across Anne and Dale's back yard. There was a subtle chill inside the house as well. Anne had turned the thermostat down as far as possible to combat the threat of a budget-blowing gas bill—as if they had a working budget. When Anne lifted a sleepy Max from his crib at the end of his afternoon nap, the tip of his nose was cold. Anne longed for the comfort of an ample bank account. She dreamt of a life in which every thought didn't revolve around their current checking balance. She thought about how much easier each minute of her day would be if she had enough money to cover all their monthly bills. She didn't dream about exotic vacations to foreign lands. She simply fantasized about how it would feel to spend freely at the grocery store, never worrying about whether the older clerk with the kind eyes would tell her that her credit card had been declined... again.

"I'm so sorry, sugar," Ruby had said just last week. "There must be a problem at the bank. Do you have another card we can try?" Anne's face had flushed with embarrassment as she dug in her purse for her debit card. She mumbled vague excuses about her husband traveling for work, she giggled nervously to hide her burning cheeks, she ignored Lila's request for a pack of gum, and she silently calculated how much money was left in their checking account. This transaction would undoubtedly cause the electric company's check to be returned for insufficient funds. Anne felt her chest constrict with panic and nausea as she wheeled the grocery cart and her children out to the parking lot. How in God's name was she facing the decision either to feed her children or to power her house?

Anne plunked Max down in his high chair and tossed a handful of Cheerios onto his tray. She could hear the increasingly annoying sounds of *Dora, the Explorer* on the TV in the family room as Lila shouted, "Backpack! Backpack!" Anne sat down at the kitchen table, covered her face with her hands, and cried.

With every tear, she counted another one of her failures. Her marriage to Dale was coming apart at the seams, their family finances were perched precariously on the brink of bankruptcy, her mother was steadily declining with Alzheimer's in a retirement home that always smelled vaguely of urine, her youngest sister had hightailed it to California to escape their crazy-ass family, and Anne hadn't spoken to Catherine in over two weeks. And now her children's noses were perpetually cold.

Although she understood her life was pretty damn good in comparison to so many others, Anne felt crushed under the weight of her burdens. It was sometimes difficult to appreciate your semi-charmed life when your checking account was continually being hit with criminally high overdraft fees for purchases you couldn't afford in the first place. And she couldn't even think about the enormous copay bill that would be arriving from the hospital soon.

When she was a senior in high school, Anne had dealt with her emotions by purging them. She'd eat herself into a sugar high, then stick her fingers down her throat to rid herself of all the sadness in her life. It was a comforting ritual, the eating, the vomiting, the crying, the exhaustion that arrived on its heels. And just to ensure she'd cleaned out all the evil, she'd take a handful of laxatives for dessert.

Eva had caught her in the bathroom one afternoon after an engaging encounter with a box of donuts and a tube of chocolate chip cookie dough. Eva had knocked loudly, shouting Anne's name.

"Are you sick?

"Must have had something bad for lunch."

"Anne, don't lie to me. Are you making yourself throw up?"

"Go away, Mom," Anne had said. "I don't feel well."

Eva had stayed outside the door. In the silence that followed the violent retching, Anne could hear her mother's breathing.

"I know what you're doing, Anne. I'm not stupid."

"You might know," Anne said. "But you certainly don't care." Snot ran down her face. It always happened. The tears, the discharge.

"I do care," Eva had countered. "I care because you're my daughter." As if that was enough.

"Just go away, Mom," Anne said again. And she had. Eva had walked away like she always did. She'd turned her cheek, ignored the mess of her skinny daughter on the bathroom floor, pretended she didn't smell the vomit lingering in the air, and had served dinner like nothing had happened. Catherine had eaten the meatloaf and mashed potatoes with two buttery dinner rolls. Big Jim heated his plate when he'd arrived home, long after his daughters had gone to bed. Anne had merely picked at her plate, had moved her peas around, had excused herself and gone to bed empty and alone.

Today, Anne wished for that oblivion, that escape. She wanted to binge on what little she found comforting in her life. She wanted to gorge on the smell of her daughter's freshly washed hair, on the sounds of the Sunday morning church choir, on the feel of Max's tiny toes. But she knew she was destined to throw it all up, to watch it splash and circle down the drain.

Anne grabbed her laptop and began looking for teaching job postings. This late in the year, very few existed. But she did find a couple of potentials within a thirty-minute drive. There was a part-time teaching aide position—one Anne knew wouldn't pay nearly enough. And there was a temporary maternity leave in Fortville, the next town over. The sixth-grade science assignment began in January and ran through the end of the year. It would be good, Anne thought, to get a foot in the door. If a permanent position opened up later, she'd have an advantage over the other applicants. She studied the online application, became overwhelmed with thoughts of daycare and high-intensity mornings and paper grading. She closed her computer, put Max in his crib, and settled herself on the family room couch for a nap instead.

25 *catherine*

It was equally foreign and comforting for Catherine to have Julie by her side for the next round of chemo. Julie had patiently waited in the lobby while Catherine's port was prepared. She'd buried herself in some homework until they were led back to Dr. Bingham's office. She'd listened intently as the doctor ran through the usual litany of questions. *How have you been feeling? Are your feet still bothering you? Is your nausea under control?* Julie watched while Dr. Bingham checked Catherine's vital signs, listened to her heart, and joked with her about her beautifully bald head. Catherine watched Julie absorb every ounce of information Dr. Bingham presented as if her own life depended on knowing each detail. And Catherine's heart ached just a bit when she thought about Michelle sitting in the same seat Julie now occupied. She was so very sad Michelle didn't know the incredible, giving human being that was Julie. She felt cheated out of sharing her girlfriend with her best friend, felt slighted at the lost opportunity to watch her two favorite females learn to appreciate and love each other.

It had been over a month since Michelle and Catherine last talked. Phone calls were ignored, and text messages were left unanswered. Fate had not yet allowed their paths to cross randomly at the grocery store or the gas station. It was almost as if Michelle had dropped off the face of the earth, greedily pulling her family along with her into some vast and dark unknown.

Catherine had recently lost herself in John Irving's *A Prayer for*

Owen Meany. It was not the first time she'd read the book, but in the absence of her best friend, a new world of pain and loss surfaced. As she drank the words like water, Owen's unnaturally high-pitched voice resonated in her head. His translucent ears glowed in the darkness of her bedroom. And her heart longed for the unconditional loyalty of a best friend who had not chosen condemnation over acceptance, one who had opted for love rather than righteousness.

Perhaps her relationship with Julie *was* an abomination of sorts. Many religious views would certainly support that claim. Catherine understood that her situation was not the norm. Even she couldn't deny questioning how her propensity toward the male anatomy now eluded her. And she also couldn't argue with the raw truth regarding her feelings for her current lover. Julie had become her entire existence. She had wound herself into Catherine's life in a way no one else had ever attempted. When Catherine took a breath, she felt an insatiable need to share it with Julie. When she closed her eyes at the end of the day, Julie's face was all she saw in the shadows, the insistent pounding of Julie's steady heartbeat was all she heard in the silence.

"Thank you for being here," Catherine said as she positioned herself in the corner of the infusion room.

"Where else would I be?" Julie asked.

As the cool liquid began to course throughout her body, Catherine gazed with gratitude and adoration at her friend and lover.

"Where's Michelle today?" sweet Jenna asked as she checked on Catherine's progress.

"She's busy," Catherine said. "I'd like for you to meet my friend, Julie."

"It's so nice to meet you," Julie said shaking Jenna's hand.

And when the introductions were over, Julie took Catherine's hand in her own. Catherine felt invincible in the grasp of Julie's warmth. Such power and might in such a beautiful package. Catherine wasn't sure what she'd done to deserve such happiness.

"I brought something for you," Julie whispered as Catherine's eyelids began sagging with fatigue.

Catherine watched as Julie pulled sheets of brightly colored stickers from her purse and began placing them on the bag that held her chemo cocktail. She smiled as Julie decorated it with small glasses of wine, sparkly bouquets of spring flowers, ballerinas adorned with pink tutus, palm trees swaying in a tropical breeze. She read the bubble letters that spelled the words *Party!* and *Fun in the Sun!*

"This isn't poison they're giving you," Julie said. "It's strength. It's healing. It should look the part."

The other patients in the infusion room watched as Julie worked her magic. Then she moved gracefully from chair to chair, sharing her collection of stickers with all those who agreed to the adventure.

"Do you have Tinkerbell?" the elderly woman next to the window asked. "She's always been my favorite."

"Faith, trust, and a little bit of Pixie Dust," Julie said. "Not only do I have Tinkerbell, but I have Ariel, too. Mermaids and fairies—there's no better combination. What's your name?"

"Jacquelyn," the woman answered. "My name is Jacquelyn." Catherine watched the interaction between the two women—one with so many years behind her, the other with so many yet to live. Young fingers deftly positioned bright rays of hope in the form of dollar-store stickers while rheumy eyes watched with gratitude. Catherine felt a pang of regret. Jacquelyn had been in the infusion room every time Catherine had been there, and yet Catherine had never bothered to ask her name. It took Julie just a few brief moments to bring a smile to the old woman's face, to bring some joy to her lonely day.

"It's nice to meet you, Jacquelyn," Julie said, gathering the old woman's hands into a gentle embrace. "I'm Julie."

"God bless you, Dear," Jacquelyn said. It was a magic moment of human connection for Catherine to witness. It was an experience that made her consider her own ties to the rest of the human race. What are we, Catherine thought, if not bound to each other? Underneath suits of skin—whether sallow and sagging or young and taut, black, white, yellow, or red—we all share a similar beating heart. Blood pumps through veins to keep us alive and drips from wounds when injured. Lungs expand, contract, expand, contract to feed gray masses of brains. Bones both brittle and strong support our external shells. Fat, skinny, attractive, ugly—none of it really mattered in the long run. Only the insides. Only that which the human eye could not see… or judge.

When Julie sat back down by Catherine's side, there was a palpable difference in the room's energy. Jenna smiled at them both as Julie held Catherine's hand.

"Thank you," Catherine whispered. "Thank you."

26 *jessica*

Even when she was very young, Jessica understood her life was different from everyone else's. Her friends had parents who took them on family vacations, who hiked through rocky mountain paths together, who curled up on the sofa for movie nights. Jessica, however, had a series of babysitters who took care of her. It was a slew of teenage girls—Daisy at the top of the list—who made her TV dinners and tucked her into bed at night. By the time Jessica was born, her parents were so far removed from the lives of their children, it was almost as if the children existed in an alternate universe.

On Jessica's tenth birthday, Big Jim, Eva, Dave, and Ellen watched the Wheaton moving van as it pulled away from their Indiana home loaded with the McPherson's belongings, the bulk and weight of a long, accumulated life together. It was headed toward Naples, Florida, and a new adventure. Dave had chosen an early retirement option from his Eli Lilly career, the boys were grown—embarking on careers and families of their own—and promises of both adventure and relaxation loomed.

"I'm not so sure about this early retirement gig," Ellen had said. "Either he's going to keel over from a heart attack the minute he stops working, or I'm going to kill him a week after he's been home."

The celebration the evening before was a birthday/going-away party. But like all other events in Jessica's young life, it wasn't really about her. The chocolate cake had her name written in purple cream cheese icing, and the obligatory *Happy Birthday* song was sung, but the true event was the adults' last evening together. They toasted with champagne and vodka martinis. They danced to James Taylor under the stars. "In my mind, I'm going to Flo-ri-da," they sang in drunken giggles, substituting "Florida" for "Carolina." They laughed and cried and made plans for frequent visits and travels abroad. They hugged and wept and said their goodbyes.

The next morning—on the first full day of Jessica's ten-year-old existence—Ellen and Dave nursed their hangovers with ibuprofen and water, loaded their RoadMaster station wagon with two suitcases, and drove south to meet the Wheaton van.

When the semi driver who was heading north fell asleep and crossed the center line, Jessica imagined that Ellen and Dave were singing *Crocodile Rock* together. They'd always loved Elton John. Or maybe it was Billy Joel. They knew every word to *Piano Man* and *Scenes from an Italian Restaurant*. Perhaps there was just a fleeting split second of fear before the darkness enveloped them.

"Dave!" Ellen might have shouted in a startled attempt to fix the inevitable. And then it would have been over in an instant.

The Tennessee Highway Patrol found bits of their belongings strewn across the highway. A black pump, a Pacers ball cap, a copy of Anne Morrow Lindbergh's *Gift from the Sea*.

The phone rang loudly that afternoon. It pierced the quiet solitude of the Mathers home with an unexpected shrillness. Big Jim was napping in his recliner, and Eva was busy cleaning up from the night before. From her bedroom retreat, Jessica could just make out the sound of wine glasses gently clinking together as Eva put them back in the cupboard. She listened to her mother hum along to Carole King's *So Far Away* on the radio, a melancholy reminder that her best friend was already miles into the next phase of her life. But the keening wail that burst from Eva's chest after the phone had been answered was a sound that eradicated all others. Jessica felt it in her toes, could taste the anguish in her own mouth.

"Nooooooo!" What fell from Eva's lips into the stillness of the afternoon was not human. It had no beginning and no end. It hung in the air like a darkening cloud, threatening rain and thunder, ominously crowding out any remaining ray of sunshine.

The bodies were transported back to Willton for the funeral. Joe and Lucas were handsome and broken as they flanked the matching set of caskets. Their red eyes were weary, confused. Joe's wife greeted friends, family, and strangers. She kept her little ones distracted with veggies and dip and small slivers of vanilla cake. "Why is Grammy still sleeping?" the toddler asked. Lucas's fiancée brought the child some butter mints.

Dave and Ellen's sons shook hands and smiled graciously at the condolences of all those in the never-ending line. Dave and Ellen's many friends mourned deeply. No one, however, felt the impact of their loss more than Big Jim and Eva. For days, weeks, months after the deaths of their friends, Eva could barely get herself dressed. Big Jim took far too many days off work. He later confessed to Eva within Jessica's earshot that he'd driven aimlessly across Indiana's back roads and looping highways attempting to make some sense of his life, of their marriage, of their shared loss.

As was the normal pattern of her life, Jessica traversed her parents' grief alone. Her sisters came home from the funeral, cried with great fervor, hugged Joe and Lucas and their pretty families, and returned just as quickly to college, to grad school. Perhaps they wanted to help Jessica, but they didn't really know her. No one did. It was possible they didn't really care. That was a skill that was never fostered in the Mathers home. Like a fingernail picking at a healing scab, they opened and re-opened each other's wounds, but they never went deeper. Sometimes Jessica longed for the electric snap of a broken bone just to experience something bigger and more powerful than any feeling her family was able to provide her.

Two weeks after the funeral, Jessica got up in the middle of the night for a glass of water. It was still summer vacation. The patio door was open, and a warm breeze wafted into the kitchen, carrying the sound of her father's grief on its balmy wings. Big Jim sat on the patio crying softly into his hands. Jessica had seen those hands on her mother's body, on Ellen's body. Those fingers had caressed and fondled and hurt. Jessica was shocked into silence. She stood rooted to the kitchen floor as she witnessed her father weeping in the night shadows. His shoulders shuddered, the white patches of hair around his temples shone in the moonlight. The sound he made was broken and unfamiliar.

Jessica was frightened, sickened, and embarrassed by her father's weakness, by his humanity. She had never been privy to that part of him. She had only known him as a larger-than-life presence, a successful businessman, a husband who touched his best friend's wife instead of his own. But this grief. It was foreign, uncomfortable, terrifying. She felt small pieces of her soul being sucked into his tear-filled space. They were pieces she was unwilling to give, parts of her she was not ready to surrender. Still thirsty and without water, Jessica turned and made her way back to the safety of her childhood bedroom.

27 *eva*

She could feel the Indiana winter moving in and settling in her old, tired bones. Eva sat silently in her bed and watched it arrive. It crept up the dead ivy and tapped on her dirty window. The birds had stopped singing, the wind had begun whistling, and Eva felt infinitely alone. She missed Big Jim, missed Ellen, missed her girls. Or at least she missed the illusion of the life she might have created had she been a better mother.

Sometimes her feeble memory gave her relief from the burdens of her past.

Sometimes it did not.

In moments of clarity, Eva thought about Ellen. Ellen had been her best friend, her confidant, her soul mate. When Big Jim couldn't meet Eva's emotional needs, Ellen had always been there. In many ways, Ellen had been a better mother to Eva's girls than Eva could have ever aspired to be.

"Ellen makes the best peanut butter and jelly sandwiches in the world!" young Catherine had always claimed. Silly girl, Eva wanted to say, she simply uses strawberry jam instead of grape jelly. There's no magic in that. I can buy strawberry jam. I can make a better sandwich. But she never did. Eva never bothered. Ellen was the one who cared, who paid attention, who knew how to give and receive kindness.

Eva missed Ellen.

But somewhere, things went drastically wrong between them. The lies, the secrets, the betrayal. Eva wanted to believe what she knew was true wasn't actually true. And then she'd seen them together. She'd walked in on Big Jim and Ellen. In her bed. In her very own bed. Eva had quietly closed the door and walked away. She'd gotten into her car and driven. This time, she didn't cry. The ache in her throat was too raw for tears.

And then, many years later, on a lonely stretch of highway in Tennessee, pieces of Ellen had been scattered on the roadside. Eva had nightmares for months afterward. She envisioned bloody limbs in trees, a severed finger—the wedding ring still intact—in a dirty puddle. Imagining was probably worse than knowing.

At least in knowing, the pictures were finite, unembellished.

Life was a journey that Eva didn't navigate well. It was a speeding train, incapable of being stopped. It was an arduous journey. Sometimes the scenery was breathtaking. Sometimes the terrain made her vomit.

Eva missed Ellen.

"Mrs. Mathers?"

The voice came from the doorway. It was a voice she heard almost every day, but one that meant nothing to her. These people took care of her now. These strangers tended to her needs. They fed her, clothed her, and helped her to the bathroom. Her life was full of strangers. Her life had always been full of strangers. Even when the strangers were her own children, her own husband, her own best friend.

Eva's fragmented mind tried desperately to piece together the broken shards of her life. So much wasted, so much to regret. Once—many, many years ago—she'd been loved. She'd married a man who loved her, one who promised to be true. They had three beautiful daughters, and they lived a pretty lie. Over time, they'd all forgotten how to love. Maybe her girls had never really known in the first place.

"Do you want to come to the dining room for your dinner tonight?"

Eva didn't want to go to the dining room. She didn't want to get out of her bed and into her waiting wheelchair. She didn't want everyone to see her try to remember how a fork worked. She wanted to eat her mashed potatoes in the privacy of her own room with *Wheel of Fortune* re-runs playing on her TV. She wanted to be invisible, to disappear, to be scattered along the side of the road.

She wanted to be anywhere but here, to be anyone but herself.

28 *catherine*

The lights in The Stitch were dim, and the background noise was loud and happy. Catherine sat with Julie in their favorite Indianapolis restaurant, sipping the blueberry martinis that were on special.

"I'm not usually a martini girl, but I must admit these are fantastic," Catherine said.

"So good," Julie replied, "that I think I'll have another!"

Julie flagged down their server and placed her order.

"Let's get some calamari, too," Catherine added.

"Perfect," Julie said, leaning across the table. The soft light reflected off her eyes, creating swirls of copper and amber. "So I've got some news to share with you."

"Good news?" Catherine asked.

"*I* think so," Julie said.

"Well, let's hear it then," Catherine smiled.

"I'm leaving Indiana University at the end of the semester," Julie said.

Catherine choked on a sip of martini.

"Is that a good choke or a bad choke?" Julie asked, smiling.

Catherine coughed. "It's an *I-don't-understand* choke," she said. "What do you mean you're leaving IU? Why? And where are you going?" Her voice grew tense as she peppered Julie with questions.

"I'm going to take those one at a time if that's okay with you," Julie said. She took a deliberate breath. "I'm leaving for us."

Catherine started to interrupt, but Julie stopped her.

"Let me finish, Catherine, please."

Catherine sat back, both hands wrapped firmly around the stem of her martini glass.

"I didn't make this decision lightly," Julie said. "It's something I've been thinking about since day one. I want our relationship to continue and to grow, and I think the best way for that to happen naturally is for me to transfer. I don't want to jeopardize your career, Catherine. Our future is too important. I've only got one more year to finish my degree, and I think it's best if I do it somewhere else."

Catherine vacillated between an overwhelming wave of love and gratitude and an anger that boiled up into her throat.

"What about what *I* think?" Catherine asked. "Why didn't you talk to me first?"

"Because I didn't want you to talk me out of it," Julie said. "That's what you're going to try to do, right? But it's already official, paperwork and everything. I'll be a student at IUPUI next year."

"That's over an hour away," Catherine said. "What about your friends? And what about your credits? Will they all transfer?"

"It's all good," Julie smiled. "Truly, Catherine. Trust me on this. I think it's the right thing to do."

Catherine felt the heat rising from her neck into her cheeks. "I'm thrilled that you're happy with your decision, Julie, but I really wish we could have discussed this together."

"We're discussing it now." Julie reached for Catherine's hands, and Catherine pulled hers away. She rested them in her lap, primly folded, fingernails digging into resistant skin.

"Now seems a little late, doesn't it?" Catherine said. "It's not a discussion now. It's an announcement. If this is about *our* relationship, I think it should have been something *we* talked about first."

"I really didn't expect this reaction from you," Julie said. "Yes, this change is about us, but my education is about me. Ultimately, this was my decision to make."

"What about your parents?" Catherine asked. "Do they know? What do they think?"

"Yes, they know. They weren't thrilled at first, but they're always supportive of me. Always."

Catherine felt the accusation in Julie's words, even if it wasn't there.

"When are we going to see each other?" Catherine asked.

"Seriously, Catherine? It's only an hour away. I'll have an apartment in Indy. I'll stay with you when I can. You'll stay with me when you can. We'll commute. People do it all the time. And most importantly, *you won't lose your job because you're dating a student!*"

Catherine couldn't debate that point. She had been concerned about their relationship being discovered by her superiors, about the dean calling her into his office for a reprimand. She'd rehearsed the discussion in her head time and time again. *Catherine, this is a warning. Our handbook clearly states our policy on faculty/student relationships...* But she still wished she'd been a part of this decision. It was a big one, a life-changer, and it felt like Julie had operated under an unfamiliar cloak of secrecy.

Their server handed Julie her drink, set a heaping dish of calamari between them, and asked if there was anything else they needed.

"No, thank you," Julie said politely while Catherine fumed. She was no longer hungry.

"This is a big deal, Julie," Catherine said. "If we're going to be together, I'd like to be a part of these kinds of decisions."

"Well, Catherine, I love you and I want to be with you... and I'm still an individual human being. Sometimes, I'm going to make decisions on my own whether you like it or not."

"This isn't about whether or not I like your decision, Julie, it's about respect. It's about communication."

"There was nothing subversive about this," Julie said. "It was a decision for me to make, and I made it. And then I shared it with you. Why is this turning into a fight? Why are you doing this?"

"Because in the end, it's about *us*. Are you going to continue to make decisions about our future without consulting me?"

"I'm just about done with this conversation, Catherine," Julie said. "I'm not going to sit here and defend a decision that was mine to make."

"But that's the point! It wasn't just yours to make!"

"Okay, seriously?" Julie said, getting up from her chair and grabbing her jacket. "I'm done here."

"Where are you going?" Catherine asked. "What are you doing?"

"I'm getting a cab and going home," Julie said.

"That's ridiculous. Let me settle up here and we'll drive home together."

"No, thank you," Julie said. "I just made another decision, Catherine. I've made a decision to go home alone."

She turned then, headed for the door, and left Catherine sitting at the table with two martinis—one half drunk, one untouched—and a cooling plate of calamari.

29 *anne*

Lila and Max were sleeping peacefully in their bedrooms when Anne clicked the TV off with the remote control.

"Dale," she said, wringing her hands nervously, "we need to talk about money."

Her husband looked at her—and maybe even a little bit through her—and Anne wondered when life had become so hard. Once upon a time, she and Dale had laughed together, had found happiness in the ordinary and mundane. At some point, their focus had shifted to responsibility, to a mortgage, to car payments, to diapers. And with that shift, they had started their journey toward becoming strangers. Every day, Dale went to work and Anne took care of the kids. On the weekends, they tended the lawn and shopped for groceries. In the evenings, they sat together in front of the television while they watched actors lead imaginary lives. They coexisted in the same house, but they no longer shared a relationship. The sound of laughter was foreign, the sound of silence, familiar. It was not the life either of them wanted, but it was what they had somehow created.

"We can't pay the bills," Anne said. She didn't know where else to begin. "There's not enough money. We're behind on the mortgage. Creditors are calling." There it was, out in the open. The hard truth sat in the space between them, finally revealed in all its horrifying glory.

To her surprise, Dale didn't yell. He didn't even seem surprised. He ran his fingers through his graying hair, took a deep breath, gathered his wits. Anne thought it was interesting that her own reaction would have been completely different. Had the tables been turned, she would have charged out of the gates with a vengeance, screaming accusations and demanding answers.

"How bad is it?" he asked.

"It's bad," she said. And then the tears came.

For the next few hours, Anne and Dale sat at the kitchen table with all their bills and bank statements spread out before them. Dale brewed a pot of coffee. Anne blew her nose until it was raw. They tapped on calculators, reviewed retirement accounts, ate bowls of Ben & Jerry's Chunky Monkey. And in the midst of their private turmoil, they looked at each other again. And in looking—really looking—there was some recognition. They saw. They worked together, lamented together. They talked. The minutes ticked away on the clock, but Anne never felt tired. She was afraid, panicked, and overwhelmed. But for the first time in a very long time, she did not feel quite so alone.

"I don't know, Annie," Dale said. "We're going to have to figure out a different way."

"I know," Anne said. "I just don't know what that means."

"We have a few options to consider," Dale said. "First, we can talk about whether or not you should go back to work."

Anne thought about the five words she'd typed onto a job application, knew this conversation was inevitable. She didn't really want to work. It wasn't that she was afraid of work—being home with her two children was far more challenging than any of her previous teaching jobs had been—but she just wasn't ready. She'd failed to fully enjoy the years she'd already been given with her kids. She hadn't planned nearly enough art projects, hadn't built enough blanket forts, hadn't read *Where the Wild Things Are* and begun a Wild Rumpus as many times as she should have.

"What about child care?" Anne asked. "We need to see if it really makes sense for me to go back." But she'd already run the numbers. She knew it was the most logical solution.

"Agreed," Dale said. "It may or may not make sense. We'll have to take a close look. Next, we might need to talk about whether or not this house is too much for us. I'm afraid that maybe we over-bought. Our home-related expenses are killing us. Between the mortgage and utilities, we're spending fifty percent of our income every month. Any financial advisor would tell us that's too much."

"But can we sell it in this market and not take a loss?" Anne asked.

"I don't know," Dale said. "We don't have a huge amount of equity. It would be close. We might be able to break even."

"And what if we can't?"

Dale ran his fingers through his hair again. His eyes were bloodshot.

"Maybe we need to talk to a lawyer," he said. "Bankruptcy would be the last thing I'd want to consider, but it might be something we have to talk about."

A small sob escaped Anne's throat. Bankruptcy. It was such an ugly word, held such dirty connotations. They were well-educated, responsible adults. They weren't the kind of people who declared bankruptcy. Anne thought about her beautiful house, about the wall colors they'd painstakingly chosen, about the window treatments she'd sewn herself. Lately, it had all begun to feel like a noose tightening around her neck. Too much to clean, too overwhelming to decorate, too expensive to maintain. But the possibility of losing it made her want to weep. Where would they go? Could she downsize her house and not downsize her self-image? Anne wondered who she was if she was not a happily-married, mother-of-two, SUV-driving, suburban housewife.

"We're in over our heads, Annie," Dale said. "And I'm sorry I let it happen. I'm sorry I wasn't more aware of what was going on. But if we don't turn it around soon, it's just going to get worse. Our credit card balances are staggering." In a gesture of loss and defeat, he pushed the bills around on the table. "We can't survive like this much longer."

Anne nodded her agreement and wiped the snot from her nose. She looked at Dale's eyes, his mouth. There was the stubble that peppered his chin as the day turned into night. She had always been so quick to judge him, to accuse him, to suspect him. And he sat by her side now without condemnation or reproach. She had married a good man. He was a much better human being than she was. They had two beautiful children. They had made their share of mistakes. They would fall. They would get back up. She shuddered at the notion of their dirty financial secrets being revealed. What if her friends found out? What would she tell Jill (who would undoubtedly be wearing Jackson on her chest during the declaration)? And Catherine? She'd struggled so hard to make their lives look perfect, to keep up with the neighbors, to drive the right cars and choose the right décor. Her life, she suddenly realized, was a big façade. What she thought mattered didn't really matter at all. Her pride, as always, had blocked out the truth. What mattered was Dale, Lila, and Max. They were here, they were healthy, they were hers. She had almost let herself forget. And she hoped she was capable of continuing to remember.

30 *jessica*

Jessica felt more than a little underdressed as she followed the hostess through the steak house to their reserved table. The lights were low, the tablecloths white, and all the male servers stood in the shadows, ready to assist in their crisply pressed tuxedos. Jessica smoothed her cotton maxi skirt with her fingers as she sat down at a table set for two.

A middle-aged server handed her a menu and asked if he could bring her a cocktail.

"Yes, please. A Manhattan on the rocks," Jessica said. She wanted a cold beer but felt uncomfortable ordering a Miller Lite in such a highbrow place.

She was halfway through her drink, enjoying watching all the elegant people surrounding her, when Dale strode across the restaurant. He was self-assured, dressed impeccably in a dark suit and pastel tie. He was handsome, Jessica noted, with his full head of dark hair, graying around the edges. Much more handsome than she'd let herself realize or remember.

He smiled when he saw her, bent down to kiss her on the cheek.

"Thanks for meeting me on such late notice," Dale said. "I'm glad it worked out."

"You're welcome," Jessica said. "I wasn't working, and I don't really have a social life, so I just had to decide whether or not to skip my nightly re-run of *The Office*."

"Well, I'm glad you were willing to make such a significant sacrifice for me," Dale said.

"What can I say?" Jessica said, sipping her Manhattan and enjoying the burn of whiskey on her throat. "I'm a giver."

"I was supposed to meet with one of my client's biggest donors tonight. Weird story. But he had to cancel, and I already had the reservation. I thought it would be fun to catch up in person. And if you've never had the shrimp cocktail here, you've never really lived."

"Thank God I get to begin living tonight," Jessica said. "But why didn't you ask Anne?"

"She has book club," Dale said. "She never misses book club. Not even for shrimp cocktail. And—truth be told—I didn't want to have dinner with Anne tonight. I wanted to have dinner with you."

Jessica sipped her drink as the waiter stopped by for Dale's drink order.

"I'll have a gin and tonic," Dale said. "And we'll start with two shrimp cocktails." They went on to order steaks, medium rare, complete with potato and asparagus sides at a price that made Jessica's heart palpitate.

"I think it's kind of weird," Jessica said as their server walked away, "that you want to have dinner with your sister-in-law instead of your wife."

"Not really weird," Dale said. "We're just going through some stuff right now. We've got some financial issues we're trying to figure out, and the conversation always goes straight there. I wanted a break from it for once."

"If you're having financial issues, an overpriced dinner date with me doesn't seem like the best move," Jessica said.

"Tax write-off," Dale said. "Let's talk a little bit about my work, and then I'll claim it."

"That doesn't sound very legit," Jessica said.

"My worry, not yours. So what do you think about donor retention software? Should we have a way to automate thank you notes, or do you think that eliminates the personal touch?" Dale asked.

Jessica laughed. "I think I couldn't possibly know less about donor retention software. But a handwritten letter is always a nice touch. It's a dying art, I think. I used to have a pen pal when I was little. I met her at summer camp, and we wrote to each other every week for almost two years. I still have those letters. It makes me happy to pull them out of my old shoebox and look at the pink and purple flowers and hearts and stars. We never really talked about anything interesting, but she was important to me. Her letters were important to me."

When the shrimp cocktail arrived, Dale stopped Jessica from grabbing the first one.

"Just a tiny bit of sauce," he advised. "Seriously. This is unlike any sauce you've ever had. Go slowly."

Jessica dipped a corner of a giant shrimp into the cocktail sauce and bit down. Tears rushed to her eyes, and her nose felt like it was on fire. She'd never tasted anything so unbelievably hot and delicious at the same time. Horseradish. Her eyes continued to tear as she reached for her water.

"Holy shit," she said. "That's incredible."

"Best in Indy," Dale said. "Legendary. People come from all over to eat the shrimp cocktail here. NFL players, rock stars, actors, race car drivers…"

"I feel like a celebrity," Jessica said. "They're probably going to want to hang my picture on the wall."

"Undoubtedly," Dale said. They placed their dinner orders and began their second round of cocktails. "So tell me, Jessica… have you thought any more about reconnecting with your sisters?"

Their dinners arrived then, steaming plates of decadence set before them. Knives passed through steaks like butter. Jessica had never eaten anything so rich. It tasted like money.

"Dale," Jessica sighed, "I think about it all the time. All my life, I've thought about it. But I'm just not ready. I don't know when I will be. I don't know if I'll ever be. I have some things to work out in my own mind and heart first."

"I respect that, Jessica," he said. "I really do. But sometimes, life doesn't wait for you. Sometimes, you just have to take a chance. I'm not telling you this to try and change your mind, but I think you should know..."

"Know what?" Jessica asked.

"About Catherine." He paused. "She has cancer."

Jessica felt her chest tighten. "What kind?" she asked in a small voice.

"Breast," Dale said. "She's going through chemo right now. She's doing remarkably well, and the rate of survival for her type of cancer is high. But she's still sick, Jessica. There are never guarantees. I just thought you should know."

Jessica sat silently, listened to herself breathe in and out, stared at the amber colored liquid in the glass before her.

"Thank you for telling me," she said quietly.

"And there's one more thing," Dale said.

"What?" Jessica asked with trepidation.

"Catherine has a girlfriend."

"A what?"

"A girlfriend. Like, a girl that she's dating."

"What are you talking about, Dale?"

"Her name is Julie. I really like her. The shit hit the fan when Anne found out, but they seem happy together."

"Are you telling me that my sister has cancer... and she's gay?" Jessica asked.

"Well, she's had boyfriends before, too, but I think this is her first girlfriend. The point is this, Jessica—life moves forward with or without you. These are your sisters."

"Jesus, Dale," Jessica laughed. "Do you have any more bombshells to drop on me?"

Jessica watched as Dale added a generous tip and signed his credit card statement. He moved with an ease and familiarity that suggested many evenings out, entertaining clients, celebrating special occasions with friends. It was an adult life that was foreign to Jessica, this assumed wealth and privilege. The memories of her parents' own wealth and privilege were hazy at best.

"Well, we spent a night in the hospital with Lila, but that's kind of par for the course with kids, I think," Dale said. "She fell off the swing set. It was pretty scary at first, but she's fine now. That's how we met Julie. Catherine came to take care of Max and brought Julie with her."

"Wow. Just wow," Jessica said. "I'm so glad Lila is okay. And Catherine…? I don't even know what to say. I do kind of wish, though, that I'd been around when Anne met Julie for the first time."

Dale laughed. "It was interesting, for sure," he said. He rearranged his silverware, looked at his plate, then stared directly into Jessica's eyes.

"Jessica, you're missing out." She started to interrupt, but he held up his hand to stop her. "Let me finish. You're missing out, your sisters are missing out, we're all missing out on each other. We are *family*. I know your childhood sucked. I know you've felt discarded. I get that. I really do. Do you know about my mom? Do you know that she killed herself when I was twelve? She died with a bottle of pills in her hand, Jessica, and I found her. All my life I've tried to figure out what I could have done to save her. I was fucking twelve years old, and she didn't care enough about me to stay. She gave birth to me, and then she just left. She didn't even leave a note. I've got nothing, Jessica. No reasons, no absolution, no answers. But her life was hers, and my life is mine, and I couldn't let her take my life when she chose to end her own. That doesn't mean it's been easy. It doesn't mean I don't wish things could have been different, that I haven't woken up many mornings wishing it was all a dream. But my mom doesn't get to dictate how I live, Jessica. Neither does yours. Neither do your sisters. What I'm saying is that I know all of you, and I know you're not all horrible people. Just broken. We're all broken. Do you know why? Because we're human. Broken humans break each other. But we can also heal each other. Which human do you want to be?"

A tear slid down Jessica's cheek and landed on her empty plate.

"It's not that easy, Dale," Jessica said.

"Of course it's not easy," Dale said. "Do you know what it is? It's a choice. Do you know what I choose, Jessica? I choose you. I choose you to be a part of our lives, of my kids' lives. That's what I choose. How about you?"

Jessica stood then, her chair scraping noisily across the tiled floor.

"I'm not ready, Dale," she said. "I'm not ready to make a choice."

He followed her outside the restaurant and to the parking lot, grabbed her hand to slow down her escape.

"Stop running, Jessica," he said. "Please."

Her mind was thick and heavy with alcohol and food as she turned to look at him. His face was open, kind. His eyes bore into hers, a silent plea. He hugged her then, wrapping her up in his arms as she trembled and cried.

She pressed her body—the one that had both failed and supported her—into her brother-in-law and allowed herself to find solace there. For a lifetime, they stood. And then she lifted her tear-streaked face from his chest and looked into his eyes.

Did he lean down into her? She couldn't be certain, although she wanted to say that he had. Regardless, she reached up to pull his face to hers and kissed him slowly, softly.

They stood, lips touching, time suspended, until he pulled his head up and away from hers.

"Jessica, no! I can't," he began.

She did not let him finish.

"God, Dale, I'm sorry," she said. "I'm sorry."

She began backing away, nervous, ashamed.

"I have to go. Thank you for dinner."

"Wait, Jessica!" he called as she hurried away. "Wait!"

But she didn't slow down, didn't look back. She unlocked her rusty Saturn and opened the door hastily, careful not to ding the sleek Mercedes in the space beside her. And then she drove away, avoiding her rearview mirror, staring nowhere else but straight ahead, thinking about nothing more than running away.

Again.

31 *anne*

Anne couldn't stop staring at the baby on Jill's nipple. It wasn't the breast she was mesmerized by, it was Jackson's size. He seemed too big to still be nursing. He almost looked like a toddler hanging there by his pink, puffy lips. Anne half-expected him to sit up and join in the conversation. She hated herself for staring—she was sure Jill was aware of her somewhat twisted fascination—but she couldn't look away. It was like passing a train wreck. You didn't really want to see the death and destruction, but your eyes were glued to the most gruesome and unnatural of details as your car drove slowly past.

They were sitting together in Willton's Brandy River Coffee House. Max, as always, was perched happily in his high chair, dissecting a chocolate chip muffin. Lila played in the corner with some of her preschool friends. Jackson sucked noisily at Jill's breast, and Anne had just refilled her coffee.

"Thanks for meeting me this morning," Anne said. "I really needed to get away from home for a bit."

"It's my pleasure," Jill said. "We don't see nearly enough of each other. It's good to catch up." Jill sipped her tea, and Anne fretted about whether her friend was going to spill the hot liquid into Jackson's curls. Such a precarious balancing act, nursing a toddler-sized baby while drinking a steaming cup of liquid. "So how's your mom doing?"

Anne never really knew how to answer that particular question. By everyone else's standards, Eva was doing relatively well. Her mental decline was slower than the doctor had anticipated, and she hadn't yet reached a sustained, angry, violent stage. Anne had heard that was the cruelest twist of fate, when your normally mild-mannered love turned into a raging, cursing lunatic. In Anne's estimation, Eva was not good, would never be good again. Of course, she remembered the Eva who had hosted elaborate dinner parties and traveled around the world. She remembered the mother who had managed, clumsily, to hold a family together despite Big Jim's continued efforts to rip it apart at the seams.

"She's about the same," Anne said. "Sometimes she knows us, sometimes she doesn't. You know what she can't do anymore, though? She can't read. I remember my mom with a book in her hands all the time. It must be excruciating to have to sacrifice the things that mean so much to you."

"Maybe she doesn't really remember what she's missing," Jill offered. "That would be some kind of blessing within the curse, huh?"

"It just sucks," Anne said. "Alzheimer's sucks. It's awful to watch it happen. No matter what tiny mercies might come and go throughout the process, it's not pretty."

"And Catherine?" Jill asked. "How is she?"

"She's doing really well," Anne said. "She seems really tired, but she just keeps going. She'll win this, I'm sure. She's too tough for cancer."

"You've got a lot on your plate right now," Jill said.

Anne thought about her mounting bills, the late mortgage payment, her unfinished job application. Afraid of tarnishing the image she'd so carefully constructed, Anne had never revealed her darkest secrets. The oversized clock above Jill's head ticked five excruciating seconds away as Anne considered her options.

"There's more, Jill," Anne said. "I haven't told anyone, but we're struggling… financially. We might have to sell the house. We just can't seem to make it work."

"Oh, honey, I'm so sorry," Jill said. "You know that's why we moved from Washington, right? It was just too expensive. We lived in an apartment there, but we knew we'd never be able to buy a house if we stayed. Jim started looking for a job in the Midwest the second I found out I was pregnant. And even when we got here, we underestimated how much having a baby would cost. It's hard being an adult sometimes, isn't it?"

Anne's jaw dropped. She had no idea why Jill and Jim had moved from Seattle—she had always assumed it was job-related, but not necessarily voluntary. "I didn't know," she said. "And do you still find it challenging here? I mean, financially?"

"Absolutely!" Jill said with an easy, unencumbered smile. "Every month, we struggle to make ends meet. We have to scrimp and save and cut coupons and turn the thermostat down. Eventually, I'm sure I'll have to go back to work. We'll never be able to send Jackson to college if I don't. But for now, I'm just enjoying my time at home with him. I'll take it for as long as I can."

Anne couldn't believe how nonchalant Jill was about her finances. No college savings? No padded checking account? Anne was convinced everyone else in the universe was financially better off than she was. There was a strange sense of comfort in the realization that she might be wrong, that there might be others who also ran their checking accounts into the ground and whose emergency savings accounts were nonexistent.

"I think that time at home for me might be coming to an end soon," Anne said. "I'm applying for teaching jobs again."

"Oh, Anne, that's wonderful!" Jill said. "But are there jobs available at this time of year?"

"Very few. But I'm looking closely at a maternity leave. I'm sure a thousand others are, too, but it's worth a shot. I don't know if I'm ready to go back yet, but I need to go back."

"I don't know if I'll ever be ready to go back to work, either," Jill admitted. "But I know it's inevitable."

"I don't even know what you do," Anne admitted.

"Marketing. Like half the rest of the world. My degree is in Marketing, and my minor is in Economics. The Economics part is pretty funny considering we're not really financially viable right now. But there are things more important than money, right?"

Anne supposed there were. But when you had no money, it seemed not only like the most important thing, it seemed like the only thing.

"So when do you find out about the maternity leave job?" Jill asked.

"Well, I haven't even finished my application yet. I'm still worried about all the logistics—you know, schedules, childcare, something to wear beyond yoga pants. The details paralyze me a little."

"Anne, I'd be happy to watch the kids for you," Jill said, pulling Jackson from her breast and refastening her nursing bra with one expert hand. She gently laid a milk-drunk Jackson into his stroller.

"What?"

"The kids. I'd love to watch them. We could use the extra money, and I know it would be easier for you to leave them with someone you know."

Anne was shell-shocked. She, herself, couldn't imagine offering to babysit someone else's children in a million years. She could barely handle the two she had.

"Do you mean that?"

"I wouldn't have said it if I didn't." Jill took a sip of her tea. "Seriously, Anne, it's a great opportunity for both of us."

"Thank you," Anne said. "Really. Thank you. That's a huge, generous offer. I don't even know what we'd be able to pay yet."

"I know whatever we decide on will be fair. Those details will work themselves out. Just know that the offer stands."

"Thank you," Anne said again. "I'll talk to Dale. He'll be thrilled. Now I just have to get the job!" She laughed nervously.

Lila was crouched in the corner, picking at an unglued corner of the wallpaper. Anne looked away quickly, uninterested in correcting her. It would have been a loud and public battle, and Anne wasn't up for it. It was just wallpaper, after all.

"There's something else I wanted to talk to you about," Anne said, a nervous lilt in her voice. "It's weird and awkward, and I'm not even sure how to start. It's about Catherine."

"You mean the cancer?"

"No," Anne said. Then she laughed in spite of herself. "My God, we sound like a soap opera: *As the Mathers House Turns.*" She said it in a deep, dramatic voice. "Are you ready for this? Turns out Catherine is gay."

"What?" The women at the table next to them turned in response to the volume of Jill's voice.

"I know, I know! It's crazy. She brought her girlfriend to the hospital after Lila fell. Her name is Julie. She was a student, but she dropped Catherine's class, so apparently, that makes everything okay."

"Holy shit," Jill laughed. "This *is* a soap opera!"

The coffee shop bustled with life. Quiches were served, tables were bussed, conversations buzzed in the air. Lila had stopped picking at the wallpaper and had moved on to bossing her friend around. Anne added more sweetener to her coffee.

"It's just so damn confusing sometimes. I mean, Catherine drives me crazy, but I do love her. And she's happier now with Julie than I've ever seen her. She's calmer, she's more present, she's more loving. That can't be all bad, can it?"

"I'm not sure that love is ever bad," Jill said.

The control freak in Anne bucked at this little nugget of truth. She wanted people to believe in what she believed in, wanted them to see her point of view. But why did she feel that way? Wanting everyone to succumb to her own way of thinking was just another manifestation of her own self-centeredness. She longed to be like Jill, to be able to embrace people despite their differences, to be able to love unconditionally. What a beautiful sentiment. And what a difficult journey for Anne. Negotiating that particular landscape required her to get out of her own comfort zone—although lately, it seemed she was being forced out of every corner of familiarity. On one hand, she wanted to be ready for new visions and new ideas, but on the other hand, she wasn't yet prepared. Whenever she and Dale took the kids camping, they spent elaborate amounts of time packing and prepping and loading every possible necessity into their backpacks and suitcases.

From marshmallows to wet wipes to hot dog skewers to hiking boots, she felt safe when she was prepared, when plans were well-established. Winging it had never been her strong suit, the unknown never her chosen path.

"Mama, I have to potty!" Lila announced loudly as she ran back to the table. Jackson jolted in his sleep at the sound of Lila's screech, but quickly settled back into his slumber.

"I'll take you, Lila," Jill said. "Your Mama can stay with the boys."

"Yay!" Lila yelled.

Anne watched her friend take her daughter by the hand and thought about how she planned to answer the questions that remained on her unfinished job application.

32 *catherine*

She wanted to blame it on the chemo. The ups, the downs, the crazy irrational thoughts and feelings she experienced, the confrontational situations she created, the weepiness and angst. But Catherine knew better. This is who she was. Who she'd always been, who she'd continue to be.

It had been four achingly long days since Julie had stormed out of The Stitch. Ninety-six hours of second-guessing and restless sleep and aching limbs, heavy with regret and angry, lingering words. She needed to call Julie, but she didn't know what to say or where to begin.

She was grading student compositions when the loud buzz of her phone broke the silence. Julie, she thought. Julie. And as she hit the green "Answer" button, she realized the face on the screen was not her dark-eyed beauty, but another one, both familiar and distant.

Michelle.

"Hello," Catherine answered awkwardly, her heart racing.

"Catherine?" the voice said. "It's Michelle."

The room before her swam, the laptop screen blurred. All else ceased to exist as the sound of her best friend's voice landed on her ears.

"Michelle. How are you?"

"I'm good. We're good. We're all good," Michelle stammered. "How are you, Catherine?"

"I'm fine," Catherine said, choosing the word she hated most in the world. Fine was a nothing word, a meh, an absence of everything important.

A Grand Canyon silence filled the space between them. Catherine imagined Michelle sitting on her family room couch, fuzzy socks on her feet, her favorite purple blanket bunched in her lap. She imagined the busy noise of her house in the background, doors slamming, kids shouting, TVs blaring. Catherine could feel Michelle's discomfort on the other end. She still knew her so well, even now.

"Catherine, I don't want this to be weird or uncomfortable. I know it's been a long time. And here's the thing... I miss you. We miss you. The kids miss you."

Catherine wanted to respond with the same, but she couldn't. She missed Michelle. She did. The void in her life was still there. The edges of the wound were no longer raw and open, but they were tender to the touch. And yet, something else existed there, too. Acceptance? Indifference? Catherine wasn't sure what to name it. She didn't mean to stay silent, but she did. In the absence of all the right words, Catherine remained quiet.

"Are you there, Catherine?"

"Yes, I'm still here, Michelle."

"I can't stop thinking about you, or about us. I miss being with you at chemo. I miss being able to text or call you to share a funny kid story. I miss sitting by you at Jake's basketball games."

Michelle continued talking, but what Catherine noticed was that Michelle never said this: I'm sorry.

"I'd like to see you. I'd like to get together and catch up. Can we do that? Is it too late?"

Was there a statute of limitations on disappointment? On betrayal? On broken promises? Catherine wasn't sure. Where did you go when everything you once held sacred was no longer? When the person you thought you knew became a stranger? When the things you believed in were so completely at odds with another's beliefs?

"Honestly, Michelle, I don't know," Catherine said. Because she truly did not know. She imagined meeting Michelle at John's Landing, their favorite bar. She imagined sharing a platter of wings, sauce on the side, like they always did. But she could not imagine the conversation that would follow, only the punctuated and awkward silences, the unspoken accusations, and the apologies that remained wishes instead.

"Not even a glass of wine?" Michelle asked. "Surely, you still drink wine?"

The levity Michelle was attempting made Catherine sad. There was so much nothingness between them. This was foreign terrain, both tricky and treacherous, an entire world buried beneath the soil.

"Do we really want to do this, Michelle?" Catherine asked. "Because the last time we talked, you showed me someone who was a stranger to me. I'm sure you feel the same way about me. At least, that's what you communicated. I don't know that we can go back. So that just leaves one direction. Forward. Are we both willing to move forward from here? Are we different people now? Are we better together? Or are we better wishing each other well and moving in different directions?"

Michelle choked back a sob. Catherine could almost see her wringing her beautiful hands, her long, elegant fingers.

"Mommy!" Catherine heard in the background.

"Not now," Tony said, shouting from another room. "Mommy's on the phone. What do you need?"

"I don't know," Michelle said. "I really don't, Catherine. But isn't it worth finding out? Aren't we worth that much?"

"I *thought* we were worth that much," Catherine said. "And then you decided we weren't. You broke my heart, Michelle. You really did. You made me re-think everything we once were. I thought we were meant to be together—no matter what. And then you walked away. I'm not sure I'm ready to go through that kind of pain again just so you can figure out how you feel about me… and about Julie. Honestly, Michelle, I'm not trying to be mean or dismissive, but I truly don't know where we go from here, knowing what we do now. Maybe we aren't supposed to stay together. Maybe there are others out there who will better serve our needs. Maybe that's the real message here."

"So your answer is no?" Michelle asked.

"My answer is a question, Michelle. My question is this: Can you love me unconditionally? Can you love me for who I am and not for who I choose to love?"

"But isn't who you choose to love part of who you are?" Michelle asked.

And that was the answer Catherine both expected and dreaded. This friend, this rock, this *Forever and Ever, Amen* piece of her heart would not be able to reconcile herself to a relationship that she couldn't name, couldn't label, couldn't judge. Perhaps time and distance would change those things, but Catherine knew that right here and now was not a place where they could move forward together. Not until Michelle was ready. And she wasn't ready. Nor was Catherine ready to be broken again. There was a trust, a safety net that had been established over the course of twenty years. And in an instant, Michelle had removed it.

"If the part of me who loves someone else is the part that's most important to you, Michelle, you're missing out on who I am, on the other 99% of me. I'm afraid that 1% will always cloud how you feel about me and who we choose to be for each other. I love you, Michelle. I will always love you. But I need you to love me, too. Wholly. And I'm not sure you can. But here's what I do know for certain: I can't let you back in and lose you again. I just can't. Maybe that's selfish. And I don't wish you anything but happiness. But I'm just not sure that happiness includes me. And Julie."

"I'm not sure, either, Catherine. But I was willing to find out."

Catherine felt her resolve strengthen. She sat up straighter in her chair.

"When you find out, Michelle, let me know."

There was no anger in her words, just a sad realization that they'd reached an impossible crossroads, that they were not the people they once believed they were.

"Goodbye, Catherine." Michelle's voice was strained from the effort of holding back tears. Catherine knew it well. She would always know that part of the friend she once believed was forever. But there were other things—deeper things—that she did not know. Catherine was not willing to let them slowly reveal themselves, to pull her into a rollercoaster of emotions that could not, in the long run, serve either of them well.

"Goodbye, Michelle."

When she disconnected her phone and her friend, Catherine wept. It was a cleansing cry, and a wall was built with every tear she wiped away. On her side of the wall was love and promise and possibility. And she knew exactly what she needed to say to Julie. The words that had seemed so elusive before were embarrassingly obvious.

When Julie answered Catherine's call on the second ring, Catherine didn't even greet her. She simply said, with humble sincerity, "I'm sorry."

33 *anne*

5:00 a.m. was awfully early to be wrangling with an uncooked turkey. Grossed out by the wet goosebump flesh of the bird, Anne waited impatiently for her coffee to brew as she stuffed her hands into the cold carcass. It was one thing to eat a turkey dinner, another thing entirely to prepare her first one. Anne wasn't convinced she'd ever be able to eat anything but mashed potatoes on Thanksgiving Day again.

Once the bird was safely in the oven, however, she sat down to relax. A warm cup of coffee, lightly sweetened with milk and sugar by her side, a book in hand, and George Winston playing in the background brought a welcome peace to and respite from the tumult of her life.

She read a chapter of the latest Anita Shreve novel and then reveled in the pre-awakening silence of her home. When she was able to quiet her own mind, Anne noticed the world around her quieted, too. She listened to the sounds of her house, the click of the grandfather clock, the rattle of the storm door in the wind. A small pang of regret pulled at her heart when she thought about this place. Even when she went back to work, they might have to sell it. Under the crushing weight of their outrageously high credit card bills, a slew of personal loans, and a hefty pile of medical bills from Lila's recent stay at the hospital, the logical path was to downsize their mortgage. There was some relief in thinking about arriving at the other end—the place where she didn't stay up at nights thinking about foreclosure and electric bills that couldn't be paid—but she knew the path to get there would not be simple or straightforward. And she was already missing her custom window coverings, her carefully selected paint colors.

One day at a time was her new mantra. And when that failed, *One hour at a time*. Sometimes, however, she had to resort to the next breath. Two breaths could be too many.

An eclectic blend of scented candles, Lysol wipes, dirty diapers, and laundry detergent smells swirled around her and settled into her bones. These would go with her. Wherever they landed, these smells and sounds and tastes would go, too. There was comfort in this thought, no matter how small.

"Mornin', Annie," Dale said, hiking up his sleep pants and simultaneously scratching his head. His hair was wild, unkempt, and lovely.

"Good morning," Anne answered. "Would you like some coffee?"

"I'll get it," Dale said. "How's the turkey?"

"It's in the oven. Let's keep our fingers crossed." She'd never been much of a cook. When people spoke of the magic and artistry of preparing food, Anne never really understood. She could follow a recipe and could generally turn something edible out, but she never really felt the lure of her stainless steel appliances and her high-end cookware.

"Have you thought any more about the house?" Dale asked as he set a fresh cup of coffee before her.

"Only every second of every day," Anne said. "It's all I can think about."

Her eyes filled with tears.

"We overbought, Annie. Plain and simple. And we're behind on our payments. We made some mistakes. We can fix them. And we won't do it again. I know it sounds dumb and sentimental, but we have each other. That's really all that matters."

"I got the job," Anne said with sad resignation.

"Oh, Anne, that's fantastic!" Dale said. "Which one? When did you find out?"

"The sixth grade science maternity leave at Fortville," Anne said. "The principal called on Monday. I accepted. I start in January."

"Congratulations," Dale said. "I'm proud of you. I know you can do this, Anne, even if you don't believe it yourself. And I'm here to help with the kids. We'll do it together. We will."

Slippered feet shuffled their way, a bed-headed toddler sleepily maneuvering them.

"I smell something," Lila said as she padded her way into the kitchen in her Hello Kitty pajamas.

"Happy Thanksgiving, sweetie pie," Anne said as her daughter climbed into her lap.

"Do I smell pie?" Lila asked.

"Nope, not yet. That's turkey in the oven."

"A turkey? With feathers?"

"No feathers," Dale laughed. "Just stuffing."

Lila satisfied herself with Dale's answer and rested her tangled curls on her mother's chest.

The holiday morning unfurled slowly and gently. Or perhaps the morning seemed slower and gentler because Anne moved that way. She smiled more, yelled less, breathed a little. As she prepared the rest of the afternoon meal, she danced to Michael Jackson and tickled Max in his high chair. She completely massacred the corn casserole (who can't make a corn casserole, for heaven's sake?), threw it in the trash can, and never gave it another thought.

At 1:00, Catherine and Julie arrived. Julie's dark hair was tied back loosely with a brown velvet ribbon. Catherine removed a gray sweater cap when she entered the house, and they both looked well-rested and happy.

After the post-hospital fight and numerous heated discussions on the phone, Catherine and Anne had reached a tentative truce, a cease-fire. Anne was beginning to realize how little control she really had over others' lives, despite her deep desire to control everything within her reach. She'd offered to host Thanksgiving, to extend an invitation to Catherine's lover as a peace offering. It was her attempt at acceptance, at reconciliation, at surrender. She'd even prepared the guest room for their arrival with clean sheets and towels and bottles of Evian. She'd tried not to think about them sleeping together in the bed, arms and legs intertwined.

"For you," Julie said as she handed Anne a bottle of Malbec. "It's one of our favorites. Hope you enjoy it, too."

"Well, let's open it and find out," Anne said.

"Everything smells wonderful," Catherine said. "I might have underestimated you."

The adults sat together, talking, drinking, and entertaining the kids when necessary. In spite of her mixed feelings about Catherine and Julie's relationship, Anne couldn't help but like Julie. She was warm, engaging, funny, smart. When Catherine and Julie touched, Anne was still taken aback. She had to push certain images from her mind, thoughts of them kissing, caressing. But when she allowed herself to see the love in the relationship instead of the physicality, Anne was in awe of how much Catherine and Julie genuinely cared for one another.

And the wine Julie brought was very drinkable. Anne was already on her second glass.

She heard Dale rattle the car keys. "I'm going to grab a couple more bottles of wine before the liquor store closes. I'll be right back."

The women gave him no argument.

Catherine settled into the couch with Lila in her lap and *Make Way for Ducklings* in her hand.

"Do you have siblings, Julie?" Anne asked.

"Nope," Julie said. "Just me. The one and only. My parents are both surgeons in Wisconsin. I had a lovely childhood—nothing but the best, really—but their careers are very demanding. Adding another kid to the mix would have thrown the entire empire out of equilibrium."

"So what brought you to Indiana?"

"Scholarship money. Pride in my ability to pay my own way through college. And I wanted to get away, to live for once without my parents making every decision for me. Imagine running from Wisconsin to Indiana for an adventure," Julie said, laughing. "But it's been the best decision of my life."

The required banter continued as everyone eased into the afternoon. Dale arrived back home with four more bottles of wine and a case of Corona.

"Mexican beer for Thanksgiving," he said. "What's more appropriate than that?"

Anne and Julie worked in the kitchen together while Catherine and Dale entertained the kids. The conversation was easy and the meal—even without the corn casserole—turned out delicious.

Both Max and Lila, stuffed full of mashed potatoes and worn out from a day full of play and laughter, were down for the night by 7:00.

"Are you ready to go see Mom?" Catherine asked.

"As ready as ever," Anne said. "Which isn't saying much."

"Do you want to go with us, Julie?" Catherine asked.

"No, thanks," Julie said. "As much as I'd like to meet your mother someday, I think the two of you should go together. I'll stay here and help Dale clean up."

The sisters reluctantly left the ease and comfort of Anne's home— Elton John playing loudly in the kitchen as Dale and Julie sang *Rocket Man* in unison—to drive to Regal Manor, brightly colored Tupperware containers of leftovers in their hands.

The automatic entrance signaled their arrival with a whoosh and a rush of warm air. They walked silently down the long hallway to Room 118, both intimately familiar with the path, the distance, the nurses' station on the left, the wheelchairs in the hallway.

"Hi, Mom," Catherine said as she walked into Eva's tiny room. Eva smiled, then turned back toward a *Seinfeld* rerun playing on her TV. Her eyes, however, seemed to be focused just to the left of the screen rather than on it.

"We brought you some turkey and green bean casserole," Anne said as she placed the containers on Eva's bedside tray. Eva looked at them without any trace of recognition.

"Here, Mom, let me help you," Anne said, placing a fork full of beans near Eva's lips. Eva didn't respond.

"You're not hungry?" Anne asked. "That's okay."

Anne set the fork back on the tray and turned to watch Jerry and Kramer banter.

"Where's Jim?" Eva asked.

"He's dead, Mom," Anne said, weary of the effort it took to keep her mother abreast of her own life.

"Oh," Eva said, turning back to the TV. For the first time since Anne could remember, Eva didn't break down into her new/old grief. She simply went back to watching Elaine and the rest of the gang.

Before the half-hour episode was over, Eva was snoring lightly with her head tilted to the side.

Anne and Catherine turned the overhead lights off and the TV volume down. Before leaving, Anne bent to kiss her mother's paper cheek.

"Happy Thanksgiving, Mom."

34 *jessica*

He phoned daily, sometimes multiple times a day. Jessica didn't answer. She called in sick to work twice, worried that he'd make his way to the Carousel Lounge, that she'd see his face in the crowd, waiting for her, forcing her to talk.

She didn't want to talk—didn't have anything to say, really—until all her plans were in place.

And ten days after Thanksgiving, they were.

Jessica sat in her empty kitchen, U-Haul loaded and waiting at the curb, cash from the sale of her Saturn in her purse. A bright red IU sweatshirt protected her from the chill in the air but did nothing to warm the cold emptiness in her heart. She fiddled with the key she was leaving for Greasy Harvey as she called Dale.

"Jessica! Jesus! I was worried about you. Are you okay?"

"Hello to you, too, Dale," Jessica said.

"You know what, Jessica?" he said, his anger pulsing through the phone line. She could feel his angst and unease spill all over her. "You don't get to just pop in and out of my life without expecting me to give a shit. It's called common courtesy. I didn't know if you were dead or alive. That's not okay."

"I'm sorry, Dale," she said, although she was more sad than sorry. She counted to one, two, took a breath. "I called to let you know that I'm moving back to California."

"What?" he asked, clearly taken aback.

"I'm leaving for California. Today. I got my old job back, and I'm going to crash with friends until I find my own place. It took me a lot of time to realize I'm not ready to be back in Indiana," Jessica said. "I thought I was, but I really wasn't. Obviously." She thought about their kiss in the parking lot, blushed at the memory of how simultaneously right and wrong it felt. "Finding you made me realize that I shouldn't have left."

"You're leaving because of me?"

"No, I'm leaving because of me. You've been good to me, Dale. Better than I deserved. But I'm not ready to be a part of my family again. I'm just not. And being here is like living with ghosts. I'm constantly worried about running into one of my sisters or someone from our past. I just need to go back and figure things out, to figure myself out. I'm no good for anyone else until I can be good for myself. And I'm not, Dale. I'm not there yet."

"Jessica," he said, "you can't keep running. That's no life. You deserve better than that. You deserve more. Can we meet? Can we talk in person?"

"No," Jessica said, her voice cracking. "I'm leaving, Dale. I'll call you when I get there, so you'll know I'm safe. You've been a good friend to me, and I appreciate that more than you know."

"Jessica, please…"

"Goodbye, Dale."

She stifled a sob as she ended the call. She was stuck between two places, between two lives. She didn't want to leave, but she couldn't stay.

Neither here nor there.

The cab of the U-Haul smelled of stale smoke, and the steering wheel was cold on her hands. Jessica steeled herself as she drove toward Willton and the Regal Manor Nursing Home. She didn't distract herself with a classic rock station or some bad nineties pop songs. Instead, she paid close attention to the harvested cornfields that sat cold and barren under a gray December sky. She allowed herself to feel the chill emanating from the windshield, the trees that had finally lost all remnants of a beautiful fall. They were stark and regal, strong and resilient. Every year, they bloomed. Every year, they relinquished their leaves to the inevitable Indiana winter winds. But they stood tall, nonetheless, and were rewarded with the spoils of spring, the green possibilities. If Jessica chose to stay, would the same happen for her? Could there be rebirth after so much loss? And more importantly, could she ever find the strength to stay?

Jessica pulled the U-Haul into the parking lot of the Regal Manor and sat staring at the red brick and brown grass. Would her mother recognize her? She was haunted by the notion that Eva asked about her every time Anne visited, but she doubted the sincerity of the request. Alzheimer's—from what little she understood—was a fickle thief, rendering its victims' past and present realities unreliable. She was unsure of what to say to her mother, this stranger who slept within the walls before her. They shared the same genetics, the same blood, but they were strangers. Mother and daughter, but no more intimately connected than the patrons who frequented the Carousel Lounge. Did Eva regret the mother she was? Did she wish things had been different? Was she even capable of understanding the past any-more? Jessica remembered that her mother had once been beautiful. But now? Jessica wasn't even sure she'd recognize the woman who'd given birth to her nearly three decades before.

I'm going in, Jessica thought, *and I'll ask for her room number. That's step one.* She did not have a step two. And as Jessica felt her hands shift the U-Haul back into drive, she realized that even step one was flawed. She pressed the gas, turned the radio on, and began her journey west. She didn't even look in the rear view mirror to see Regal Manor grow smaller and smaller until it was nothing more than a hazy memory.

35 *catherine*

Christmas morning crept in with a hush. Tangled legs and arms stretched, moved, awakened.

"Merry Christmas," Julie said, a gentle hand skimming Catherine's cheek, tracing the laugh lines around her eyes.

"Merry Christmas to you."

They lay in silence together for a while as the morning light began inching through the spaces between the blinds and the window. In the stillness, Catherine recalled a Christmas more than thirty-five years before, another that had dawned with silent anticipation. She had begged Big Jim and Eva for a Baby Alive doll.

"I'll take care of her!" she promised. "I'll keep her clean all by myself!"

And when Catherine had snuck down the stairs that Christmas morning, there she was—perfectly brand new and smelling of synthetic materials.

Catherine thought she'd fall in love with her baby doll, the one she'd named Jenny. She had plans to carry her everywhere, sleep with her every night, sing songs to her during the day. But it didn't happen that way. When Jenny arrived, Catherine didn't know what to do or how to feel. She mixed the powdered food, fed her doll with the tiny spoon, and waited to be enamored. But then she had to change the diaper. It was a disgusting mess, and cleaning the doll was even worse. She'd held Jenny under the faucet, trying to direct the water into her mouth without soaking the rest of her. The water ran from Jenny's bottom into the sink as it washed out the remaining food. Catherine had determined that it was far more entertaining to flip Jenny upside down and watch the water spew from her mouth instead. Before the original supply of food was depleted, Catherine was done with Jenny. She'd tucked her under the bed and promptly forgotten about her.

"I'm glad you're here," Catherine said, looking into Julie's dark eyes.

"Me, too."

They kissed then, a luxuriously slow, sensuous encounter. Catherine's heart beat faster, her body tingled.

The morning unfolded with coffee and breakfast casserole—one Julie had prepared the previous day. They unwrapped each other's gifts—a cashmere hat, scarf, and glove set from Julie to Catherine; a leather backpack from Catherine to Julie. After a third cup of coffee was poured, Julie produced another present—a small box, beautifully wrapped in foil paper and curled ribbons.

"What's this?" Catherine asked.

"One more. For you."

Catherine gasped when she opened the jeweler's box and saw the ring. It was an understated, antique gold band with a repeating pattern of diamonds and emeralds.

"Julie?"

"It was my great-grandmother's," Julie said.

Catherine shook her head, unable to speak.

"No, listen, Cat," Julie interrupted. "It was mine. Now it's yours. There's nothing more I want to give you right now than this ring. It means the world to me. And so do you."

"Julie, I can't take this…"

"Yes, you can," Julie said. "If it makes you feel better, I discussed it with my parents first. Please don't argue about this, Catherine. I didn't make this decision lightly. I love you. I want you to have this piece of me, of my history. Nothing would make me happier than seeing you wear it. Nothing. This… and you… I've never been more sure about anything in my life."

The ring fit perfectly on Catherine's left pinky finger. She held her hand up to the Christmas lights and watched the emeralds dance.

"I love it," Catherine said. Tears fell from her eyes. "And I love you. So much. Thank you, Julie. For this, for you, for everything. I have never been happier. I can't imagine ever being happier."

"That goes both ways, you know. I don't want to think about life without you. Ever."

"Then let's not think about it," Catherine said as she pulled her cashmere hat onto her bald head. Sometimes it was easier not to think about things you couldn't see.

"I bet Anne and Dale are having a fantastic Christmas morning," Julie said.

"Yes, if Anne allows herself to have some fun. Christmas with kids is an entirely different experience, I suppose."

"I'm looking forward to joining them this afternoon. I hope Max loves his trains," Julie said.

Max turned one shortly after Thanksgiving, and Julie had convinced Catherine to buy a Thomas the Tank Engine train table. Although he wasn't quite sure what to make of his birthday gift (after all, what one-year-old gets excited about a table?), they'd also purchased tracks and trains for Christmas—including Max's favorite, Peter Sam.

"I'm guessing he sleeps with Peter Sam tonight," Catherine said. Of course, she'd also insisted they add the "Catherine" car to her nephew's new collection.

The gift they thought Lila would like best was a Boogie Board Writing Tablet. She loved coloring, that girl. And electronics. They'd chosen the pink floral version for a pink-loving girl and had wrapped it in pink Christmas paper. It had been fun shopping together for the kids. And for a brief moment, Catherine had wondered what it might be like to raise a child with Julie. Then she promptly remembered her disastrous affair with Baby Alive.

"What time are we going to Dale and Anne's?" Julie asked.

"We're supposed to gather around 3:00. If we get there at 3:02, Anne might just explode."

"You two are so mean to each other sometimes," Julie said. "You always expect the worst. Sometimes I think when people treat each other that way, that's what they get: the worst of each other."

Catherine stopped to think about Julie's words and recognized the truth within them. She did seem always to expect the worst from Anne. Somehow, she and Anne had both fallen into a familiar pattern of thinking the worst of each other. When she allowed herself to be more judicious, Catherine was able to admire the life that Anne had created for herself, the work that went into raising and nurturing a family.

"You might be right. It's just so familiar to both of us—swing, deflect, swing, deflect. We Mathers are all about self-defense and self-preservation."

"Here's my advice," Julie said. "Choose differently. You girls never really had a family. Make one now. Be there for each other. I've met you both, and I like you both. Maybe if you give it a chance, you'll learn to like each other, too."

"Maybe…" Catherine said as she began stretching her creaky joints to rise. She had to admit that she'd been enjoying her sister's company lately—the meals together, the nursing home visits, the talks that dipped below the surface. It felt like they'd all reached a different level in both their relationships with each other and in their individual lives. Maybe they could create something from the nothingness that had defined their relationship for decades.

Maybe.

Reflecting on her relationship with her sister—and her history of failed relationships in general—reminded Catherine of the news she'd forgotten to share with Julie. Catherine had spoken with Jenna last week about some medication adjustments, and Jenna had sadly informed her that Jacquelyn, the older chemo patient who was so charmed by Julie, had passed.

"Julie," Catherine said, "I know the timing isn't great, but you also know my memory isn't great these days. Chemo brain." Catherine smiled gently. "I found out from Jenna last week that Jacquelyn died."

"I'm so sorry, Catherine," Julie said. "That makes me so sad. How does it make you feel? Is it scary for you?"

Catherine wasn't frightened by Jacquelyn's death, she was sad.

"It's just… she was there, and then she wasn't. It's crazy, really. We spent all that time together, all those intimate hours. We sat in that same corner week after week. And I never talked to her, never even knew her name until you asked her. I don't know if she was married, if she had kids, if she had grandkids. I don't know anything about her. But I could have. I could have known every detail of her life. Maybe she was a famous artist, or a beloved doctor, or a badass lawyer. Maybe she was the first person in her family to go to college. What if she walked in protest marches in the Sixties? She might have had the best peanut butter cookie recipe on the planet. She was a person. A living, breathing human being with a past and a present and a future. She had a story to tell. I could have known her, might have even grown to love her. But I didn't bother. And now it's too late. How fucked up is that?"

"It's not fucked up," Julie said. "It's just a missed opportunity. Life is full of them, don't you think? But Catherine, think about your sister, your brother-in-law, your niece and nephew. You don't want them to be a missed opportunity, too, do you?"

Catherine thought about her whole family, about Big Jim, about Eva, about Jessica. Their entire existence was a missed opportunity. At least until now. Maybe Julie was right—maybe it didn't have to continue to be that way. Perhaps it was as simple as flipping a switch, of choosing differently.

After all, she'd chosen differently with Julie, had chosen to follow her heart, had chosen vulnerability over the safe and secure. And that had been a good choice. It had been, in fact, the best choice she'd ever made.

36 *jessica*

Tues, Dec 27, 7:55 p.m. (Jessica)
Arrived in CA a couple weeks ago. Still need some time. Can I have your email?

Tues, Dec 27, 8:17 p.m. (Dale)
Call me tomorrow?

Tues, Dec 27, 8:29 p.m. (Jessica)
I'd rather email. For now at least.

Jessica Mathers
Back in CA
January 15, 2011

Dear Dale,
   It's been a while. I know. Thanks for not pressuring me to talk. Here's what I have to begin with, though... I'm sorry I kissed you. So very sorry. I was wrong, it was wrong. I can't take it back. I'm sorry. Meeting you again put me in a strange place, and I was kind of an emotional mess. I just got lost for a bit. I'm trying not to be lost anymore.
   I'm sorry it took me so long to communicate at all. But it's

better that I waited. I'm feeling less anxious and more settled now.

It's good to be back. Good and bad and scary and exciting all rolled into one. I guess I should say I'm glad to be here, mostly.

Turns out my roommate, Beth, also has a boyfriend. His name is Ted. So really, I have two roommates, Beth and Ted. BeTed. TeBeth. (That's Hollywood style. I know I'm in LA, but whatever.) So far, it's not been too bad, but it's a bit cozy. Beth eats a lot of tuna. It always smells nasty in our apartment. Ted keeps trying to fix me up with a friend of his, but the guy's got an annoying laugh that I can't get past.

I found a new waitressing job. And so far, it doesn't even require me to take my clothes off. (That's a joke! Are you laughing?) I'm settling in. Figuring it out as I go. Maybe someday soon, I'll have a plan that extends beyond my posted work schedule. Not yet, though.

How are you? Did you make quota in December? Did you guys decide to sell the house? Did Anne start her new job? How are the kids? Hug them for me, please (even though they don't know who I am).

Peace and Love,
Jessica

37 *anne*

It was working. Sort of. Day by day, they were stumbling into a routine. Anne got the kids up and dressed. Dale fed them while she showered. He dropped them off at Jill's in the morning; she picked them up after school. By the time they all got to the dinner table, however, they were done. Picking, fighting, arguing, whining—everyone except Max. It was tough, this new routine. Lila was clingy at night. Max's nose dripped continuously.

The realtor had suggested they put the house on the market as soon as possible, so Anne and Dale spent their weekends touching up paint and making donation trips to Goodwill. They weren't sure where they were going to live if the house sold quickly, but they hadn't gotten around to tackling that detail. Not yet.

Anne's colleagues at school were helpful and supportive, but the students were downright wild. Their hormones raged, tears fell regularly, fistfights were always a possibility. She often felt more like a babysitter than a teacher.

"Seriously, Meredith…" Anne said to one of her colleagues. "If Lila and Max act like this as teenagers, I might send them to live with someone else for awhile."

"The crazy waxes and wanes," Meredith said. "They're still coming down from their winter break high. And you're fresh blood." She smiled. "They'll get into a routine soon. They're not so bad, really. In fact, you might even fall in love with a few of them. This age is pretty special if you're willing to look past their mood swings and fashion faux pas."

"I can't look past anything right now," Anne admitted. "I can't even focus my eyes, I'm so tired. I feel like I'm swimming upstream. And sometimes, I'm not even keeping my head above water."

"That gets easier, too," Meredith said. "Give yourself some time. This 'working mother' gig is new for you. Cut yourself a little slack. The new job, the kids, the house, your mom—you've got plenty on your plate right now. You know if you need anything, all you have to do is ask, right?"

"Right," Anne smiled, grateful for the gesture. She knew, however, that she'd never ask for help, would never show that kind of weakness. Martyrdom was her chosen path—always had been. There was no need to consider an alternative at this point.

But Dale bore the brunt of her fatigue and sadness and frustration. Night after night, Anne blamed him for everything—their rocky marriage, their disobedient daughter, the home sale, the stress.

"This was not my dream!" Anne yelled after the kids had gone to bed. "I wanted to stay home with our children! You were the one who was going to take care of us. That was our plan. Now we're barely—barely—holding it all together! Damn it, Dale! Why couldn't you make this work?"

Dale never argued back, much to Anne's surprise. She knew she was being completely irrational and altogether unfair. None of this was Dale's fault alone. Most of it, if she was completely honest, was hers. She'd wanted the custom home, the big cars, the professional landscaping. She'd wanted a second baby when they were both just getting used to the first. She always pushed, then pushed a little more to get her way. Enabler, Anne thought. That's what Dale was. He should have pushed back, should have stood up to her.

In her more rational moments, she realized how ridiculous and mean and vindictive she was. But her rational moments were few and far between. The contentedness she'd felt throughout the holidays had been packed away with the Christmas decorations. This new normal was eating her alive, bit by bit.

"We'll get through, Anne," Dale said, dodging the icy stares and the angry words. "This is the worst of it. Once we sell the house, we'll start again. Relieving this financial burden will be huge for us. Huge." He scrubbed the dishes and folded the laundry. He cleaned the toilets and made the kids' beds.

Anne slept when she could and cried away many of her waking hours. When the weekends came, she and Dale worked on the house side by side, but as strangers. Anne's favorite time of day was when she was in the car by herself, delivering Goodwill items, picking up fast food for the kids, running to the grocery store. It was the one time she felt free and unburdened by the demands of her home and her family. But deep inside, she knew she wasn't really free and unburdened. She was a wife and a mother and a teacher and an underwater homeowner. There was nothing about her that was unburdened, nothing that even hinted at relief any time soon. She also knew innately that things were bound to get worse before they got better.

What she didn't know, what she couldn't possibly comprehend— not yet—was the meaning of worse.

38 *dale*

Dale Jackley
Re: Back in CA
January 20, 2011

Dear Jessica,

It was really good to hear from you. I wish you wouldn't have waited so long. I miss knowing that you're here, but I'm glad you're settling in to your new-old life. And the kiss? Don't think another thing about it. It happened—we can't change that—but it doesn't ever have to be mentioned again.

I'm glad to hear you found a job and that your roommates are working out (mostly!). Things here are crazy, but okay. Anne's job seems to be going well, but she's stressed out. There's a lot of tension, but I know it will pass. If you look at the list of biggest life stressors, we've cornered the market on a few of them. Anne's never been one to deal with change very well. We'll get through it, though. I might take up smoking, but we'll get through it. (Ha!)

The kids are great! They really love going to Jill's during the day. When I drop them off in the morning, they can't wait to get inside. Max loves Jackson. It will be fun when they're old enough to play trains together. That's Max's latest obsession, thanks to Julie and Catherine. Lila is still loving school and still bossing everyone around. She comes by that pretty honestly, I guess.

The house hasn't sold yet, but we've had a couple of showings. Those are the absolute worst! We run around like maniacs trying to make beds and pick up toys and make sure there aren't any dirty diapers smelling the place up. Then the realtor comes by with the prospective buyers for about five minutes and they decide the colors aren't right or the house is facing the wrong direction or they don't like the cabinets. It's crazy.

Speaking of crazy, it's time to get the kids to bed, so I have to run. Great hearing from you. I hope it won't be so long next time.

Love,
Dale

39 *catherine*

"It's kind of surreal," Catherine admitted. Julie was driving her to St. Mark's Oncology Care Center for her final round of chemo. The February sky was cold and gray, but nothing could dampen Catherine's spirit today. "This routine has become such a part of my life, it feels a little strange now that it's ending."

She looked at Julie in the driver's seat of the Volvo, marveled at her careful "ten and two" hands.

"It's really ending, isn't it?"

That beautiful smile spread across Julie's face.

"It is, Cat," she said. "It really is. Welcome to the rest of your life."

They pulled in to the center's parking lot and donned their knit hats and gloves. The wind bit at their faces as they made their way through the automatic doors. An instrumental version of Billy Joel's *She Got a Way* played throughout the waiting area.

"Hello, ladies!" Front Desk Betty (as Catherine and Julie affectionately called her) pushed a clipboard toward Catherine. "Big day for you, Professor!"

"Big day, indeed," Catherine concurred.

She signed releases, paid her outstanding balance—the portion insurance didn't cover. She met with Dr. Bingham, talked with him about the medications she'd take for the next year, about the scheduled removal of her port. When she was hooked up to her chemo treatment for the final time, she allowed her thoughts to drift to her father.

She was young, no more than five, and the Mathers family was at the beach. Eva sat in the shade of an umbrella with baby Anne, who crawled to the edge of the blanket time and time again, shoving fistfuls of sand into her mouth. The ocean was calm, it kissed the shore with a whisper and retreated gently. Catherine sat at the edge of the water watching the tiny crabs surface and dig. Big Jim approached her loudly, roughly, the way he approached everything in life.

"Come on, Cat," he said. "Let's swim."

But Catherine didn't want to swim. She was content to sit, to feel the waves on her toes and the sand between her fingers.

"No thanks, Daddy," she said.

"Oh, come on!" her father bellowed. "It's not every day we get to swim in the ocean."

Catherine had no interest in swimming in the ocean. She had tasted the salt on her fingertips and imagined the life that lived in those blue waters. It was not her place to swim, it was theirs—the fish, the sharks, the crabs. She preferred the clear blue of the community pool where she could wear her Speedo goggles and see everything as clearly as if she were on dry land.

Her father, however, was waiting for her, so she went. He scooped her up in his arms and traipsed into the sea. As the water rose above his knees, his hips, and to his bare belly, Catherine clung to him more tightly. She knew if he let her go, the sand was too far down for her feet to touch. Her heart raced, and she dug her sloppily painted fingernails into his strong, hairy arms.

"That's good, Daddy," she said. Her racing heart caused her voice to shake. "That's far enough."

"Nonsense, little girl," he said, making her feel small and silly. "You can swim. The ocean is just a giant swimming pool. No need to be afraid."

He had peeled her hands from his body and held her at arm's length.

"No, Daddy! Please!"

But he laughed. And with a quick movement, he had tossed her into the salty blue.

Catherine would never forget the feeling of flying backwards, briefly, suspended between the safety of her father's arms and certain death. She yelped, tried to catch her breath, but it was too late. The waters enveloped her, and she gulped a mouthful of salt and sea. She felt herself sinking down, felt her toes hit the sand below. She'd opened her eyes instinctually, tried to focus through the watery haze. When she looked up, she saw light above the water's surface, and she kicked, flailed, fought to find the sky. When she surfaced, frantically, she coughed, sputtered, cried out.

"Swim to me, Cat!" Big Jim had called. "I'm right here."

He was a few strokes away, but it might as well have been a million miles. She had no choice but to swim, to kick, to fight her way back to him.

And she did.

Her first chemo felt a great deal like her reluctant introduction to the ocean. The fear, the breathlessness, the feeling of being disconnected from all that was safe and known. But here she was, her face about to break the water's surface, her father's arms within reach. She had made it.

"What are you thinking about?" Julie asked.

"The ocean," Catherine said. "My father."

"We should go to the ocean," Julie said dreamily. "As a celebration."

Catherine looked at her lover as Julie placed a palm tree sticker on her chemo bag. At that moment, there was nothing Catherine wanted more than to lie on the beach with her beautiful Julie, to read in the sand, to hold hands and drink wine and watch the sun burn itself out in the sea.

"Yes," Catherine said. "Yes."

She closed her eyes then and drifted into a peaceful sleep. Her dreams were of dolphins and sand castles instead of the deep black unknown. Even her subconscious had gained some perspective.

"Cat, Cat..." She woke to a gentle nudge, beautiful black hair cascading over her face. "Cat, sweetie, you're done."

Done. She was done. It was over. Though with cancer, she knew, it was never really over. There was always a possibility of relapse. But today, she was done. She had made it.

Julie leaned in and brushed Catherine's lips with a tender kiss. As Catherine sat up, she couldn't help but notice Jacquelyn's chair, now occupied by an older man.

Once her IVs were removed, and the congratulations bestowed upon her by the nurses and her fellow patients, Catherine and Julie walked to the lunch bell hanging on the wall. Traditionally, those who finished their last round of chemo rang the bell upon their departure.

Catherine pulled on the chain, ringing once, twice.

"Ring it with me," Catherine said to Julie. And together, three more rings. Shouts of congratulations, clapping, smiles.

Julie hugged her tightly, whispered in her ear.

"This is our new beginning," she said. "Welcome to your big, bright, beautiful future."

40 *anne*

The day began like any other.

After Dale changed Max's diaper, he sat his sixteen-month-old son on the family room floor to play and made his way to the kitchen where he began cutting bananas and boiling the water for their favorite breakfast oatmeal.

Anne scurried throughout the house in her modest heels, watching the morning unfold, clicking as she went. She bent quickly to kiss the soft of Max's cheek, left him playing contentedly with his Duplos, and called a harried, "Goodbye! Love you!" to Dale.

Precisely what happened in the following moments neither could quite recall. A folder containing Anne's meeting notes was forgotten, the phone rang, Lila emerged groggily from her pink Parisian bedroom, some coffee was spilled.

In the garage, Anne started the Suburban, Guster blaring from the speakers, the diplomatic approach to a troubled student and his demanding mother cycled through her head. *Mrs. Delacorte, we need to talk about Joey's ability to appropriately redirect his anger.*

Anne backed from the garage into the driveway, remembered her forgotten folder, threw the truck into park, ran back into the house for her evidence (*1. On January 10th, Joey threw his math book at the wall. 2. On February 8th, Joey threatened to stick Thea's finger in the electric pencil sharpener...*), climbed once again into the driver's seat (a little trickle of sweat now rolling down the back of her neck), and refastened her seatbelt.

Max, in his Winnie the Pooh pajama top—the one with a cheery, "Hello, Friend!" emblazoned across the front in cartoon bubble letters—toddled into the driveway, the early March cement shockingly cold on his tender feet.

His parents didn't witness this last journey, but they both imagined it again—then again—until it became as real and impenetrable as the slabs of granite that comprised the countertops in their overpriced kitchen.

In the hazy Valium dreams that followed, Anne heard Max's gravelly voice calling, "Mama! Kisses!" as he ran behind the wheels of the Suburban, the one whose consumer safety ratings ensured her children would be most protected in the event of an accident. When they had first found out they were expecting Max, Anne and Dale had spent the extra money for a vehicle bigger than they needed. There were Cheerios on the floor, toys and books scattered throughout the back, Lila's Baby Lulu bows strewn about.

When Anne felt the heavy tires back over something, she was more annoyed than concerned. What had the kids left out this time? A scooter? An oversized plastic baseball bat? Lila and Max had been so excited for their first taste of spring—it was always that way after a brutal Indiana winter, the promise of warmth baiting everyone with hope and a premature need to wear shorts—they'd been outside as much as Anne would allow. She had to ask, then beg, then threaten them back inside when their noses were red and cold and it was time for dinner and baths.

And so Anne kept driving, the "For Sale" sign in their front yard flashing across her rearview mirror. She felt the second bump as the front tires went up and over. She turned the wheel to angle out onto the street, and that's when she saw.

A language invented by fallible humans cannot adequately describe the scene of a miniature, unmoving body in a Winnie the Pooh pajama top, auburn curls tumbling like a gentle ocean surf in the morning breeze. *Hello, Friend.*

Anne threw open the door and stumbled to her ruined son. All that remained in her was one keening wail, animal-like in its intensity, Max's name tethered to the end of it like a kite.

She knew instinctively that she should not move him. And she also knew instinctively that it no longer mattered. So she chose to grab him up into her mother-arms, crushing his heart to her own as if she might somehow restart its steady, reliable cadence. In two small seconds—two out of the millions she'd been given—everything was irrevocably changed.

Dale appeared at the wide open front door, summoned, most likely, by Anne's primal scream. She watched him run toward them, his mouth open, noticed the blood blooming across her freshly pressed work blouse.

"Oh, my God, Anne! What have you done? What have you done?"

Anne didn't know whether Dale regretted the impact of those words after they were spoken, but they pinned her down like an anvil around her neck. The "you" in that question, the implied blame, the accusation was something she could not hold. In the days and weeks to come, the noose of guilt around her neck tightened, tightened.

Dale pried Max from Anne's arms. The Suburban's tires had not touched their son's face, had not damaged his perfect skull, the ever-expanding brain with all its firing synapses, suddenly silenced. But Max's chest—that place where the life pulsed in and out—was crushed, the protective shield of his butterfly-wing ribs no match for the six-thousand-pound vehicle, the one idling carelessly at the end of the driveway, oblivious to the bananas browning in the kitchen.

after

"No one ever told me that grief felt so like fear."
—C.S. Lewis

"Forgiveness is the fragrance that the violet sheds
on the heel that has crushed it."
—Mark Twain

41 *dale*

Choosing the outfit your toddler should be buried in is an impossible undertaking. Not because an outfit cannot be chosen—there are certainly enough pairs of Baby Gap khakis and rugby striped neckties shorter than Dale's forearm—but because making that choice under the inherent circumstances is an aberration, an unnatural detour in life's journey.

Dale stood with Anne in front of Max's closet. They were both motionless, nearly emotionless. Nothing remained within them. There were Max's frog overalls, the Easter outfit Anne had bought just two weeks before—the one that matched the madras pattern of Lila's new dress. There was his owl sweater, the corduroy pants.

Anne sat down in the spot where she was just standing, and Dale noticed something clutched in her hand. Peter Sam, Max's favorite train. She held it out to him like an offering.

"Yes," Dale said. "That. Peter Sam. Yes."

It was all the conversation they were capable of so far, these staccato bursts of shared understanding. He gently took his wife's arm and led her back to their bed. She curled up into the dirty sheets, the ones that were beginning to smell of sweat and overuse. Catherine would choose the outfit. Catherine could choose the outfit. Dale could not.

Catherine and Julie arrived later that afternoon. They entered quietly, reverently. Julie took Lila to McDonald's, let her play in the indoor playground. Catherine stayed with Anne, stroked her sister's hair, coaxed her into the shower where she could wash away the dirt and grit of the past forty-eight hours. Dale watched as his wife was led through the act of living, as his sister-in-law reminded Anne how to walk, how to breathe, how to exist.

He knew the Valium was dulling her senses along with the sharp edges of her pain, but he was worried that without help, Anne would not remember how to live. She was nearly catatonic at times. He missed the tears, the vocal anguish. When she was crying and screaming and wailing, he knew she was, at least, still alive.

"Time, Dale," Catherine assured him. She poured them both a Scotch on the rocks and sat down on the couch. "She needs time. Lots of it, I'm sure. We're here—Julie and I. We're here for whatever you need."

Dale choked, set his Scotch on the table, a sob escaping from deep in his gut.

"Oh, God, Catherine," he cried. "Max… Max…"

She held him then, like a baby in her arms. He fell into her, the weight of his body pressed to her chest and in her lap. For an eternity, perhaps, he cried. And then, he stopped.

"We need to pick an outfit," he said.

Catherine understood. So they went back to Max's closet where Catherine chose a pair of tiny tan slacks, a blue and white checkered Oxford cloth shirt, some argyle socks, an impossibly small pair of slip-on shoes.

"This is Max," Catherine said. "My handsome nephew. Right here."

The doorbell rang throughout the evening as friends and neighbors and Tot Moms arrived with casseroles, cakes, breads, cookies, whole hams. Dale took the food in his hands, delivered it to Catherine and Julie in the kitchen. Anne remained in bed. Lila was excited to see some of her friends arrive with their parents.

"My brother died," she said to her classmate, Sarah. "He's in heaven now. With Jesus."

Sarah nodded. "That's what Mommy said."

"He's not coming back," Lila continued. "We'll never see him again.

Well, except for the funeral tomorrow. We'll see him there. And some-day in heaven. But he'll still be dead."

Dale winced at his daughter's blunt words, but also realized what she was repeating was exactly what they'd conveyed to her. He won-dered how much of this she would remember after experiencing it at such a tender age. Would she remember Max at all? Or would her memories consist of hazy, dreamy waves of semi-recall? Max's laugh, the smell of his freshly shampooed hair, the feel of his tiny hand in her own?

"Want to come play in my room?" Lila asked her friend.

Sarah's mother intervened.

"We can't stay today, sweetie, but I'll bring Sarah back soon."

"Mom!" Sarah protested.

"If there's anything you need," Sarah's mom said to Dale, "... any-thing at all."

The moms and dads all said the same thing. There was really noth-ing better to say. There were no words to help any of them traverse this path.

Shelby Mattison, the Jackleys' favorite neighborhood babysitter, arrived a short time later to take Lila to the playground. Shelby was quiet and visibly uncomfortable around Dale. There was no way to bridge the silence between them, and words were inadequate. Her young arms had held Max, her hands had fed him. Now their beloved babysitter only had one child to tend. Now Dale and Anne only had one child to tend. Dale handed Lila's backpack to Shelby, noticed her eyes brim with tears. But he could not offer her comfort.

"Thank you," Dale said because he was grateful. Grateful for the people bringing his family food, taking care of his daughter, sur-rounding his family with love, supporting them when they could not stand on their own.

42 *jessica*

She had not answered her phone.

He'd called back. And then he'd called again. Jessica watched Dale's name flash across her screen, listened to her phone buzz until it went silent.

"Call me, Jessica," Dale said on her voicemail. "Please."

His voice sounded strange, distant. Something was wrong, Jessica was certain. Had Anne read their emails? Found out about the kiss? Had Eva passed? A multitude of possibilities swirled through her imagination.

The phone buzzed again. A good human being would answer, she thought. A good friend would be there. She waited, though, until the buzz was nearly silent before she pressed the button that would connect her to Dale. She wasn't a good human being, after all. She was just human.

"Hello?"

"Jessica…" Dale's voice cracked.

"What's wrong, Dale?" she asked. "I know something's wrong. You're scaring me."

He choked back a sob, and she heard him swallow.

"Jessica, it's Max," he said.

She thought about Lila's hospital stay last autumn, wondered briefly what kind of accident could befall a toddler. A tumble down the stairs? A broken bone? Stitches?

"There was an accident," Dale said. "Max was hit by a car."

Jessica stopped breathing.

"And Anne was driving."

She waited, perched on the edge of shock and disbelief. What was Dale saying? How in the world did any of this make sense?

"Is he...?" Jessica asked, the work "okay" lingering in the space between.

"He's dead," Dale said. "Max is dead."

Everything stopped for a moment. The ticking of the kitchen clock, the hum of the refrigerator, the game show Beth and Ted were half-watching in the next room, Jessica's heart.

"Dale," she whispered. And there was nothing more she could say. He cried on the other end. She imagined him, phone to his ear, hand over his eyes, sitting slumped at the kitchen table. He was blocking out all the light, she was certain. Because there was no light, there was only darkness.

A series of visions ran through her mind: Max playing baseball, Max starting school, Max going to the Prom, Max heading to college, Max getting married, Max becoming a father. But these were broken promises now. They were nothing more than wisps of cloud on a windy day, shifting, changing, incapable of being held, slipping through outstretched fingers.

"Dale," she whispered again.

"I bought a plane ticket for you," he said. "The funeral is Saturday. Please come home, Jessica. I need you. We need you."

"Dale," she said again, stupidly.

"I have to go," he said. "Check your email."

After they disconnected the call, she opened her email and found her ticket. Her flight left at 7:00 the following morning. She was scheduled to work tomorrow evening, but she knew she could call in sick.

Could she go? Should she go?

On one hand, Jessica felt the right thing to do was to be there for Dale, for her sisters. On the other hand, she wondered if her presence would create more heartache. Perhaps it was best for everyone to traverse their own grief before she forced herself back into their lives. The only one who really needed her there was Dale. The only one who would notice her absence was Dale. If Jessica showed up uninvited and unannounced into Anne's own private hell, wouldn't that make things worse? Far worse? Wouldn't she open wounds that could not currently be tended? Would Anne simply bleed out from so much trauma?

A bird landed on the windowsill and began pecking at his reflection in the glass. *Peck, peck, peck.* Jessica covered her ears. *Peck, peck, peck.* The noise was louder than it should have been and infinitely more jarring. How could such a tiny creature create such a cacophony? Her head ached. She closed the curtain, left the kitchen, found solace in the comfort and quiet of her bedroom where she sat in the dark and wept.

43 *catherine*

Julie and Catherine arrived at the funeral home seconds behind the Jackleys. Catherine parked near the front door and watched as Dale, Anne, and Lila exited Dale's Volvo. No one could bear even to look at the Suburban any more. Later, it would be traded for something much smaller and more economical, a Honda Civic four-door with its high safety ratings and low price tag. It was lost on no one that only one car seat was needed now, and a single row of seats would more than suffice.

Lila twirled in her purple floral dress. Julie had taken Lila shopping the evening before, had let her pick out whatever she wanted.

"Do you think it's appropriate?" Dale had asked.

"I don't think there's anything appropriate about what's happening tomorrow and the day after," Julie had replied, her voice soft with respect and strong with conviction. "She's a little girl. I think whatever she wants to wear is what she should wear."

And no one argued.

Over the past few days, Catherine had watched as her lover did everything that needed to be done, but that no one could necessarily articulate. Julie knew when Lila needed an outing, heated up a meal when the rest of them had forgotten to eat. In this fog of grief, Catherine felt anchored by the strength of her partner, and so very grateful for her unassuming presence.

The Sanders Funeral Home was cool and quiet when they entered.

Mr. Sanders—grandson of the founding father—met them at the door. Already, the entry was overflowing with flower arrangements, the scent sharp and piercing, an assault on their senses.

Anne read some of the cards as she moved from vase to vase. Catherine noticed that Anne had not yet cried today. Numbed with Valium, fatigue, and hunger, she had been eerily stoic.

"I got a new dress," Lila announced to Mr. Sanders.

He crouched down so he was eye-to-eye with her. "And you look beautiful."

"Daddy says I get to see Baby Max today," she said. "But he's still dead."

"Yes, honey, he is." Mr. Sanders stood to address the adults. "Are you ready to go in?"

Anne followed first, then Dale. Catherine took Lila by the hand and motioned gently for Julie to join them as they were all led into the showing room.

The casket, so shockingly small, was at the front of the room flanked by floral arrangements with sashes that read, "Our Boy" and "Little Brother." The distance was a million miles, and they walked it, together, step by step.

And then.

There he was. That precious baby boy. Unnaturally pale against his checkered shirt, Peter Sam resting beneath one tiny hand.

Anne and Dale knelt before him, heads bowed, shoulders shaking.

"Hi, Baby Max!" Lila said. Dale scooped her up in his arms and held her close. She reached down into the casket to touch her brother's face.

"Daddy, he's so cold. Where's his blankie?"

Catherine felt an ache in her chest worse than any cancer pain. Anne had been sleeping with Max's worn, frayed blankie. Dale had asked if they should bury the blanket with Max, but Anne couldn't let it go. The night before, when Catherine and Julie had checked on Catherine's sleeping sister, they'd found Anne clutching the blanket to her face with both hands.

"We're keeping his blankie with us," Dale said.

"But Daddy, it's Max's blankie," Lila argued.

"She's right," Anne whispered. "You're right, Lila-Bear. Max needs his blankie."

Julie turned, unasked, and drove back to the Jackley home. When she returned with the tattered blue blanket, Lila ran to the casket and tucked it beside Max's pale head.

"There you go, Max. Now you won't be so cold."

When Mr. Sanders opened the parlor doors to welcome the waiting guests, the line already snaked out the door and into the cool March air. Fathers, mothers, children, neighbors, high school and college friends, church acquaintances... they'd all come to stand with Anne and Dale, to share a small piece of a grief too heavy to bear. Family pictures were placed around the funeral home—Max's birth, his first steps, his first birthday party. A video montage played on various screens throughout the building. Julie had facilitated all of this. With Dale's direction and Catherine's help, she'd chosen pictures, set them to music, created a memorial for a boy whose life had only just begun.

Julie took Catherine's hand and they stood together, a witness to an unnamable grief.

44 *dale*

Dale Jackley
The Other Side
March 21, 2011

Dear Jessica,

I wish you would have come to Max's funeral. I was angry, but now I'm not. I'm sure you had your reasons. Who am I to judge? But I missed you.

I've found that the only way to the other side is through. So that's what I'm doing. I'm making my way through. I went back to work last week—just part-time. I'm worried about leaving Anne alone, and I need to take care of Lila. Anne's just not ready to do it yet. She's not ready to do much of anything yet.

I worry so much about her, Jess. I know that grief takes time—maybe more time than I can even wrap my brain around. And I don't think we'll ever completely be out of it. Max was a part of us, and now he's not. It's too much, really, for any parent to fathom.

We're seeing a counselor, but only because I'm making Anne go. She barely eats. You wouldn't even recognize her, she's lost so much weight. I have to force her to shower. She hasn't gone back to work. I don't know if she ever will.

Oh, and did I mention the house is in foreclosure? We

took it off the market because we couldn't bear the thought of strangers traipsing through Max's room. Everything fell apart at the seams when we lost Max. Everything. But the house? I don't even care. We'll stay here until they force us to leave, and then we'll figure out what's next. When you've lost what's most important, nothing else seems to matter.

Moment by moment is all I can do right now. Thank God for Jill who takes care of our sweet Lila when her Mom and I are unable. And so often, we're unable.

Love,
Dale

45 *catherine*

Julie didn't bring much when she moved in at the end of April, but all Catherine really needed and wanted was Julie herself. After Max died, Julie had sublet her apartment in Indianapolis. Time had suddenly become this precious, precarious gift, and neither was willing to second-guess how much remained. It was an easy transition, living together. They quickly fell into a routine of coffee, the morning paper, work, school, dinner, and wine.

Catherine made the drive to Willton at least once a week now. Julie's easy commute to Indianapolis made Catherine realize how selfish she'd been with her time and her unwillingness to traverse the miles that separated her from her family. She visited Eva, visited Anne, tried to ensure the fragile pieces of her family were held together. Eva grew quieter with each passing visit. She no longer asked about Jessica or Big Jim. Instead, she stared at her small TV, watching, but not comprehending. The doctors said her physical health was generally good, and Catherine wondered how long her mother would live in this unreachable shell, this island of oblivion. The nurses moved Eva frequently so she wouldn't get bedsores, and they fed her baby-like foods because she'd forgotten how to chew. Catherine thought about the promising life Max once had before him and the inequity of death. God help her, but she wished her mother's life—this pointless existence—could have been breathed back into her nephew.

And then there was Anne. She had retreated to a place no one could quite reach—not Dale, not Catherine, not even Lila. Anne had mastered the art of doing just enough to survive—showering occasionally, eating enough to sustain (but not nourish), brushing her teeth. She even read Lila a bedtime story now and then, and often curled up beside her when she was done, holding her daughter too tightly against her chest, staying in Lila's bed all night. But there was a hollow indifference in Anne's eyes that frightened Catherine. Faithfully, though, Catherine visited, took her sister out to dinner, played with her niece, checked on her brother-in-law. She clung desperately to the belief that time would eventually bring her sister back around, maybe not to the person she once was, but at least to a person who could figure out how to exist and function on this earth.

On her last visit home, Catherine had driven by the Mathers' family home. The sprawling ranch from her childhood looked smaller than she'd remembered. The flowering pears that lined the street—the ones Big Jim had planted when they first bought the house—were huge towers of soon-to-be green. Those trees had been alive longer than the Mathers sisters had. They'd weathered snow and ice storms, summer heat, and high winds. And still, they stood tall, roots firmly planted in the ground. Humans, Catherine thought, were so much more fragile.

The basketball goal where Catherine had honed her skills had long since been taken down. But she could vividly recall shooting free throws in that driveway until it was too dark to see. And she'd jogged up and down these streets, dribbling with her right hand, and then her left, sharpening her ball-handling skills for the next season's opponents.

Basketball, really, had been what saved Catherine from an isolated and lonely existence. She'd learned how to create something of her own when nothing had been given her. She feared, though, that Anne had not learned that same valuable lesson—had not figured out how to choose the good amidst the bad. Catherine remembered looking at her younger sister in the crowd as her senior year team cut down the Sectional nets. Anne had looked so lost, so lonely. Catherine saw a yearning in her sister's eyes that betrayed her tough outer shell. But

Catherine was seventeen, and she had not bothered to reach out. She left for college the next year, had left her family behind.

As she sat idling in front of the house, a young woman emerged from the front door.

"Can I help you?" she asked.

"Oh, no, thank you. I'm sorry to bother you. I was born in this house many, many years ago."

"Really?" the woman asked, genuinely interested. "Would you like to come in? Look around?"

A small boy appeared at the woman's side, clutching his mother's leg.

"I'd be happy to have you!"

Catherine looked at the toddler's face, his messy hair. She knew she could not step foot in that house, not now. Maybe not ever.

"No, thank you. Thank you so much. But I'm late for a meeting, so I need to get going."

"Stop by any time!" the woman called as Catherine rolled up her window.

But Catherine wouldn't stop again.

As she drove away, she watched the pear trees grow smaller and smaller in her rear view mirror until she could no longer see them. They became invisible, just like her sister.

46 *anne*

Showering was a necessity, but even so, it was a chore. Everything, in fact, was a chore. Breathing, most of all.

As a child, Anne remembered her propensity for dramatic tantrums. Her favorite trick, when she didn't get her way, was holding her breath until she passed out. Eva used to walk away, leaving Anne to wake up on the floor alone and confused. Big Jim would throw cold water in her face. Catherine would sometimes sit beside her, staring strangely at her when she awoke as if she was an alien from another world. It was an ineffective tactic because her parents never caved to her childhood whims, but it made her feel like she was in control of something—even if it was only her ability to fall, temporarily unconscious, to the floor.

She thought about how careless she was with that oxygen. She'd been young, reckless. She hadn't realized how precious those breaths were, the ones she willingly withheld. Anne would give anything now—anything—for the chance to breathe those precious puffs of air into Max's useless lungs.

But she knew life didn't work that way. Anne wasn't sure of much, but she knew for certain Max was not coming back. The past month had made her question everything—her purpose on this earth, her ability to raise her daughter, the viability of her marriage, the belief in her God. Especially the belief in her God. Before, He was the one who held it all together with an invisible string and a master plan.

But the string had broken and Anne doubted now that there ever was a plan.

The house was in foreclosure now: this she knew. She also knew she had a $750,000 life insurance policy that would leave her husband and daughter some financial peace. She didn't think about what else that money might leave them.

Instead, the day Max was lowered into the ground kept cycling through her head. His tiny casket, sealed forever shut, contained her precious boy, his blankie, Peter Sam, and half her heart. Anne didn't know how to survive with half a heart. In fact, she considered it near impossible. She'd sat in a folding chair in the sunshine, daffodils blooming around the base of the tree to her left. Dale's arm was around her shoulders, Lila sat quietly on his lap. One of Lila's preschool teachers—the one pursuing her Master's in Vocal Performance—sang *Baby Mine* as Max's casket was placed in the soft spring ground. Who had chosen that song? When the music ended, Father Daniel handed Anne a yellow tulip. She understood she was supposed to throw it into the hole, a final goodbye to her boy. She looked down at her hands, saw that her cuticles were bleeding. She had not realized she'd been chewing through her skin and fingernails. There was no semblance of pain. Perhaps, she'd thought, a body can only recognize and process so much at once.

"Honey, Lila would like you to read her a bedtime story." Dale's voice echoed in the quiet of her bedroom.

"Okay," she said because that was what she was supposed to say.

She walked to her daughter's pink bedroom, careful not to glance into Max's. She caught a glimpse of the hand-painted "Max" sign out of the corner of her eye, but she kept walking.

"Will you read *Time for Bed* tonight, Mama, please?" Lila requested.

Obediently, Anne removed the book from the shelf, sat in the rocker, let Lila climb into her lap.

"It's time for bed, little mouse, little mouse. Darkness is falling all over the house."

She read the words only, distanced herself from the experience.

She could not allow herself to feel anything in this moment, or she would not get through this moment. She inhaled the scent of Lila's strawberry soap, grateful to Dale for keeping their daughter safe and fed and clean.

"I love you, Lila-Bear," Anne said.

"I love you, too, Mama."

Anne turned the Eiffel Tower nightlight on and gently closed the door.

She walked to Max's room, hesitated, and entered. His Johnson's lavender baby lotion scent settled into her senses. The stars and moon mobile above his crib was still and silent. Anne walked to the crib, lowered the rail, and climbed into his bed. It wasn't an easy task, but she couldn't imagine being anywhere else but here. Scrunched into a small, empty shell of herself, she breathed in the slightly sour smell where his damp breath had settled into the sheet. She laid her head where his once rested and fell into a dark and weighted sleep.

47 *eva*

It was a dream she'd had many times before. What were those called? Recurrent? She shivered when she woke, the memory fresh. Eva was ice skating on a frozen Lake Tippecanoe, her girls trailing behind like ducklings. The lake was Norman Rockwellesque, with a fresh layer of snow resting on the tree branches. In an instant, however, the ice gave way, and Eva was plunged into the frigid waters below. She felt her limbs go numb in the cold. She instinctively opened her eyes and looked frantically through the blue waters that enveloped her. When she tried to surface, she couldn't find the opening her own body had made. With her face pressed to the ice above her, she pounded with her hands, trying to get the girls' attention. But they skated around her, laughing, oblivious to the hole in the lake and their mother drowning silently beneath the surface.

"Mrs. Mathers," a voice said. "Are you awake?"

Was she awake? Her mind was foggy, her eyes adjusting to the dim light of the room.

The nurse touched Eva's head, brushed her wispy hair from her forehead.

"Are you feeling better?"

Had she been feeling badly? She wasn't sure how to answer any of these questions.

The nurse, it seemed, didn't really need an answer. She went about her business, took Eva's temperature, changed the pad underneath her.

Eva was expertly rolled from one side of the bed to the other, and she did not protest. Protesting, she thought, was futile. In this place, what needed to happen happened, whether Eva agreed to it or not.

It was much like her own home had been in that way. Life went on around and about her, and she had little control over how it all played out. Big Jim worked and played and drank and philandered. The girls grew up and away.

I failed at being a wife, Eva thought. *I failed at being a mother. I have failed adulthood.* A childhood fraught with booze and anger and punishment continued to define her and her ability to rise above. She was burdened by the weight of being unwanted, by the chains of not enough, of never enough.

"Give us this day our daily bread and forgive us our trespasses," Eva whispered, the words, seared into her memory, a soothing balm on her tired, cracked lips.

Some overcome adversity, some sink into it. Eva had wanted to be strong and courageous, but it was not part of her composition. She'd wanted to be a good mother, to be a better mother than her own, but she could not quite figure out how to rise above. Couldn't? Wouldn't? Eva felt herself slipping deeper, deeper, as she fought for air, for redemption.

48 *jessica*

Jessica Mathers
Re: The Other Side
April 18, 2011

Dear Dale,

I don't know what to say other than I'm sorry. I know it's too little, too late. I understand that it's hollow. I get that it's the resounding chorus of my life. I'm sorry, I'm sorry, I'm sorry. But I am.

I know I let you down. But I couldn't be there. I couldn't put my sisters into that position when they needed to grieve. I couldn't put the spotlight on me, on my return. Anne deserved that much. We may never see eye-to-eye on this, but I think more than she needed me, Anne needed me to stay gone.

I'm worried about her, too, Dale. I am. I'm worried about all of you. And I feel completely helpless. What can I do for you? What can I do for Anne? What can I do for Lila?

What happens when you lose the house? Where will you go? Jesus, Dale, how did all of this happen? All of it?

Please tell me what you want from me. I will do my best to be what you need.

Love,
Jessica

49 *anne*

Mother's Day was near. Dale had planned a luncheon for the three of them at a fancy hotel. It was a day Anne did not want to celebrate, not now, not ever. But she could not find the words to convey this feeling, so she smiled and nodded when he suggested his big idea.

"Julie wants to take Lila shopping for a new dress," Dale said. "Is that okay with you?"

"That will be fun for her," Anne said.

Today, she planned to visit Max's grave. She hadn't been since the funeral, couldn't bear to think about the damp mound of dirt with whispers of grass beginning to grow from it. New life above, no life below. It was a cruel and senseless torment, having a baby in the ground.

When she drove through the Our Lady of Peace cemetery gates, her breath came in ragged spurts. She tried to keep the sounds of her own life quiet, careful not to disturb those who no longer had breath to enjoy. The trees were glorious in their spring birth, bright greens against cerulean skies.

And then, she was there.

Anne sat in the Honda for a long time. It was small and tidy and smelled of new leather. There was Big Jim's grave. But she wasn't there to see him.

The granite headstone was in place. The words "Our Angel" carved in stone. And Max's birth and death dates, so close. Too close. Was he really an angel? Anne couldn't know. She'd prayed for some sign, some divine intervention, some message that he was okay. But all she'd received in return was silence and an irrepressible ache. Throughout her church-going years, she'd heard the stories of people who'd received direct messages from God, but God had never spoken to Anne, despite her urgent pleas. So she was left to wonder, to guess, to second-guess.

After an eternity, Anne got out of the car. On unsure legs, she walked to her son's grave. She ran her fingers across the cool granite, followed the marbled lines in the rock.

"Oh, Max," she whispered. "Oh, Max. I'm so, so sorry."

The pain in her chest was a bomb, ticking. She laid down on the ground, her hand on the base of the headstone and wept into the dirt. She was tethered to this place for life. Her own world had begun—and would invariably end—in Willton, Indiana. How could it be otherwise? How could she ever leave this place where her son came screaming, red-faced, and wet-haired into the world? Where he took his first steps? Said his first words? Where his body—damaged beyond repair—rested in the ground?

She stayed with Max until the dampness of the earth soaked into her clothes and skin. This place felt more like home than home, where her husband and daughter awaited her return.

Later that day, still wearing her wet, dirty clothes, Anne drove to Regal Manor. She had not visited her mother since Max's death.

The room was dark and quiet when she arrived. A vintage *All in the Family* episode cast a warm glow on her mother's face. Eva's eyes were closed, her mouth moving ever so slightly to the rhythm of her dream.

Anne glanced past her sleeping mother. Eva's chest rose and fell unevenly, a single breath occasionally bursting forth with ambition. On the nightstand sat pictures of her grandchildren, professional photos of Lila and Max. Max's laughing face beamed at his mother across the room. Anne rose, unsteadily, and walked to Max. She took the framed photo in her hand, brushing her fingers lightly across

Max's cheek. Anne lifted the photo, placed it into her purse. When her fingers released their grip, she felt the half-full bottle of Valium there, an invitation, a promise. Anne walked to the door, turned back for a moment, and blew Eva a kiss goodbye.

50 *dale*

He was drowning. The riptide had him in its tenacious grip, pulling, dragging him farther from the shore. Dale knew what he needed to do to survive—stop fighting, stop flailing, let the water drag him out until it released him, then swim slowly back, cutting through the current that so ruthlessly ripped him from safety.

He knew in his head what to do, but the tide kept beckoning, and his instinct to fight was strong. *True strength*, Dale thought, *is in the surrender*. It's in admitting defeat, raising the white flag, doing whatever it takes—regardless of fear or fatigue or ego—to break the pattern and swim home a different way.

While Lila was at Jill's and Anne slept another day in her altered, untouchable state, Dale visited all the local grocery stores and gathered their empty, unused boxes. He bought giant rolls of packing tape from The Home Depot, and he began assembling the containers that would soon contain all the physical remnants of their lives. Books, dishes, DVDs, electronics, appliances, photo albums, socks, trinkets once treasured that now held little meaning. He wrapped them all carefully, packed them away quietly, and assigned labels. *Good China, Extra Blankets, High School/College Yearbooks*—these were the names he gave the stacks that grew silently throughout the house like stalagmites.

"Daddy, why are you putting all our things in boxes?" Lila asked when she returned home.

"Because we're going to move to a new house," Dale explained.

"But I like this house," Lila said. "This is my house."

"I know you do, sweetie. I do, too. But we're going to move to another house soon—one that's a little bit smaller, where we won't need so much stuff."

"But I like my stuff," Lila said.

"I know. And you'll still have all the stuff you love the most. Mommy and I will make sure of that."

"Will Mommy be Mommy again after we move?" Lila asked, absent-mindedly rearranging the Barbies on the kitchen table.

Dale swallowed a wave of salt water, fought for another breath and the will to keep moving his weary limbs.

"I hope so, Lila," Dale said. "Mommy is still very sad about Max. We're all very sad about Max. She needs time to rest and get better. We can give her some time, can't we?"

"She's taking a long time," Lila said. "I miss her. And I miss Max. What if he comes back to this house and we're not here?"

"Oh, Lila-Bug," Dale said, "Max isn't coming back to us."

"I know you say that," Lila said, "but what if you're wrong?"

"I'm not wrong, Honey. Max will always be in our hearts, but he's not coming back to live with us."

Lila moved Barbie's stiff arms up and down, straightened the doll's shirt.

"Will my new bedroom be pink?" she asked.

"If you want it to be pink, it will be pink," Dale said.

"Okay," Lila said. "Then I'll move."

Dale watched his daughter play contentedly with her plastic dolls and thought about how simple life could be in the midst of such complication. You pack boxes, you give your house back to the bank, you move to an apartment and paint the walls pink. You do all those things because there are no other choices. When life's biggest decisions have been made for you, there is little left to contemplate.

He closed another box, the loud screech of the packing tape

strangely satisfying in his ears. Then he prepared a plate of grapes and cheese that his wife would leave untouched and delivered it to her bedroom.

51 *catherine*

"Let's go," Julie said. "Just the two of us for a long weekend. It will be good for you, don't you think? Some ocean air, the sun, a little bit of sand between your toes? You have a break before summer session begins, right? Let's just do it, Catherine. What do you say?"

Physically, Catherine was feeling stronger every day. Her hair was growing back, the crushing fatigue had dissipated, and her workload no longer seemed like a near-death sentence. But emotionally, she was a mess—missing her nephew and all the promise he once held, worried about her sister, her brother-in-law, her niece's scarred future. Lila would always be the girl whose mom ran over her baby brother. Catherine could already hear the unfiltered elementary school questions, the mean junior high taunts.

Anne was another story altogether. She'd become an empty cicada shell clinging to a tree, ready to blow away with a strong wind. Could Catherine really leave her now? Could she leave any of them?

"You're recovering, too, Catherine," Julie said. "You have to put your own oxygen mask on before you can help others. If you don't take care of yourself, you're not going to be any good to anyone else. It's just a long weekend."

So Catherine—perhaps against her better judgment—agreed. Once the semester ended and her grades had been recorded, she and Julie rented a tiny, beachfront house on St. George Island, packed the car, and drove fifteen hours south.

The house, with its pale yellow walls and starfish paintings, was perfect. And the sound of the surf instantly put Catherine at ease—a feeling she'd almost forgotten. They didn't bother to unpack before they walked down to the ocean, their feet sinking into the powdery, white sand.

"Yes," Catherine said, "as usual, you were right. This was exactly what I needed."

Julie took Catherine's hand as they stared out to sea together.

"God, Catherine, it's just been so much. Too much. The world needs to slow down a bit, don't you think?"

Catherine sat down in the sand, motioned for Julie to sit beside her. She rested her head on Julie's shoulder, breathed in the scent of the salt water and Julie's strawberry shampoo.

"I think I'm glad you're here to share it with me, the good and the bad," Catherine said. "I don't know if I would have made it alone."

"We're not meant to go it alone," Julie said.

"I can't stop thinking about Max," Catherine said. "About his little body in the ground, alone. I know that's strange and maybe even gruesome, but it wakes me up at night."

"I can't imagine anything more awful than a child's unexpected and accidental death," Julie said. "Well, any child's death, for that matter. It's just not the way life is supposed to work."

"Life never really works out the way we think it's going to, does it?" Catherine asked. She turned to face Julie. "Sometimes that's a good thing."

They kissed then, lips tender and soft. The waves crashed at their feet, and Catherine thought, *this. This is what matters. This is what we have. Here. Now. Nothing more.*

The days crept into the nights too quickly. They ate Apalachicola Bay oysters, drank wine in plastic glasses crusty with sand, applied sunscreen to each other's shoulders. And before they knew it, four days had come and gone. A world away, their former lives awaited: summer semester, visits to Regal Manor, helping Dale pack for the move.

"I'm not ready to go back," Catherine said to Julie as they loaded suitcases into the car.

"I could stay forever," Julie said. "I really could. When it's time for retirement options, we need to keep this one in mind."

Even now, it still took Catherine aback when Julie talked about their future with such assurance and ease. Catherine had never shared a real future with anyone, had never dreamt of growing old with someone else's hand in her own. But with Julie, it was all different and promising and right. They might never be able to marry legally, but it didn't matter. Rings and legal papers were nothing substantial. What mattered wasn't physical.

It was after midnight on the drive home, and Julie was sleeping soundly in the passenger's seat. Catherine's phone vibrated on the console, and she knew immediately that something was wrong. Her heart seized when she saw Dale's phone number flash across her phone screen.

"Dale?" she answered frantically. "It's so late. What is it?"

"It's your Mom," Dale said, his voice shaking. "Are you on your way home?"

52 *dale*

Dale Jackley
Thank You
May 30, 2011

Dear Jessica,

Thank you. A million times, thank you. If you hadn't co-signed our lease for us, I don't know what we would have done. The foreclosure has already ruined our credit, so no one would even consider our applications.

You know you will never have to pay a dime, don't you? We won't ruin you, too. I promise you that.

God, this is all so humiliating and humbling and shitty. What's happening to us? To our family? I don't know if we'll recover from all this. I truly don't. All I can manage right now is today, this hour.

I hate emailing this next bit of news to you, but I understand you still don't want to talk. Your Mom, Jessica—she's in the cardiac ICU. She had a heart attack and survived, and that's all I really know right now. Catherine is on her way home from Florida, and Anne is, well... Anne.

I will keep you updated as I know more. And, of course, you're always welcome to call if and when you're ready.

Love,
Dale

53 *catherine*

Eva's heart attack had left her weak and incapacitated, but alive. Ten days after she arrived in the ICU, she was sent back to Regal Manor to continue biding her time. Catherine had visited when she could, which wasn't very often. Summer classes kept her busy and tied to Indiana University. But when she could manage the drive, Catherine drove. And she stayed, spending time at her mother's bedside like she hadn't before, holding Eva's bony hand, talking about subjects she'd not dared to broach. *Not so brave*, Catherine thought, *now that my mom can't participate in the conversation*. Not so brave, but necessary.

"Your mom's been resting peacefully today," the night nurse said. Catherine noticed the name on her tag: JoAnn.

JoAnn refilled Eva's water pitcher and dimmed the lights.

"If you need anything, let me know," she said.

"Thank you," Catherine said. "We should be fine."

Eva's eyes were closed, her mouth slightly open. Shallow breaths escaped, made mute by the sound of hallway activity.

"Where's Ruth?" Catherine heard a demanding voice shout. Anne had mentioned Ruth's mom before. She smiled slightly, connecting the dots.

"I'm glad you're resting, Mom," Catherine said as she sat beside Eva. "It's the best thing for you right now. Your cardiologist is happy with the stents. That's good news."

The one-sided conversation began slowly, awkwardly. Catherine rubbed Eva's cool arm, marveling at the similarities in the shapes of their fingers, the topography of their hands.

"I've been thinking a lot, Mom. I've been thinking about you and Dad, about Max, about Anne and Jessica. And I've been thinking about Michelle." She paused. "It's funny, I think, the way we humans relate to each other. I mean, I wonder what your relationship with Dad was like. Did you love him, Mom? From day one? Up until the end? Did you truly feel a connection with him, or did you stay because you didn't know where else to go? There's so much I don't know about you—sometimes it takes me by surprise to call you 'Mom.' We were never really good at family, were we? When I look back, it seems we all kind of existed independently. Those thoughts make me sad. We could have been so much more."

The glow of the TV flickered on Eva's face.

"I feel like we're really good at walking around with holes in our hearts. I've got one in the shape of you, one in the shape of Dad, one in the shape of Jessica. And I don't really look at or touch them. They're just there, in the background like shadows. Does that make any sense?"

Catherine laid her left hand next to Eva's. She traced the similar lines with her right index finger, marking the genetic path from one point to the next.

"I used to wish we were a big, happy, loud family like the Bradys," Catherine admitted. "But we were about as different from the Bradys as we could be. And I used to wish Dad was warm and loving, like Pa Ingalls." Catherine smiled sadly at her childhood memories. "Maybe I watched too much TV."

"You know Michelle and I had a friendship break-up, don't you? It's been hard, Mom. Harder than I thought it would be. She was the family I never felt I really had. I think, maybe, I lived vicariously through her and her family. I loved the loud, crazy, constant activity at her house. It made me feel whole. Sure, we used to disagree about lots of things—politics, religion, the best sitcoms…" Catherine paused again. "But when I started dating Julie, Michelle made me feel like I'd changed, like I was somehow a different person, a worse person.

And what do you do with that?" Catherine asked rhetorically. "What do you do when someone challenges who you are as a human being? When they make you feel less than? It was a crossroads for us. And I don't think we can ever go back. Something broke in me when I thought what was unconditional suddenly became conditional."

Eva sighed in her sleep, shifted her weight ever so slightly.

"Was it like that with you and Dad?" Catherine asked. "Did you once love him and then fall out of love? And did you stay because there was nowhere else to go? How does it feel when someone vows to be true forever… and then isn't? Did you become so broken that there was nothing left of you to give? Or did your own mom do that to you? I know your childhood was rough, but you never gave us details. We just weren't the kind of family to share those intimacies. Was she the one who broke you?"

A great, gaping silence filled the room as the hallway noise quieted and the residents began settling in for the night.

"We've been so selfish, all of us. It's easy to see that now that Max is gone. We all miss him so much. Sure, we loved him while he was here, but it wasn't enough. We didn't appreciate him. We didn't appreciate us. Anne and I have been so worried about everything we don't have— everything we didn't have—that we failed to even notice what was right before us. And Jessica. Thinking about Jessica breaks my heart in two, Mom. It really does. We just let her go. Just like that. She walked out, and we never bothered to try and get her back. She was just a baby when she went, not even twenty. We were the adults then—all of us. How in the world did we just let her go? If we've felt disconnected and alone, imagine how she feels…"

A weight settled in Catherine's chest, heavy and dense. She rubbed the softness of her own head where the hair was just long enough to lie flat.

"I'm going to find her, Mom. Julie is going to help me. I don't know if Jessica will come back or not, but I have to try. We can't just keep losing one another forever, can we? What kind of life is that? What kind of lives have we chosen?"

Eva's eyes fluttered open in a haze of confusion.

"Hello, Mom," Catherine said softly.

Eva looked at Catherine, unsmiling, uncomprehending.

"Hello," she said, no trace of recognition in her face. "Do I know you?"

54 *anne*

There were moments when she understood how she *should* act. There were times she was willing to play the part, to step back into her life, to hold her daughter. Even those times, however, felt false. Anne knew she should be figuring out how to exist within these new parameters, these Max-empty days, but it was a choice she was not yet fully ready to make.

She knew there was an apartment, there were packed boxes, there was a moving date on the calendar. She'd seen the thick stack of paperwork from the sheriff announcing the sale of their home. That ream of paper would have once been the end of her, but the end of her had already come and gone, rendering the papers worthless and ineffective. So the bank was taking her house. So they were moving into an apartment. So their finances were shot, their credit ruined. And Max was still in the ground.

On her better days, Anne understood the importance of keeping Lila close, of appreciating the precious gift her daughter was. And yet, she couldn't quite figure out how to traverse those feelings, often holding her daughter tightly, tightly, until the air was squeezed from her resistant lungs, until she ran to her father crying for a reprieve.

Anne couldn't quite get it right.

She was going back to work when school resumed in August. She'd have to decorate her classroom, prepare her lesson plans, dress herself every day. She'd have to talk and interact and smile and nod and grade papers and monitor lunch. She'd have to participate in life again. Anne wasn't sure how that was going to happen, but it was on the calendar. Her return-to-life was scheduled for August 15, ready or not. And Anne was not ready.

Dale seemed ready. He was uncharacteristically cheerful about Anne's return to school. He mentioned more often than necessary that it was going to be good for her, for Lila, for all of them. He believed this was what the family needed—routine, a fresh start, a new school year. He told Anne time and time again, "You can do it, Anne. I know you can. Max would want you to be happy. Max would want us to move forward."

But Dale didn't know what Max wanted. How could he possibly know what their dead toddler would think about Anne's return to teaching? Dale knew what *he* wanted, Anne thought. That was not the same thing.

She did not resist where time was leading her, though. The days until her August 15 start day were startlingly few. The remaining white blocks on the calendar loomed before her like gaping holes, ready to suck her into oblivion.

Ready or not.

55 *dale*

The move happened the last week of July. Friends came with trucks and beer and able backs. The expense of hiring professional movers was out of the question, but when you were the father of a recently buried son, everyone wanted to help. It had not been difficult to gather volunteers.

Dale rambled on vaguely about hospital bills and funeral expenses, about downsizing, about the sanctuary of a home where Max had not laughed, where his fingerprints didn't need to be wiped from walls. But Dale was certain people knew the truth. The sheriff's sale had been advertised in the local paper. And Willton was not a big town. He could not, however, bring himself to care about what his neighbors thought of his financial demise. Dale—the salesman who formerly couldn't sleep at night until he was on track to make more than 110% of his monthly quota—couldn't bring himself to care about much of anything beyond making it through the next day, the next hour.

His correspondence with Jessica had become more frequent, although they still weren't speaking in person. Dale understood her silence now in a way he never would have before. He understood the need for a safe place, a familiar place, and email was Jessica's safe place with him. He gave her space, and she gave him support. She emailed at least once a day, checking on him, on her sisters, on Lila.

Oh, Lila. Sweet, sad Lila. She bounced off the walls one minute and sobbed in his arms the next. It was all so much for someone so little—Max, the move, her mother's quiet withdrawal.

"I don't want to be the only one," she whispered to Dale before bed one evening. The moon shone through the cracks of her window blinds, and Dale had just finished reading *Where the Wild Things Are* at Lila's request. He'd choked over the name Max again and again, bravely trying to keep the right tenor when describing the wild rumpus. Lila had pointed to the illustration on the book's front cover. "Now this is the only Max I know."

Once the dust settled, Dale intended to find a counselor for his daughter, one who was trained to help her sort through the fragile intricacies of her young life. *As soon as we're settled in the apartment,* he promised himself. *We'll figure out how to move forward once we have our feet on solid ground again.*

In two short weeks, Anne was returning to her teaching job. Before Max's death, the school had offered Anne a full-time position, and she had gratefully accepted. Now he wondered if the administration regretted that decision, if they were as concerned as he was about having his broken wife teach their impressionable middle schoolers. But on the other hand, he harbored a secret hope that returning to some semblance of normalcy would bring Anne back, would force her into living again. *Fake it until you make it,* he thought. That's all he wanted his wife to accomplish.

56 *jessica*

She was a coward. This she understood. Not to be able to pick up the phone and call her brother-in-law was selfish at best, pathetic at worst. None of what was happening in Dale's life was about her.

And yet it was.

Isn't that what we all do? she thought. *As human beings, aren't we all a bit narcissistic at our core? Doesn't everything that moves in and out of our lives get filtered through our own experiences, our own beliefs? Isn't it, ultimately, our job to figure out how to traverse it all with some sense of grace?*

Jessica, however, was feeling far from graceful. She felt frantic most days, heart racing, chest pounding, brain swirling. She could not figure out how to put together the pieces of her own life and place, and that left her feeling that anything she might offer up to anyone else was woefully inadequate.

She was happy to sign the lease for Dale and Anne—thrilled, actually. It was something she could easily do, something that required nothing more than her good credit. It was a desperate offering, a manic yell of *Yes! Yes! Take what you need from me!* Money had never been important to Jessica. Beyond the basics, she didn't need much. And as a child, she'd had an abundance of money and an empty existence. Love was what she wanted. Love and acceptance. Those things were much harder to come by.

As Jessica fried some breakfast eggs, Beth and Ted came spilling out of the second bedroom, hair tousled, clothes askew. The eggs popped and crackled in the pan, a background noise to her room-mates' laughter.

"Morning, Jess!" Beth smiled, her eyes still droopy with sleep.

"Good morning," Jessica replied. She liked when Beth called her Jess. It made her feel like she belonged to someone. The shortening of a name was akin to a hug, the familiarity warm and comforting. Jessica really enjoyed Beth's company, but their moments together were few and far between. Ted was Beth's focus, Beth's life. Jessica was on the periphery. She stood in her well-worn position on the outside looking in, unable to infiltrate herself successfully into another's life. It was not a position of self-pity, but rather one of paralysis.

Moving from state to state was easy for Jessica. Miles were made for traversing. It was the more intricate distances—the interpersonal journeys—that waylaid her every time.

57 *catherine*

L ife was funny. At times, it came in slow, undulating waves, nearly
lulling you into a heavy sleep. Other times, it raced at you like a
runaway train, screeching, shrieking, horn blowing frantic warning
calls. Catherine could not get off the track.

She had fantasized for a brief moment that perhaps she would have
a chance to rest, now that the chemo was complete. She dreamt about
long, leisurely days of recovery, of slow awakenings and hot coffee.
But the days were clipped and hasty. She had things to do, places to
go, essays to grade, family members to mend. Turning in her summer
grades had felt like a monumental achievement, like she'd crossed the
finish line of a hundred-mile run. She did not know how it had all
come together in time.

August sat heavy on her body and her heart. The day of Dale and
Anne's foreclosure, come and gone. She could not bear to check the
paper for news of the sheriff's sale. She did not want to know how
much was paid for the memory of Max, for lives that would never
again be whole. Anne and Dale had settled into the apartment, a tiny
space adorned with shockingly white walls and a quiet hush. She'd
spoken to Lila on the phone just the night before.

"Lila-Bear! It's almost time for school to start! Are you excited?"

"Yes, Aunt Cat! Jill says it's going to be so much fun!" Catherine
could hear her niece's raspy breath, the phone held too close to her
tiny ear. "Jill says I'll get to finger paint!"

"That's the best part of preschool, for sure!" Catherine said. "That and snacks."

"There'll be snacks?" Lila gasped. "Jill didn't tell me about snacks!"

An ache settled in Catherine's chest to hear Lila talk about Jill when it was Anne who should be center stage in Lila's life. But Anne was incapable of taking care of herself, let alone anyone else. Anne was returning to a teaching position in less than two weeks, and Catherine was terrified at the prospect of her sister being in charge of other children. Did the administration know how unstable Anne was right now? Of course they didn't. No one truly knew but Dale, Catherine, Julie, Jill. Everyone was still taking care of the Jackley family, bringing meals, hiring housekeepers, organizing cabinets, and stocking toilet paper. Everyone wanted something to do, something to keep them moving. No one wanted in too close, though. No one was able to look too deeply into the Jackley family dynamic. It was too much. Too much for anyone. Getting close was scary, unsettling. A dead child in this home meant that dead children could happen. That it *did* happen. No one was safe, no one immune.

Over the summer, through the darkest of days, Catherine had grown fiercely protective of her sister in a way she'd never before experienced. *Maybe this is what family feels like*, she often thought. This need to take care of business, to circle the wagons, to do what needed to be done, to come out swinging in a show of solidarity. Was it loving Julie that allowed her to feel this way? Or was it losing Max? Perhaps a combination of the two. Whatever the cause, Catherine had risen to the occasion with a ferocity. She changed the Jackleys' sheets, stocked the refrigerator with healthy food, visited Eva regularly, got updates from Jill, took Lila to dinner so Dale could go to bed early—could join his wife who'd retreated to her bedroom in the early afternoon.

She knew Dale was hoping Anne's work would bring about a miracle, that being responsible for other children would bring Anne back to the land of the living. Catherine understood there was no alternative way of believing for Dale. He was holding on to his wife by a thread. A strong wind could send her flying through the clouds and away from him forever. It was a possibility he could not entertain.

"Get some sleep, love," Julie said time and time again. "You must rest."

"I will soon," Catherine said. "I promise. Just one more phone call."

And so she forged ahead while Julie prepared for her first semester at IUPUI. Catherine watched Julie bring home maps and books and a couple new logoed shirts. Julie was an IUPUI Jaguar now, sleek, speedy, beautiful. Cohabitating had been the best decision they could have made. Nothing inspired and calmed Catherine more than seeing Julie's face in the morning and sleeping beside her, arms and legs tangled, at night. She was Catherine's reminder—in the face of all that had been lost—of life, of love, of hope.

Of family.

58 *anne*

Twenty-eight expectant faces stared at her. She stood at the front of the classroom, appropriately dressed, hair done, make-up applied. How had that all happened? She vaguely recalled a kiss goodbye from Dale, and one from Lila. Familiar faces greeted her at the school, welcomed her back with hesitant voices and pity-filled eyes.

"Whatever you need…" Meredith had said, hugging her awkwardly. "Anything. Don't hesitate to ask." It was a common refrain. Everyone knew Anne needed something, but no one was quite sure what that was, not even Anne. Of course, there were moments of clarity, tiny slivers of time when it seemed she might be able to breathe normally again. But thoughts of Max and the memory of that day always, without fail, pulled her back underwater. Sometimes the pain was so intense, she thought her ribs would crack under the pressure.

"Good morning!" Anne said, smiling at her class. "Welcome to your first day! My name is Mrs. Jackley, and we've got a busy year ahead." She wondered how many of her students knew she was the teacher who ran over her own child. Her opening lines fell from her mouth with ease and clarity, almost as if she'd rehearsed them. But she hadn't rehearsed anything. Her life was on auto-pilot, and she never really knew what was coming next. Except for the hurt, the despair. Those were constant. Her unwanted friends, her dark companions. Grief was a shadow that clung to her, its stench overwhelming her senses, its heaviness crushing her, slowly, slowly.

Dale was so much better at living than she was. He could make meals, clean the house, care for Lila, tuck their living daughter in at night. He went to work, he unpacked boxes, he made their new apartment feel like a home. Maybe not *her* home, but someone's. He still smiled at Anne, still told her he loved her. Despite. God, how could anyone love her? How could anyone forgive her? How could she ever forgive herself?

It was only 8:00 a.m., and Anne wasn't sure how she was going to get through the day. Somehow, though, she did. And then she got through the next one, and the one after that. For two weeks, she continued waking up, getting dressed, going to work, and finding her way home. She talked with colleagues, hugged her daughter, graded papers, and slept with the aid of powerful pills. And then, one day in early September, she stopped.

Anne woke earlier than usual that morning, the dark outside still clinging to the edges of the trees like a tattered cloak. She donned her fleece robe, walked the small distance from the bedroom to the family room, and stood before the sliding doors that opened on to a small, concrete patio. She could feel the chill through the glass, and when she laid her open palm against the surface, she shivered. Autumn had always been her favorite season—she and Catherine had shared an affinity for falling leaves and bulky sweaters. Visiting pumpkin patches with Lila and Max, sipping hot cider, and pushing the double stroller through the mazes of orange and brown used to be one of her most highly anticipated pastimes. The yellows and reds had entranced her. And although she'd never admit it back then—especially to Catherine—she'd loved visiting her alma mater, the beautiful Indiana University campus, in autumn when the trees boasted of their beauty.

This morning, though, autumn was different. It felt like the end of something, and the chill did not excite her. Instead, it settled into her bones, crackling, freezing. She thought about Max in the cold, hardening ground, and she knew. He needed her. He needed her more than anyone here needed her. Even Lila. Lila deserved happiness and joy, not a life anchored by a mother who was no longer whole. Dale could remarry. Someone would love him more fully and more completely than Anne could. Someone else's heart would be big enough to let him in. Hers, on the other hand, continued shrinking. She was afraid that soon, nothing would remain but an empty, hollow shell.

Father, forgive me, she prayed. But that Father had abandoned her back in the spring, taking her only son with Him.

Anne walked to the kitchen and took her favorite coffee mug from the cupboard. She traced the lines of the calla lilies that adorned it. She filled it with the remains of a bottle of Cabernet Sauvignon and reached into the pocket of her robe. There was the bottle of Valium she'd hidden from Dale. He'd kept tabs on her medication, but he didn't know about this one. It was her secret. Hers alone. Anne's fingers wrapped around the outside of the plastic tube as if grasping a lover's hand.

Today, she thought. *Today is the day.*

And she smiled at the notion of holding Max once more.

59 *dale*

He did not like the beeps and buzzes of the hospital room or the steady flow of traffic. In Dale's opinion, the hospital should be a sacred place, a quiet sanctuary in which to recover, or to say farewell.

But Anne's room was not silent, and all Dale wanted was for his wife to rest peacefully, to regain her strength, her sanity, and her will to live. By the grace of a God he'd long ago given up, and by the expertise of a team of quick-thinking emergency room doctors, his wife had survived her attempt to end her own life with prescription drugs and wine. Dale had not fared nearly as well. He'd called Jill that morning, broken down and desperate. The night before Anne took the Valium, he'd slept on the couch. He'd gotten Lila up in the morning, had sat her down at the breakfast table in front of a bowl of oatmeal flavored with cinnamon and sugar. Then he'd gone to wake Anne.

"Please come get Lila right now," he'd quietly begged Jill, fumbling with his phone, clearing Anne's mouth, and listening for the breaths that were still coming in shallow spurts. It seemed there was too much time in between each. "Take her to school. It's Anne. She overdosed, Jill. The EMTs are on the way. I can't have Lila here when they arrive." Jill had let herself in to the Jackleys' house mere minutes ahead of the EMTs, her hair disheveled, her pajama pants wrinkled.

"You're not even dressed, silly!" Lila had said as Jill whooshed her off into the car, briefly looking over her shoulder with pained concern.

"Love you, Lila!" Dale said. "I'll call you, Jill."

And then he'd returned to his wife and waited for the EMTs to arrive, praying, begging. After they'd reached the hospital, after the doctors assured him that Anne was going to live, he called Catherine, then Jessica. Neither of them answered, but Dale left them both messages.

On Jessica's voice mail, he'd said, "Jessica, it's Dale. We need you to come home. Your sister overdosed, and no matter what's happened in the past, you three need to figure out a way to move forward. Enough with the bullshit. Enough. Call me."

He was angry, angrier than he'd ever been before, angrier than he assumed he should be. He'd leaned over Anne's bed and whispered in her sleeping ear, "Goddammit, Anne! What the fuck were you thinking? This is not okay. Not okay in any way, shape, or form. Lila needs you. I need you. This world needs you. You have no right to check out now. No fucking right."

He'd broken down, crying then. "Jesus, Anne, do you think I don't miss him? Do you think that every single second of my life I don't wish that morning had played out differently? That I'd made him sit at the table to eat his bananas two minutes earlier? That I'd double-checked the door to make sure it was locked? Do you think you're the only one who cries herself to sleep at night remembering the way he smelled, the way he smiled? This grief is not yours alone! You can't claim it for yourself! And you cannot—cannot—create more of it for the rest of us. Goddammit, Anne, I love you! Do you not understand that? Do you think that's something that comes and goes? That it's conditional? Because it's not." He'd stopped then, wiping his nose and swallowing his sobs.

"Anne, don't leave me. Please don't leave me. I cannot walk through this life alone. And there is no one I want beside me but you. No one. Do you believe me, Anne? Do you believe how much I love and need you?"

She had not responded in her drug-induced sleep, but Dale had to believe she'd heard. A tear, tiny as a spattered rain drop, slipped from her eye and disappeared down her cheek.

"Don't go," he'd said again. Just to make sure she understood.

60 *catherine*

Catherine had always thought Anne was too afraid of death and pain to kill herself. She'd considered her younger sister a bit of a coward. Of course, they'd all worried about the possibility in the long days after Max's death, but Catherine would never have believed Anne had the chutzpah to do it. Anne had always been weak, a follower. And ending your own life required a strength Anne did not possess. Catherine was still shocked as she sat beside her sister's hospital bed, watching her breath move in and out, in and out.

Life was so precarious, she thought. So fragile. One moment here, the next moment, somewhere else. Somewhere no one really understood, despite the insistent claims of those who believed wholeheartedly in a heaven and a hell beyond this life. But they'd experienced hell right here on earth when they'd put Max in the ground. If there was something worse than that, Catherine could not imagine it.

Catherine looked at her sleeping sister and considered what life would be like without Anne. Even though they'd never managed to create a kinship or a close sisterly relationship, Catherine realized how big a space Anne would leave behind if she chose to go. She couldn't erase the image in her mind that Dale had described. He'd found his wife in their bedroom blue-lipped and covered in her own Cabernet-stained vomit. The vomiting, the doctors had told him, had most likely saved Anne. Her body had expelled enough poison, had purged the worst of the toxins she'd hoped would end her.

Julie walked into Anne's hospital room with her backpack slung over one shoulder.

"Hello, Cat," she said to Catherine, her voice soft and gentle.

"Hi," Catherine said, sighing with contentedness at the sight of her friend and lover.

"How's she doing?"

"Good. Better."

"I'm so glad to hear that," Julie said. "Where's Dale?"

"Picking Lila up from Jill's. He's bringing her to visit later tonight."

"Any word on when Anne's going home?"

"Not yet," Catherine said.

"And you? When are you coming home?" Julie brushed Catherine's cheek with a kiss.

"In time for dinner. But I have a ton of grading to do tonight," she said apologetically.

"No worries," Julie said. "I've got a paper to write, too. We'll order in some Chinese and hunker down together."

"Sounds perfect," Catherine said. And she meant it. Her life with Julie was about as close to perfect as she could imagine, hills and valleys and all.

The week prior, Catherine had been formally recognized by a student as his most influential professor. Because she taught him during the most intense rounds of her chemotherapy, the award was even more touching and unexpected.

I made it, Catherine thought. *I survived breast cancer, chemo, work, losing Michelle, finding Julie, losing Max, finding Anne.* She marveled at the tenacity of the human body and spirit, while she grieved the broken parts of her sister. She was not going to lose Anne again, was not willing to let her go as she had before.

Catherine credited Julie with giving her a new outlook on life. Julie and cancer. Catherine had even begun to soften around the edges with Eva. The cold, disconnected past seemed more and more like a cloudy memory, and Catherine was able to view Eva as she was: sick, frail, confused, alone. The mother to whom she had surrendered so much power was a weak and fragile shell, ready to crack under the weight of age and memory. Catherine's job, she understood, was to help see her mother through her end days with the love and compassion she was never given as a child. It wasn't an eye for an eye that motivated her now, it was the next right thing. So many wrongs had been committed, but the next moment could be different if that's what she chose. And it seemed obvious to her as she sat by her broken sister's hospital bed that a soft, forgiving heart was the only logical choice.

61 *jessica*

She played Dale's message again. She'd played it at least a hundred times. By now, she knew it by heart, but she still needed to hear his voice. It was strong, commanding. Jessica had been drawn to Dale's kindness, but she did not know this side of him. And she liked this side of him, the part that called her to action, the part that demanded more from her than she'd expected from herself. No one had ever been that model for her before. No one had cared enough to call her out on her own selfish bullshit.

Jessica was astounded by the ongoing tragedy in her family: Eva, Max, Anne. Even Beth weighed in on all that had recently transpired.

"Damn, Jess, it's like a family curse. What do you think will happen next? What are you going to do?"

She stepped outside into the California air. It was hot, heavy, unusually warm for a September afternoon. The memory of a cool autumn childhood morning tugged at her chest as the heat bore down on her.

When Dale first left his message, Jessica had begun packing. That's what she'd always done in a crisis—move, run, pack, go. But this felt different. She was not driven by panic or fear this time, but by something deeper and more stable. Jessica knew she was going home, but she wasn't running full tilt back into her past. In fact, she moved slowly, contemplating her next steps with forethought.

Anne was going to live. Dale had made that clear. Jessica would not lose her unknown nephew and her sister within the same year. Dale would not lose his son and his wife. But Anne needed to find her life again, and Jessica knew that she would be a part of that journey. Perhaps she would be welcome, perhaps she would not. But she would be there nonetheless. She would show up. Showing up was always the first step.

Jessica breathed in deeply. She loved the air in L.A., the hint of sea, a whisper of danger and excitement. But she also yearned for Indiana where the scent of fresh grass clippings and after-rain asphalt comforted her. When she closed her eyes, Jessica could still vividly recall running through cornfields with her young, unsupervised grade school friends. She remembered the cobwebs hitting her face, the plant leaves slicing into her scabby legs.

But it was the milkweed pods in the field down the street from her house that had always been her favorite. She loved splitting them open to reveal the damp, downy fluff in autumn. She'd read as a child that milkweed was poisonous to many creatures, but the monarch was immune to its toxins. The orange and black monarch butterfly that lived so briefly but covered thousands of miles during its fall migration to Mexico, to California, to where she was standing right this moment. Jessica had watched those winged beauties with reverence and awe, marveling at their metamorphosis. For Jessica, they were beauty and strength personified. They were the embodiment of a majestic life, short, powerful, purposeful.

In second grade, Miss Blackwell had instructed the class to create a bug collection. Never one to be squeamish about such things, Jessica had eagerly searched for and pinned a variety of insects onto her Styrofoam display board. She picked straight pins with tiny, bright balls on the ends, alternating the colors into a rainbow. But when she caught her monarch butterfly—the crowning glory of her collection— she was hesitant and anxious. She held it in her hand for a long time, feeling the near weightlessness of its magnificent wings. She thought about the journey this one would never take, the skies it would never discover. With tears dripping onto her three-legged grasshopper, she pinned the monarch with her blue-tipped spear and watched, horrified, as its wings beat furiously, fruitlessly against a force greater than its own body and spirit.

Jessica gazed out across the L.A. sky, took her phone from her pocket, searched her contacts for the number Dale had long ago provided, took a deep breath, and hit *call*.

After a single ring, a voice on the other end—both unknown and somehow still familiar—answered quietly, "Hello?"

Jessica's heart skipped a beat.

"Hello?" the voice asked again, a bit more impatiently this time.

Jessica paused, gathering strength, listening to the unmistakable hospital noises that echoed in the background.

"Hello," she replied. "Catherine? It's me... Jessica."

And she waited, tense and anxious, the silence between them a spider's thread, invisible, tethered to each with a promise of possibility.

acknowledgments

When a book takes four years to come to fruition, there are many who become part of your journey. And then there are those who make the journey possible, who clear the path so you don't trip over the roots, who keep the woodland creatures at bay while you continue to put one foot in front of the other... or something like that.

This section is for you.

First and foremost, to my beloved husband, Chris, who picked me out of high school Pop-Swing Choir two and a half decades ago when I was a hot mess of teenage angst and drama and hormones. Twenty-eight years and four teenagers later, I'm a middle-aged mess of angst and drama and hormones, and you're still here. Steady. Faithful. Holding us all together, cooking amazing meals, and burning up the dance floor. Thank you for being everything to me. Thank you for giving everything to me.

Sam, Gus, Mary Claire, and George, you'll always be the best works I'll ever produce. You are each better human beings than I could ever hope to be. It's been my greatest pleasure and privilege to walk you through this world.

To Mom, my first fan, the one who has always, unconditionally, had my back. Thank you for showing me how far strength, independence, a perfect Keoke coffee, and a kick-ass sense of humor will carry you.

And to Carrie, my other mother. To Bob, who has cared for us all so lovingly. To Kevin, Andy, Amber, Josh, Jackson, and Jocey, too. And to Jean and Dave, the best in-laws a girl could wish for. And to the rest of the Willis family who loves and laughs and lifts a glass with great gusto.

Where would I be without my girls? The ones whose couches are my homes away from home? Whose wine cellars are fair game? The ones who cook for me, laugh with me, and take my middle-of-the-night calls? I'm looking at you, Andi Speigelberg, Katy Allen, Libby Sigler, Heather Carson, Mary Robison, Debbie Dyson, Heather Spinner, Jenny Godby, Lou Kachur, Kirsten DeHaai, and Jennifer Atkins.

And to you, Rachel Macy Stafford, who first found my words online and felt compelled enough to share them with your kind and loyal followers. Your generosity changed the trajectory of my writing life. But more importantly, your friendship changed me. I am a better writer because of the opportunities you opened for me, but I am a better human being because of you. Thank you for seeing what I couldn't. Thank you for believing with such conviction. I am so grateful these two Hoosier girls decided to share a dinner together in Alabama.

Then there are those writer friends who have become, simply, friends… who also happen to write. Thank goodness our love of words brought us together, Sherry Stanfa-Stanley, Karen Lynch, Tricia Booker, Logan Fisher, Dawn Pier, Amy Ferris, Michelle Peters, and Kristin VanderHey Shaw.

Thank you to those who slogged through my first drafts and told me they were good, despite. I appreciate you, Debbie Dyson, Sherry Stanfa-Stanley, Beth Batka, Nicole Ross, Mary Robison, Andi Spiegelberg, and Jeryl Mitsch.

And to those who have been such cheerleaders, such supporters, and such friends: Liz Farrelly, Nicole Ross, Jeryl Mitsch, Kay Brocato, Amy Corey, Jessica Bex, Joyce Dreesen, Andrea Maurer, Mandy Sheckles, Molly Godby, Mara Winter, Kelly DiBenedetto, Amy Rowe, and JoDee Waltz.

A huge thank you to each and every one of you who has so loyally read my blog and my essays and my articles and my online ramblings. Writing isn't always easy. Writing into a void is harder. Thank you for giving my words a soft place to land.

Thank you to those who first deemed my words publication-worthy. To Mary Wynne Cox at Indy's Child who gave me such an amazing platform for so many years. To Jessica Smock and Stephanie Sprenger for including me in the lovely *My Other Ex: Women's True Stories of Loving and Losing Friends* and to Mickey Nelson and Eve Batey for giving me pages in *Nothing but the Truth So Help Me God: 73 Women on Life's Transitions*. Thank you, Jen Pastiloff Taleghany, for so graciously giving some tender words a home on The Manifest-Station. And thank you, Mamalode, for featuring my stories. BlogHer, I'm still a little giddy about being named a 2015 Voice of the Year. So much thanks.

To two of the most amazing photographers I know: Christie Turnbull who always makes me look so much better in pictures than I do in person, and Beth Batka who inspired the imagery of this novel with her haunting milkweed pod photo.

To T. Greenwood, author and editor extraordinaire. Thank you for helping guide this book into something so much better than I could have ever created on my own. And to the indomitable Connie May Fowler and Richard McCann who offered such support, such wisdom, such kindness. I am forever indebted.

Brooke Warner, thank you for saying yes. And Lauren Wise, so much thanks for keeping this train on the tracks.

Crystal Patriarche and Taylor Vargecko, where would I be without you tirelessly singing my praises? So much gratitude.

And a shout-out to Brandi Carlile whose beloved music was the backdrop to many hours of writing.

To stand on the shoulders of such giants, to be held in the arms of such angels.

I am so incredibly lucky.

I am so grateful.

kickstarter backer acknowledgments

The publication of this book was made possible by a successful Kickstarter campaign and the incredibly generous support and backing of Katy & Eric Allen; Charlie Anderson; Charles & Marcia Anderson; April; Tim & Jennifer Atkins; Sayuri B.; Chris & Amy Baggott; Angela Barnett; Elizabeth Batka; Becca; Betty Becker; Beth; Jenny Bivans; Ashley Brewer; Jill Helgason Broome; Eileen Carmody Byman; Lisa Cadigan; Angela Carr; Carrie, Kevin, & Family; Kurtis & Heather Carson; Christian; Cindy & Morey Cohen; Michelle Conner; Amy Corey; Teal Cracraft; Kirsten DeHaai; Scott & Erin Dorsey; Kathy Dowling; Joyce Dreesen; Anne Dunlavy; Debbie Dyson; James Emmert; Jill Curry Ginn; Jason & Molly Godby; Jennifer Godby; Mary Catherine Grau; Greg & Mary; Mangala Hasanadka; Angela & David Heinig; Sherry Hitch; Becky Thayer Holl; Tricia Inniger; Tom Jennings; Jill; Karen; Melissa L.; Jennifer White Lee; Andy Lenzy; Shelley Lidy; Amber Marie List; Liz; Jennifer Machala; Lisa Mack; Andrea Maurer; Jen McDonald; Mick & Mimi McKee; Mike; Jeryl Mitsch; Nancy; Eva Nehring; Rachel Nielson; Jodi Nixon; Dawn Pier; Sandy R.; Cynthia Ragona; Rosie Reast; The Rimer Family; Scott & Mary Robison; Nicole Ross; Amy Rowe; Megan Sabine; Julie Ruppert Schulte; Amy Sherer; Libby Sigler; Angela Solis; Kristie Smith; Bonnie Spiegelberg; Andrea & Scott Spiegelberg; Craig & Heather Spinner;

Chris Splater; Rachel Macy Stafford; Sherry Stanfa-Stanley; Sherry Dyson Stepp; Chris Vetters; Mary Warner; Jayme Wasserstrom; Theresa Wilcox; Kim Williams; Dave & Jean Willis; and those who chose to remain anonymous. I am so very grateful to each and every one of you.

about the author

© Christie Turnbull Photography

Katrina Anne Willis was named a 2011 Midwest Writers Fellow, a 2013 Listen to Your Mother participant, and a 2015 BlogHer Voice of the Year. She has been anthologized in *My Other Ex: Women's True Stories of Losing and Leaving Friends* (2014) and *Nothing but the Truth So Help Me God: 73 Women on Life's Transitions* (2014). Her work has appeared on a variety of sites, including the Manifest-Station, Mamalode, Indy's Child, BlogHer, Hands Free Mama, and Momastery. A Hoosier at heart, Katrina currently lives in Northwest Ohio with her husband and four teenagers, and she writes semi-regularly at www.katrinaannewillis.com. This is her first novel.

SELECTED TITLES FROM SHE WRITES PRESS

She Writes Press is an independent publishing company
founded to serve women writers everywhere.
Visit us at www.shewritespress.com.

The S-Word by Paolina Milana
$16.95, 978-1-63152-927-6
An insider's account of growing up with a schizophrenic mother, and
the disastrous toll the illness—and her Sicilian Catholic family's code of
secrecy—takes upon her young life.

How to Grow an Addict by J.A. Wright
$16.95, 978-1-63152-991-7
Raised by an abusive father, a detached mother, and a loving aunt and
uncle, Randall Grange is built for addiction. By twenty-three, she knows
that together, pills and booze have the power to cure just about any problem she could possibly have . . . right?

The Belief in Angels by J. Dylan Yates
$16.95, 978-1-938314-64-3
From the Majdonek death camp to a volatile hippie household on the East
Coast, this narrative of tragedy, survival, and hope spans more than fifty
years, from the 1920s to the 1970s.

Pieces by Maria Kostaki
$16.95, 978-1-63152-966-5
After five years of living with her grandparents in Cold War-era Moscow,
Sasha finds herself suddenly living in Athens, Greece—caught between
her psychologically abusive mother and violent stepfather.

Our Love Could Light the World by Anne Leigh Parrish
$15.95, 978-1-938314-44-5
Twelve stories depicting a dysfunctional and chaotic—yet lovable—family
that has to band together in order to survive.

The Rooms Are Filled by Jessica Null Vealitzek
$16.95, 978-1-938314-58-2
The coming-of-age story of two outcasts—a nine-year-old boy who just lost
his father, and a closeted young woman—brought together by circumstance.

Trespassers by Andrea Miles
$16.95, 978-1-63152-903-0
Sexual abuse survivor Melanie must make a choice: choose forgiveness
and begin to heal from her emotional wounds, or exact revenge for the
crimes committed against her—even if it destroys her family.